Her Eagle Was a Seagull...

By
Curtis Westerman

 **New Generation Publishing**

To My Cornish Maid Carol Ann

Eagles may be handsome birds.

However Seagulls are not only handsome they're successful.

Edwina, page 140.

Chapter One

07:26 Monday 14th May 1951.

Leaving the damp chill of the early morning mist behind them, six Royal Navy Wrens in full uniform ran carrying their holdalls into Plymouth's North Road Railway Station. The porter glanced at their papers and informed them they had just one minute to catch the Penzance train. Laughing and chattering, they ran up the platform and yanked open the first carriage door they came to. They piled in, still chattering and laughing. Suddenly they went quiet; they had noticed that this non corridor train carriage had an occupant.

AC1 Paul Edward Weston, minus his tunic, shoes, collar and tie, which he'd removed for comfort, was lying fast asleep on the seat with even his trouser belt undone. Something he deeply regretted doing later.

Weston had arrived at Plymouth station at five o'clock that morning after being wrongly routed via Crewe and Birmingham by the staff at Liverpool Lime Street station. Consequently, he was worn out and sick of changing trains. The porter told him the Penzance stopping train was waiting for its locomotive in the station, but it wouldn't be leaving until seven thirty. Weston saw this as a golden opportunity to catch up on his missed sleep. He made himself as comfortable as he could. The loud noises the girls made while crowding into the carriage hadn't wakened him. It actually took a kiss on his lips from the petty officer Wren in charge to bring him round. He slowly opened his eyes and a second later he was sitting bolt upright, fully realising he was cornered, trapped would be a better word, in a non corridor carriage like a fly in a spider's web. At that very moment, as if to quell any thoughts he may have had about leaving the train, it began to move.

'Hello, sleeping beauty,' the petty officer Wren said, smiling. 'My name's Sonia, what's your name?' The other girls looked on, grinning.

Weston, now wishing he hadn't removed some of his clothes and undone his belt, pulled his trousers up higher and didn't answer.

'Very well, I don't care I'm going to call you Brylcream. Say hello to Brylcream girls, don't you think he's handsome? What do you think girls shall we have his pants off and see what he's hiding in there?' Weston took a tight hold on his trousers and awaited the onslaught.

His Guardian Angel looked on, pleased with the situation. Her charge was extremely shy of girls, so this chance meeting with the Wrens could only be good for him. He could only learn and gain from this hands-on experience. He was certainly going to need all the knowledge of women he could get before being thrown in at the deep end with the experienced ladies of Bravemouth.

The Wrens dropped upon Weston like a swarm of locusts. It was all over within a few seconds.

'Right girls hold him,' Sonia said. Two of the girls sat on Weston's chest and the other three girls held him down. Within a couple of minutes Weston had been stripped. They stood back and looked at him. The petty officer Wren, smiling, took his.........in her hand, which despite all that had happened to him had risen to the occasion.

This was a shock for Weston, who'd not even had a girl friend. The very moment her hand closed around his.........Weston's entire body began to shake and tingle with feelings he had never experienced before.

'We can all have a go at shagging him, in turn,' Sonia said, throwing her panties aside and looking at her friends, 'but I'm going first.' Rebecca the Guardian Angel looked on, pleased that the new powers she'd bestowed upon Weston were working. They had certainly enabled Weston to go from being a shy virgin into a fully accomplished stud in one unplanned bout of sexual intercourse.

So began the strange new life Paul Edward Weston discovered was going to be his norm from this day onwards.

Chapter Two

Friday 11th May 1951. Three days earlier.

The strange events which were making such a huge upheaval in Paul Edward Weston's life began when God's chief trouble shooter materialised in the Head of the Earth Department's office. Jeremy, the Head of the Earth Department, got to his feet, knowing only too well that this was Archangel Morwenna.

'A personal visit from you is indeed a great honour, Archangel Morwenna,' he managed to say, his trembling voice breaking the eerie silence. 'Would you care to sit and how can I help you?'

She gave him a sideways quizzical glance and, pushing him aside, she chose to sit in his personal chair.

'You may call me Morwenna and please don't stand on ceremony, sit down.' She nodded to the hard chair he kept for underlings the other side of his desk.

'May I inquire the reason for your visit, Morwenna?'

'Yes, indeed you may,' she snapped, her attitude changing. 'The Good Lord's displeased with the Earth Department. The crux of the matter is, what are you doing, or to put it bluntly, what have you done in regard to answering the prayers of Mrs April Ferrimins and her so-called friends? I'm waiting, Jeremy,' she set her eyes on him. 'What have you done?' Jeremy flushed with embarrassment, his department had achieved nothing positive in that particular quest and she would know at once if he lied; he would have to tell her the truth.

'We've searched every corner of the Earth, Morwenna, I've sent my most able Angels out on this quest and all have failed. The Good Lord's set us an impossible task this time and why in heaven does he want to answer this stupid woman and her friend's prayers for anyway?'

'I don't know why, Jerry. The Good Lord has these fads every now and again; it's not up to us to criticise. As for the task being impossible, I don't agree, the Good Lord wouldn't set a task that couldn't be completed. Somewhere out there, there's a person who resembles this Mrs Ferrimins' long lost love? Do you have anyone out on the task at the moment?'

'Yes, I have one of my brightest workers on the task, Angel Rebecca.' He coughed to clear his throat, feeling uncomfortable by his answer. 'She's very reliable, despite her outrageous behaviour, and I thought it would help her to earn her wings.'

'Rebecca, not that excuse for an Angel; the one who overeats and prefers to play a guitar to her harp?'

'I'm afraid so, Morwenna, but she did pass her Guardian Angel exams with honours.' He noticed a look of disapproval pass over the Archangel's face. 'I shall have her recalled at once.' He took a deep breath and thought, poor Angel Rebecca, she will never earn her wings now.

Angel Rebecca was exactly like the Archangel had described her; she was an out-and-out rebel, albeit an extremely nice one. Rebecca was what would be known in human terms as a tomboy or a think-for-yourself girl. Nevertheless, despite all her faults, she had worked extremely hard at her exams and to everyone's surprise she passed with honours to become a Guardian Angel, first class. However, before she could claim and wear her wings, she not only had to be trustworthy, but she had to complete a first class assignment.

Rebecca was well aware that lots of the other Angels had failed dismally in the particular task she had been given. She also knew she had only been given this task to get her out of the Head of the Earth Department's hair. However, this had made her more determined than ever to succeed.

Filled with the joys of spring, Rebecca skipped up the winding petal strewn path to the Earth office.

'Watch this,' she shouted to her friends sitting on the lawn.' She attempted to do a cartwheel, but her action failed dismally and she finished up flat on her bottom, much to her friends' amusement.

Ignoring their laughter, she pushed open the door to the Head of Department's office without knocking and walked in. She froze in midstride at the sight of Archangel Morwenna.

'Sorry Chief, er, sir, I wasn't aware…sorry, your Archness… I didn't realise, ever so sorry.'

'Rebecca, don't go away, I was about to recall you, I want to give you a break from your tiresome task.'

'Thank you for your concern, sir. However, I've completed my, as you call it, tiresome assignment, sir.'

'You have?' The Head of Department looked at her in amazement. However, there were questions in his eyes. 'This is wonderful news Rebecca, the Good Lord will be pleased.' He looked over the top of his glasses in an inquisitorial manner. 'Sure you have the right man?'

'Yes, sir, an Englishman by the name of Paul Edward Weston, this man fulfils all the Good Lord's requirements, take a look, sir.' She waved her hand at the blank office wall. A picture of a tall young man with tousled hair appeared. 'Compare him with the German gentleman, Ernst Metzler, sir.' She waved her hand again and a second picture of a young man appeared. 'They are as alike as two peas in a pod, sir. They even have the same birthmark, sir.' She waved her hand again and a close up of the two men's naked torsos appeared, revealing, just below the navels on both men, a raised bird in flight shaped birthmark.

'Yes you are right, these two men are identical in every way,' Archangel Morwenna said. 'You have done well to succeed where the others have failed, Angel Rebecca.' Archangel Morwenna got to her feet. 'This certainly lets me and you off the hook, Jeremy. Plus this means promotion for you, Rebecca, well done.' She shot a sideways glance at the Head of Department. 'I want Guardian Angel first class Rebecca to be appointed Paul Edward Weston's Guardian Angel; that young man is going to be your sole responsibility from this moment. I think congratulations are in order. Yes, my dear you may collect your wings and wear them with pride, you've proved yourself a worthy Guardian.'

'Thank you very much, your Archness and... and ... and you too, sir.'

'I wouldn't give thanks if I were you, Rebecca,' the Head of the Earth Department said. 'Your life from this day on is going to be nothing but hard work and I want you to throw that stupid guitar away, put yourself on a diet and start behaving like a real Angel. You heard the Archangel, the Good Lord's put you in charge of the poor young man who is going to take on and satisfy the ladies of Bravemouth, his name is Paul Edward Weston. That poor fellow is being sent by God to a town in Cornwall called Bravemouth, he's being sent in answer to the prayers of a certain Mrs April Ferrimins and her friends who are all members of some stupidly named "Five Leaf Clover Club". Neither Archangel Morwenna or myself agree with this assignment, to put it mildly; this woman and her friends only want a man to gratify their sexual needs. Why the Good Lord is answering their prayers is a mystery.'

Archangel Morwenna stood and fluttered her wings.

'I must go Jerry, I can't wait to give the Good Lord the news about Angel Rebecca's success. Good luck Rebecca, hope your new wings will be strong enough.' She gave Rebecca's rotund figure a searching look with a smile on her lips. 'The Head of the Earth Department will see you later and give you your orders.' She raised her arms and the next moment there was a flash of bright light and she was gone.

'Wish she wouldn't arrive and leave like that,' the Head of the Earth Department said, and Rebecca, don't forget you must endow your charge with all the new powers he is going to need. Such as being able to heal quickly and the ability to satisfy any woman who looks into his eyes, with the exception of any young ladies which he himself loves.'

Rebecca, wondering what she had let herself in for, thanked the Head of the Earth Department and left his office to collect her wings.

Chapter Three

Friday 11th May 1951.

At the very moment Rebecca had left to collect her wings, an old but sleek black painted motor yacht named "Mother's Boys" was passing between the two castles guarding Bravemouth harbour. It sailed up the harbour and anchored behind a classical white motor yacht, under the wooded slopes of the East Side of the harbour. Its crew, a mismatch of two young and two older men, were summoned to the owner's cabin for a briefing. The owner was Mrs Ruby Kingsley, a fifty-year-old attractive red headed woman. She'd arrived in Bravemouth to execute her plan of kidnapping the wife of millionaire Michael Ferrimins and to hold her ransom for £75,000. This 'JOB' as she called it was to be her first since she'd fallen out with her criminal husband. However, now she'd had another look at her gang as they filed into her cabin, she began to have second thoughts. The two younger men were her sons, albeit by different fathers and were as opposite as chalk and cheese. Dennis her eldest son was tall and thin, while her other son Graham was grossly overweight; he must have weighed at least twenty stone or 280 lb. Laurel and Hardy will never be dead while Dennis and Graham are alive, she thought as she looked at them; they're certainly not the brightest sparklers in the packet. The others were two most unscrupulous types she'd picked up in the London underworld. Charles was a small well-spoken weasel of a man. The other was Harry, a tall heavily built cockney with tiny eyes and brown hair; it was rumoured, but not substantiated, that he had murdered someone in his dark past.

Mrs Ruby Kingsley went over her plan with them in

fine detail several times. Afterwards, to put the first part of her plan into operation, she sent her thin son Dennis ashore wearing an RAF uniform. Mrs Ruby Kingsley was well aware of the fact that there was quite a lot of RAF boys in Bravemouth and, knowing that the RAF were forever changing their personnel, she knew no one would question him. His orders were to rent a holiday home for a few days as close to the Ferrimins' household as possible, so he could watch what was happening there and report back to his mother. She herself planned to take up residence in the Bravemouth hotel, where Dennis could report to her daily. The other three members of the gang were to return with the yacht to a creek near Falmouth where she had rented a house. When they got there they were to start work on a large white van she'd procured to make it look like the ambulance she planned to use for the kidnapping. The police, she figured out, would find it hard to stop and question an ambulance.

Chapter Four

Friday 11th May 1951 12:30pm.

April Ferrimins was in a terrible mood. Nigel, her new boyfriend, a naval officer she'd met in the yacht club and who had promised so much, had failed her dismally at the first jump. The poor fellow had the effrontery to have a heart attack while making love to her. Consequently, in April's eyes, he was to blame for a day she'd really looked forward to being ruined.

Returning home still angry with the world in general, she sat sulking, feeling like a cat which had lost a mouse, in the taxi outside her home waiting for the driver to open the door for her. She handed him a five pound note without speaking and ran down the path to the front door of her house holding her dress, which she'd not found time to button up together. In her impetuosity to open the door she dropped her keys and instead of picking them up she kicked them into the side garden and proceeded to bang with her fists on the door. Her daily help opened the door and April actually fell into the hall, her shoulder catching a picture on the wall which dropped to the floor.

'Bloody hell, that's all I need,' she said, glaring at Kathleen, her daily help, who'd been vacuuming the floor. 'Put that picture back Kathy and it's about time you were finished in here, it's turned twelve o'clock.'

Kathleen gave her employer a scurrilous look, which took in April's unkempt appearance, while she picked up the picture. Wherever she's been, she left in a flaming hurry, she thought, she's no bra or for that matter any underclothes on. Wonder what's happened.

'Careful, Kathy, that frame's old and I like that picture, it holds special memories for me.' The picture

17

was of five young ladies dressed in bathing suits standing together on a beach, a brass plate on the frame read "The Five Leaf Clovers. Summer holidays Falmouth 1935."

April Ferrimins, with her shoulder length straight blond hair, large green eyes, long legs and good looks, was most men's perfect woman. Wherever she went, men would stare at her with unbridled lust. Nevertheless, despite her looks, the few extra marital affairs she'd been engaged in since she'd moved from the colonies to live amongst her friends in Bravemouth had been disasters.

April stood over Kathleen, until she replaced the picture to her satisfaction and, without another word, she ran down the stairs to her bedroom. Her house like all the others in the area had been built with the views of the harbour in mind; consequently the bedrooms were placed downstairs and the reception rooms above. Holding back her tears of disappointment, she tore the unbuttoned dress from her body and threw it on the floor. Frustrated to the point of screaming, she yet again went over the morning's events in her mind. Oh Lord please help me, she thought, oh why, why did Nigel have to go the same way, he's the fourth man this month. I've been cursed I know I have. She relieved her feelings by taking a vicious kick at her ruined dress. I'm as beautiful as ever, so why don't I enjoy myself, why do all the men I get now let me down? I don't know what to think, why do they lose their erections when they get into bed with me? Still I can't be bothered worrying about Nigel and his heart. I'm going to accept Edwina's invitation to go riding with her.

She dressed again, this time in her riding clothes. She ran up the stairs to the hall. Her daily help was still there cleaning the windows. However, April was far too cross with the world in general to exchange small

18

talk with her. Wanting time to think, she walked across her large drawing room, opened the French windows and stepped out into the relative cool of the wide veranda of her harbour side home.

Chapter Five

Friday 11th May 1951 12:45pm.

Dennis, or Stan Laurel, as his mother thought of him, wasn't as unintelligent as she thought. He wasted no time in renting a small empty holiday home in the road above and overlooking Mrs Ferrimins' home. However, his mind full of intrigue about this Mrs April Ferrimins, he made up his mind to try to see her. To this end he walked down the road to Rowanberry House with the intention of knocking on the door and asking her the whereabouts of some fictitious person. However, his plans changed when he saw the ring of keys, with a label stating Rowanberry House, lying where April had kicked them. He picked them up and ran back to the rented holiday home to phone his mother. She was over the moon at this stroke of luck and she told him to go into town and have the keys duplicated at once and to replace the originals where he'd found them. She couldn't believe her luck.

He took them to the local iron mongers, where the owner, without asking any questions concerning the keys, duplicated them all.

Later in that afternoon he stood by April's garden gate and threw the original keys onto the lawn where he had found them. That was when another stroke of luck came his way. He met, albeit by accident, Mrs Ferrimins' daily help, Kathleen. She had come out to see what he was up to; before she could ask him he disarmed her by smiling broadly.

'Who lives in this big house?' he asked her.

'Mrs high and mighty herself lives here: Mrs bloody April snobby Ferrimins.' Dennis, without even trying, was being given all the facts he needed to know,

including the fact that all the houses like Mrs
Ferrimins' home, built overlooking the harbour, were
called upside down houses. They had their bedrooms
downstairs and the living quarters above to catch the
view. Kathleen even let him know which bedroom Mrs
Ferrimins slept in.

Chapter six

Friday 11th May 1951.

April, feeling low in spirit, was sitting on her veranda looking over but not seeing the beautiful harbour of Bravemouth. Her mind a seething whirlpool of unanswered questions. I'm going to have one more go at praying, she thought, sighing deeply, even though I know it will be a waste of time.

She closed her eyes and once again repeated her prayer. Hoping and hoping this time it would be answered.

''Tis that woman, Missus Todmarsh-Rivers, she be here to see ee Madam,' her daily help announced in her rich Cornish accent.

'Kathleen, I will not tell you again. You must say Mrs Todmarsh-Rivers is here to see you, madam.' She sighed. 'Thank you Kathleen, show her out to the veranda will you? Seeing the weather's so pleasant, you can serve our coffee out here.'

Jemima Todmarsh-Rivers looked as if she'd just stepped from the cover of Vogue magazine, her dark shoulder length hair left loose and wearing a tight red silk shirt a black skirt and black high heeled shoes.

Jemima and April had been the closest of friends for many years. They smiled and greeted one another with meaningful hugs and kisses.

'I didn't expect to see you today, Jemmy darling.'

'I thought I'd pop down for a word or two, I saw you go by in the taxi at noon, what happened to your romp, sorry your rendezvous, with that naval fellow? Why are you dressed for riding? Why aren't you wearing one of those new designer dresses I thought you bought especially for today?'

'It was awful, Jemmy. Nigel the selfish bastard had a heart attack. I walked out on him. I've been cursed, he's now the fifth man who's let me down. I left the hotel at once, phoned for an ambulance for him and took the taxi home. That's another of my affairs washed down the drain. I'm fed up, Jemmy, I don't know what's gone wrong with me. I'm sure I've been cursed. Oh to hell with him, I don't want to talk about it.'

Although opposite in colouring, Jemima with her dark eyes and hair and April with her green eyes and fair hair, they were both tall beautiful women. They were probably two of the finest products of the public and finishing school system of upper crust Britain in the pre-war years. They stood looking over to the far side of the harbour towards a lovely classical white motor yacht.

'Was there no way you could have made it to the cocktail party aboard her on Wednesday, Jemmy?'

'No, sorry darling, it was out of our hands. David is in the air force and he had to accept the invitation to the Group Captain's get together, it was as good as a direct order.'

'Couldn't he have gone alone? He's a big boy now.'

'No, be reasonable, April. I had no choice in the matter; the Group Captain's wife was expecting me.'

'Jemmy darling, I missed you.'

'I don't think so; April Berkshire's never missed anyone.' (Her friend always called April by her maiden name.) 'However, may I be presumptuous and inquire how you came by the invitation? I wasn't aware that you knew anyone with a luxury motor yacht.'

'Admiral Noel Firnback brought them over personally. Apparently, he knows Michael rather well; they served together during the war. He'd apparently met a mutual friend at some reunion or other who told him Michael and I had moved to Bravemouth.'

'An Admiral indeed, was he a tall dark handsome pirate kind of a man?'

'Good grief no darling, just the opposite, he was a short plump old man. Typical retired officer. The old fart actually took me in his arms and tried to kiss me, his hands were everywhere. He reeked of whisky and tobacco. I've grown to hate old men, Jemmy.' The daily help brought out the coffee. The conversation lapsed while she placed the tray on the table.

'Leave it Kathleen, I shall pour,' April said. 'You can get on with your duties, you've a lot to do.'

The young woman stuck her tongue out behind her employer's back and left.

'I really wanted you to come to the yacht, darling. You would insist on marrying David for love and now look at you, penniless and married to the air force. Why didn't you marry for money, like the rest of the "Five Leaf Clovers"?'

'What, and be like you lot, looking for sex in every man you meet and going to bed every night with an old man, I don't think so, and forget money Daddy's got plenty. Ugh, I cannot stand old men they always seem to have bad breath, makes my skin creep when I think about it. Regarding me marrying David for love? What about yourself, what would you have done if your handsome Ernst hadn't returned to Germany in 1939? Would you have married for love?'

Jemima had touched on April's one and only weak spot. April's eyes filled with the deep emotion she always felt whenever her lost love was mentioned.

'Poor Ernst. You're right, I certainly loved that man. Do you know, even after all these years, I can still see him in my mind's eye, his long unruly hair falling across his lovely face.' She looked at her friend and shook her head. 'Wasn't it tragic? Why did he have to

24

be shot down and killed, over his beloved England? War's so horrid; people in love on opposite sides, through no fault of their own. He loved everything British you know. I called him my Eagle, because he had a birthmark of that shape on his tummy. Plus he was only happy when he was skiing down the steepest pistes, climbing the highest peaks, gliding or flying. If he'd asked me, before he'd left for Germany, even though I was still at the Swiss finishing school, I would have married him. However, he didn't and it's all water under the bridge now.' Jemima had heard this story many times before and, realising she'd gone too far, kept quiet and looked across the harbour while she gathered her thoughts.

'I didn't mean to upset you, April darling. Come along sweetie, shall we change the subject? Tell me? Who did you take to the yacht Cocktail party with you in the end?'

April wiped away a tear before answering.

'Edwina, she's over from the states for a few weeks and Lucy and Judy also came.'

'Sorry I didn't know Edwina was in Bravemouth,' Jemima said, 'I bet the yacht crew enjoyed having you lot of beautiful nymphomaniacs on the loose. All four of you were stupid marrying those old decrepit men. Everything was fine and dandy, while you in the colonies with those young attachés and officers flying in and out on a regular basis to satisfy your needs. However, things are very different now you're in Bravemouth.'

'Jemmy, don't go on, and we are not nymphomaniacs, we just enjoy sex. It was great fun on the yacht, even if there were no young studs around. Pity you missed it. Don't you think it's wonderful, that Edwina, Judy, Lucy, and us two, can say we are still friends after all these years. We did have some fantastic

25

times during our boarding school days. I shall never forget those wonderful holidays we spent at your family home in Falmouth. Remember the time your mother bought each of us a ring.'

'Of course, I wear mine all the time.' She held her hand out and they compared their eighteen-carat gold signet rings with the cloverleaf motif.

'Do the others wear theirs?'

'I think so, you can ask Edwina, she'll be here shortly. By the way I missed you at church on Sunday, we all prayed together for an uplift to our mediocre lives.'

'I've never heard such rubbish, what mediocre lives? Michael's away in London most of the time, so you're more or less a free agent and you're all millionaires. The only things you lot are short of is a full and meaningful sex life?'

'Well, Jemmy, you may think what you like, but we all prayed for an uplift to our lives, I think we need one, our lives are meaningless without sexual gratification.'

Here we go again, Jemima thought. I'd better change the subject.

'Where is Edwina?'

'I'm not sure, I've not seen her since I returned from you know where. Perhaps she walked up to get my car from the garage; she came down by train, her car's being exchanged for a new one. She'll be here in a moment. She's arranged to go riding at Judy's stables later. I'm going to accompany her now, seeing I've nothing better to do.'

They heard April's daily open the front door and the next moment her sister Edwina, together with two other women, came out onto the terrace.

'I walked into Judy and Lucy in town,' Edwina said, speaking in a deep husky voice, 'so I invited them back for drinks, April darling. Hello, Jemmy, good to see you again, so the whole gang's here, isn't this simply spiffing.' April and Jemmy gave their friends the usual hug and kiss greeting. Edwina was dressed like April in a white long sleeved frilly fronted blouse, tight riding trousers and knee length polished tan boots. Although not quite as tall as her sister, she was still a beautiful woman. The only exception between them was her long red hair, which at the moment she had tied back in a ponytail.

'Edwina, what do you think about convening a meeting of the Clover club, this is the first time we've all been together for months?' Judy said. She was an Amazon of a woman dressed in a pair of dark slacks and a sleeveless button down white top which was not fully fastened.

'Yes of course, what a good idea,' Edwina said. 'Will you take the minutes, Lucy?'

'Yes, but remember this, I've not got last year's minutes, we shall have to take them as read and I shall need paper and a pen.'

'I'll get you a pen and some paper, Lucy,' April said.

Lucy Carrington-Townley was a small, tiny petite woman with large dark eyes and short black hair worn in a page boy style. She was dressed in a short breast revealingly white sundress and high heeled white sandals.

'I wasn't aware you were over from the states, Eddy,' Jemima said. 'How's your husband keeping and how's the high life in London?'

'London's fine,' Edwina said. 'However, my husband, Franklin Junior, what a bloody title for a useless American fart. He only uses that appendage between his legs for peeing now.'

'Edwina, don't talk about your beloved husband like that,' April said.

'Why not, it's the truth and what beloved husband?'

'Stop it Eddy, it's in very poor taste,' April said, her face turning red.

'Bollocks, April, and why aren't you wearing one of those new dresses you bought especially for today? What happened?'

'I'll tell you all about it on the way to Judy's. I've decided to go riding with you after all.' Edwina smiled and poured herself a cup of coffee.

'Martinis all round ladies?' April said. 'Good, I'll go and make them.' She walked towards the French windows.

'Jemmy, perhaps you're the person to help me?' Edwina said sitting down. 'I want, no I need, a good man, I feel so bloody horny in this heat. Will your David be free for a romp with me this afternoon?'

'No he bloody well will not! How dare you, you rotten egg? Don't you go near him, Edwina! You keep away from my David.'

'Why, Jemmy? Do you think he'd let me…?'

'Why not, he's only a man, what chance would he have, with a scheming bitch like you?'

'Edwina, stop it, don't be so horrid to Jemima,' Lucy said.

'Keep out of this and mind your own business, Lucy. So you think I'm a scheming bitch do you, Jemmy?' Edwina snarled, giving her friend a cold look. 'You lot can all go to hell, I know what I need and it's a bloody good fucking and I mean a real good fucking, but I suppose I shall have to settle for a wild gallop across the meadows on one of your stallions, Judy.' Her face changed, she smiled mischievously. 'That is unless your Monte is free this afternoon.'

'Monte?' Judy laughed. 'That would be a bloody waste of time; he's gone over the top queer now, he's into bondage, whips and handcuffs, and all that rubbish,

28

without my participation in his stupid sex games of course.'

'Do you know, girls?' Edwina said sighing. 'I'm sick of being in the company of old men. I think what we all need is a young, preferably handsome virile untiring stud. Got any ideas girls? How's your George performing at the moment, Lucy?'

'My George? He'd be no good to you Eddy, he's got a soft five inches in the middle of his tassel. He's done nothing for me for years.'

'Five inches in the middle, why, how long is it?'

'It might make three inches, fully roused, but it's not been that way for years.' They laughed.

'Sure there are no sexy young men around here, Jemmy?' Edwina asked, this time using a more friendly tone.

'Yes I'm absolutely sure, they are all spoken for in Bravemouth darling. You could try praying like April, for what good it does. I'm surprised you didn't find someone to fit the bill on the yacht.'

'No hopes of that my dear darling,' Edwina said, mockingly. 'The entire crew were in my opinion puffs, not real men and as far as praying goes I've tried that and it's a bloody waste of time.'

'I'm not so sure about that Eddy,' April said, returning with the Martinis. 'I pray all the time.'

'Still at it are you, April?' Edwina snapped. 'I must say those nuns at the boarding school have a lot to answer for.'

'Now Eddy don't you go on,' April said, 'you know I've always been religious, however I do agree with all that's been said about old men. Michael's far too old for me, he's rushing headlong into sixty-five; he still thinks he can still manage sex, but he doesn't give me satisfaction. I want a man like Eddy said, a young man, one not too experienced in the ways of life, someone I

29

can take in hand. I'm sick and tired of these sordid affairs I've been having.'

'You will find no one like that in Bravemouth,' Jemima said.

'I'm going to keep on praying until my prayers are answered,' April said.

'Looks to me, only your David is available at the moment, Jemmy,' Edwina said.

'My David's definitely not available, especially to you, Edwina,' Jemima snapped.

Chapter Seven

Friday 11th May 1951.

The Head of the Earth Department returned with the Good Lord's orders for Rebecca, regarding Paul Edward Weston's mission.

'Send Paul Edward Weston's Guardian Angel to see me at once,' he said to his secretary.

Angel Rebecca, for once without her guitar and for the first time wearing her wings, walked into his office.

'Thank you for being so prompt Rebecca, take a seat while I explain in detail what the Good Lord wants you to do. To begin with, I've been told to inform you that you have been given unequivocal authority over everything and everyone on this mission, no other Guardian Angel will interfere with your work. Your number one task will be, as always, to make sure nothing inappropriate happens to your charge: Paul Edward Weston. He's going to be upsetting some very rich and powerful men. They certainly won't approve of him having sexual affairs with their wives. Which after all is the only reason God is sending him there.'

'Wives? Wives in the plural, sir, I thought he was only being sent to Mrs April Ferrimins, sir?'

'No, no, no, he's also being sent to gratify the needs of her three friends as well. They are all members of some fraternity club know as the "Five Leaf Clovers".'

'Why of all the people in the world has the Good Lord chosen Paul Edward Weston for this task, he's so shy?'

'Simple Rebecca, because he looks like Ernst Metzler, April Ferrimins' long lost love; there is no other reason. Shy of women or not, he is now the Good Lord's chosen one. The Good Lord also wants you to

31

give him all the powers he will need to make him an untiring woman-pleasing stud. Your first task is to get him redirected from his Northern Ireland posting to the RAF base in Bravemouth, Cornwall. After you have sorted that out, endow him with his new powers and report back to me. I have also just been informed that a gang of criminals have just arrived in Bravemouth aboard a yacht. They plan to kidnap this Mrs Ferrimins and hold her for ransom. So you will probably have that to contend with as well. Good luck with your mission Rebecca.'

Rebecca set to work at once in the RAF personnel offices. Within a few minutes new orders had been sent out redirecting Weston to the RAF base in Bravemouth.

'The first part of your orders has been carried out, sir,' Angel Rebecca said, reporting back. 'Paul Edward Weston has been given his new powers and he's been redirected to Bravemouth.'

'That's all for now then Rebecca, report back to me at regular intervals. Go now to Bravemouth and work out how you're going to introduce you're lowly airman into the restricted life of these upper class women.'

Chapter Eight

Friday 11th May 1951.

Rebecca wandered around the Cornish town of Bravemouth, its beautiful natural harbour guarded by two castles where the river Bravy joined the sea. She found Rowanberry House without a lot of difficulty and, hoping to learn something about the ladies of Bravemouth, she made herself comfortable by sitting on the rail that ran around the Ferrimins' terrace. She became enthralled listening to April and her four friends talking. She sincerely hoped to hear something that would help her get Weston to mix with these upper crust women. *I suppose the first thing I should do is to find out who's who among this lot?*

The five ladies were sitting around a table and it didn't take her long to work out who they were; the good looking blonde was obviously April and the equally good looking red head her sister, Edwina.

'Have you paper and a pen, Lucy?' Edwina inquired. Lucy nodded.

So that's it; the small one is Lucy and the big one Judy.

That just leaves the dark haired one in the red shirt, she must be Jemima. Rebecca was now able to put a name to each one.

'Good we'll make a start,' Edwina said. 'I declare this, our twenty-fifth meeting of the "Five Leaf Clover club", open. I propose we regard last year's minutes as read. Will one of you second my proposal?' The lady with the pen and paper put her hand up.

'Good, thank you, Lucy, are there any questions?'

'It was suggested last year that we should hold a séance,' Judy, the large well-proportioned woman, said.

'Thank you, Judy,' Edwina said. 'But for goodness sake, why on Earth should we hold a séance?'

'No reason at all Eddy,' Judy said. 'I think this would be an ideal opportunity and it could be a good laugh.'

'I don't want to go indoors and sit in the dark,' Jemima said.

'We can hold it out here, Jemima,' Judy said. 'We don't have to be in the dark. Edwina, you're the senior by a few months, so you can act as the medium.'

Edwina sat at the end of the table, while the other four under Judy's direction sat either side, holding hands.

'Right, stop giggling,' Edwina said. 'That means you, Lucy, come along girls, concentrate.'

'I'll make a start on the minutes by putting the time and place down,' Lucy said. 'Take note it is exactly one o'clock Friday 11th May and the meeting is taking place on April's terrace.'

If they are going to hold a séance, Rebecca thought, I can use this to my advantage. She rushed into Edwina's mind, who suddenly went white and collapsed with her head on the table.

'Stop playing about Eddy,' April said.

'Look at her,' Judy said, 'she's as white as a sheet?' However, before Judy could answer, Rebecca put them all into a deep dreamless sleep while she delved in their minds. She soon discovered all she wanted to know, regarding Weston being introduced into their way of life.

Her work there was now finished; however, just to let the ladies know they'd disturbed something in the spirit world, she told each in turn to undress and then to sleep on until three o'clock.

'Well that was a right old waste of time, nothing happened,' said Judy, sitting up and opening her eyes.

34

'I don't know about that, look its three o'clock,' Lucy said, looking at her watch. 'We've been asleep for over two hours, and where the hell are my clothes I'm naked, no we are all bloody naked?'

'I'm naked too, I don't like this, I had my new silk shirt on, oh look at it now, take you feet off it, April,' Jemima said, her face quite ashen.

'We've lost a full two hours and we are all naked. I think we've dabbled into something that should have been well and truly left alone,' April said.

'Is the meeting closed,' Lucy said, slipping her sundress back on.

Edwina, who was still fully dressed, came round and stared at them.

'What on Earth's happened, why are you naked, are we having this séance are not?' she said.

'Shall I put what happened in the minutes?' Lucy asked.

'Yes put it all in, that's if you can remember it, I can't,' Jemima said. 'You never know it might stop us from dabbling into the unknown again next year.'

'I'm going home,' said Judy, struggling to fasten her top. 'Are you coming, Lucy? There's a meddlesome spirit around this house and I don't want it attaching itself to me. Thank you for the drinks, April darling, will I be seeing you and Eddy at the farm later?'

'Yes, of course,' Edwina said, 'I think we both need a good gallop on one of your stallions across the meadows, are you joining us, Jemmy?'

'No thank you, I think I shall stop here and keep my eye on David.'

With kisses and hugs all round, Judy and Lucy left.

Rebecca had really hit the jackpot; she'd discovered during her probing that Jemima's husband was the commanding officer of the RAF Marine Craft Base in Bravemouth. She'd also discovered that April needed some work doing, which her daily help couldn't manage. I'm going to get Jemima's husband to send Weston to do those jobs for her. Her old lost love and Weston are so alike, her eyes will do the rest.

'Will David be in his office in the morning, Jemmy?' April asked.

'Yes, he's in the office most Saturday mornings, why?'

'I'm going to see him, I want to ask him to send one of his boys to do those jobs for me, why I didn't think of him before amazes me. You know I've asked every handyman in Bravemouth to do those jobs, but they are all too busy. I'm playing tennis with Lucy in the morning so I will call in on my way to the club.'

'You can always ask him, I suppose,' Jemima said, questioning whether her best friend, like Edwina, had some ulterior motive in seeing her husband.

Chapter Nine

The following morning, Squadron Leader, ex-Battle of Britain pilot, David Todmarsh-Rivers, the commanding officer of the RAF Marine Craft Unit in Bravemouth, entered his office and dropped thankfully into his chair. He lit his first cigarette of the day and drew the smoke in deeply; this was an enjoyable ritual he'd indulged in for many years, his first "fag," as he called it. He was a handsome man of around thirty-nine years, six foot tall with dark brown eyes and thick dark wavy hair turning grey at the temples, giving him a most distinguished, almost theatrical appearance.

He reluctantly stubbed his cigarette into the ashtray and lifted from the in-tray the personnel files of the four new men who were being posted into his unit.

He read through them all and he threw the last one on top of the others in his out-tray. Written across it was: AC1 Paul Edward Weston No2486777. Scowling, he picked it up and read through it again. He glanced at his watch, it was eleven o'clock. Sighing deeply, he thought bloody long morning, thank goodness it's Saturday, and only half day, if it gets any hotter.

Rebecca drifted around the squadron leaders office; she'd gone there to make doubly sure he sent Paul Edward Weston to April Ferrimins' home the following Monday. She'd watched him scowl, and she wondered why. It was only when he read through Weston's file one of his clerks knocked and opened his office door.

'Excuse me, sir, sorry to disturb you, sir.'

'Yes, Wittingham?'

'Mrs Ferrimins is here to see you, sir.'

Rebecca wasn't surprised to see him leap from his

desk, adjust his tie and quickly run a comb through his hair before she came in.

April breezed in wearing an extremely short, low cut white tennis dress, ankle socks and tennis shoes. The promiscuous way she was showing her body, plus her vivacious personality, filled the office.

'April darling? Good grief. I didn't expect...you look... er... w-what can I do for you? Like a coffee?'

'No thank you, David darling.' She bent forward, pushing her breasts up and staring into his eyes. 'I've only a brief moment, David, Lucy's waiting outside in her car.' She laughed. 'Holding up the traffic I imagine, we are on our way to the tennis club.'

I didn't think you'd be sweeping chimneys in that get up, he thought, letting his eyes move from her face to her breasts then on to her extra long suntanned legs, which in that short dress, went up and up forever. Hell, he thought, you might be my wife's best friend, but you do strange things to me, I could really shag you rotten, April. That was the moment he noticed the clerk was still standing in the door enjoying the view.

'Get out, Wittingham, and close the bloody door,' he bellowed.

'That was rather harsh of you, David,' April said, 'the poor boy was doing no harm.' He ignored April's protestation.

'Jemmy tells me that you enjoyed yourselves last week on the classic yacht, April.'

'Yes, we had the most spiffing time, pity poor Jemmy missed out.'

'Quite. Quite, sorry about that, nevertheless Jemmy had to accompany me, it was most important. What can I do for you, April?'

'Darling David, excuse me disturbing you at your work, but Jemmy suggested that I should ask you,' she lied. 'Could you possibly spare one of your little men to do some ever so tedious tasks for me, around the home.' She walked across to the window and looked out over the river. 'Love the view from here, darling.'

It's not as good as the view I'm getting from here, he thought, hell I could really shag you, April. She smiled as if she could read his mind and she slipped her arm around his shoulders.

'You know the sort of things, David darling, horrid jobs, such as moving furniture around, taking carpets up, putting things away in the attic etc, jobs my daily can't manage. I really miss having a man about the house, but of course my Michael would be next to useless if he were here. He hates to dirty his hands.'

David the brave RAF squadron leader, who had fought against German bombers and fighters in his Spitfire without even experiencing fear, was now well and truly scared. His body had slipped out of his control and he couldn't stop it responding to her. He like most men had always wanted to make love with her, but no she was taboo, she was his wife's best friend? He fell back into his chair picked up a piece of paper and fanned his face.

'Yes of course, anything for you, April, well anything within my power, will Monday be alright?'

She purposely undid the top two buttons of her dress, allowing more of her cleavage to show, before leaning over his desk and kissing him full on the lips.

'Thank you ever so much, David darling, you are a true friend, will I be seeing you and Jemmy at the yacht club later?' She turned away, disappointed that all her efforts had failed to arouse him, perhaps she really was losing her charm with men?

'No afraid not, April, we are away visiting Jemmy's family in Falmouth until Sunday evening.'

She's not leaving like this, Rebecca thought. Show this teasing woman what a real man is like, she suggested to his mind.

He leapt to his feet, and April willingly offered herself into his strong arms. He pressed her down on his desk and kissed her long and hard. That was the moment the enormity of what he was doing struck him and he let her go.

'David, David, oh, David, I didn't expect that, you've taken my breath away. I don't know what to say. You are all man, you beast, I don't know you are a very naughty boy.' She straightened her hair, adjusted her breasts and brushed her dress down. 'Must say I enjoyed being kissed by you, David, it was super, even though you are my best friend's husband. Do you know you've got me all excited, you beast. I'd much rather go to bed with you now than play tennis.'

Wondering why he'd lost his iron control, he dropped into his chair. He'd have rather been in a dog fight with two German fighters than try and explain to his wife what he'd done.

'I'm sorry, April, I don't know what came over me? I do love Jemima dearly, you know. Gosh, April, I'm really sorry. I hope I didn't hurt you. Whatever you do, don't tell Jemmy, I must have had a brainstorm, or something.'

'That was no brainstorm, David, you've wanted to do that for a long time. I can tell from the way a man looks at me.' She smiled. 'Don't let it worry you. I thought it rather nice of you; I never dreamt I'd get a kiss from Jemmy's man of iron. Relax, David. I wouldn't hurt my best friend.' She stood in the doorway and laughed. 'Until Monday, David, but don't forget, I now hold an IOU on you for you to do something for me in payment for that kiss. However, for the time being, what time on Monday do you think you will be sending this little man over?'

'It'll be after lunch, shall we say sometime around

one thirty.'

'After lunch Monday, I shall be waiting, you, you beast.' She blew him a kiss.

He followed her out into the street and opened the car door for her. April smiled and for her friend's benefit she gave him a peck of a kiss on the cheek before climbing in.

'Care to join us in a game, David?' Lucy said. 'I could do your backhand a little good.' Lucy was sitting in the driver's seat; she was also dressed in a short white tennis dress. She smiled seductively. 'If you don't want to play tennis, we could always try something else, I'm very adaptable.' She tittered, 'What do you think, April?'

April looked David straight in the eye, pursed her lips and blew him a kiss.

'There's a lot of traffic backed up behind you, Lucy,' he said, ignoring the girls' backchat. 'Perhaps you'd better move on.'

'Stop the buggers from speeding through the town,' Lucy snapped.

He didn't like to hear a woman swear, so he quietly closed the car door.

'Goodbye ladies have a good game. Are you playing together?'

'No of course not, David,' Lucy said. 'We have partners waiting at the tennis club, male of course.' They waved goodbye and moved on.

He stood and watched until the car went around the corner.

'It's time I went home,' he said out loud, looking at his watch before walking back into the base.

'Mr Greenwith, keep your staff under control?' he said scowling at the two clerks who were holding their hands near their chests. He knew the clerks weren't talking about juicy melons. 'Have these men nothing

41

better to do?'

Warrant Officer Greenwich, a small bald headed man with a shrewd mind and cold grey eyes, didn't answer. The air force had been his life and he knew enough about officers not to answer back when he could see they were angry. He waited for the C/O to carry on.

'One of those new men we're expecting, AC1 Weston, did you read through his file? Makes bloody interesting reading, seems to be a bit of clever bugger to me, I don't think we want or need his type here.'

'I've not read it, sir,' Mr Greenwith said, lying, 'but I will.'

'I'm away for the weekend, Mr Greenwith, you know where to find me?'

'Yes, sir.'

Picking up his hat and tunic the C/O walked out into the street without uttering another word.

Mr Greenwith looked at his clerks.

'Well, he's left the door open, what are you two waiting for? It's the weekend, get yourselves away.' The clerks quickly vacated their desks. Alone in the office, Mr Greenwith sat down and once again he read through the file of AC1 P E Weston. Mm, private school education. I'm surprised he's not gone on to university, he thought. It's like "Toddymarsh" says, you appear to be a most intriguing young man, AC1 Weston. He coughed to clear his throat; the W/O suffered from chronic catarrh. I can't wait for Monday; I want to meet you, AC1 Paul Edward Weston. I wonder how you'll get on with our squadron leader. He locked the files in his desk drawer, put on his hat and walked out into the street. Behind him the sign on the window said "RAF Marine Craft Unit 1201 Bravemouth." He turned smartly on his heel and marched away.

Chapter Ten

Saturday 12th May 1951.

That's it I've now got everything organised regarding Weston and the ladies of Bravemouth, Rebecca thought. He will be sent to the Ferrimins' household on Monday afternoon. So until then I'm going to practice my new powers on someone. She wandered around the town until she chanced upon the local vicar smoking a cigarette in the church vestry. Needing to test her new powers thoroughly, she hypnotised him and to test her skills she told him to take all his clothes off. What Rebecca didn't know was the vicar was smoking a cigarette to pass the time while he waited for one of his parishioners – the lady in charge of the church flowers, Mrs Heimer. He wanted to discuss the rest of the year's church flower arrangements with her.

Mrs Heimer was a large but quite attractive woman, the type you always find helping out in schools and church jumble sales. Even though the vicar had never encouraged her, he still found the attention she gave him quite flattering. The vicar came round from Rebecca's induced hypnotic trance to discover he was stark naked. Wondering what had happened to him, he picked up his clothes from the floor and was about to dress when Mrs Heimer walked in.

'My sweet love you do know my feelings for you,' she shouted. 'You're ready and waiting for me.' She ran across and took him tightly into her arms.

Rebecca looked on, thinking this is another mess I've made, still no real harm's been done thank goodness. I must remember to check the minds of people in the future. Rebecca will never forget the horrified look on the vicar's face as his naked body disappeared under the folds of Mrs Heimer's floral dress.

I suppose I'd better report to the Head of Department and get another ticking off, Rebecca thought, I must make sure I get it right before Weston arrives.

Chapter Eleven

Monday 14th May 8:45am.

The Penzance train began to slow as it approached Polcastle station. This was where Weston changed trains for Bravemouth.

The Wrens also knew Weston had to leave the train here. Consequently, they were showing their anger with Sonia the petty officer for monopolizing Weston for the whole journey.

While the girls were busy arguing about who was going to have Weston next, he saw a meagre chance to get his clothes; he leaped up and grabbed his trousers and before the girls could stop him he backed himself against the carriage door, where he held them off while he put his trousers on. The train pulled into Polcastle station and stopped.

The cool morning mist which had shrouded the entire county of Cornwall since first light was now clearing and the station could be seen in its true glory. The profusion of flower baskets hanging from the canopy were filled with multicoloured spring blooms. These were covered in dew and glistening like diamonds. While on a closely mown grass bank the other side of the tracks, the name Polcastle stood out clearly, written in bright red tulips, surrounded by primroses.

'That's it Dave, close the bloody doors and I'll send it out again,' the Station Master shouted. 'I don't want them to blame me for it being late.'

He was about to blow his whistle and bring the flag down when a carriage door opened with a loud crash and a bedraggled half naked man covered in what could only be lipstick stumbled out on to the platform.

Several young ladies, Royal Navy Wrens minus tunics, followed him out carrying what could only be his kit.

'What's going on, Dave?' the Station Master shouted to the porter.

'Don't know George, but I'll bloody well find out.' The porter ran up to the young man who had sat himself on a platform seat. 'You stupid fool, you could have been killed, this train was about to leave. Hell boy, what's this, good grief you're covered in lipstick.'

'Tell me something I don't know,' the young man gasped. 'I've been more or less raped by those bloody Wrens, I couldn't get away from them, it's a non corridor carriage. He opened his kit bag, which one of the Wrens had thrown onto the platform, took out a flannel and towel and began to clean the lipstick from his chest face and neck.

'What's your name boy and have you got a ticket?' the porter said.

'Of course I've got a bloody ticket, it's about all I have got, I used to be AC1 Paul Edward Weston, now after being mauled with those girls I don't know who I am. Is this Polcastle station? They wouldn't let me get off the train, I had to fight my way out. They said I couldn't leave until I'd shagged them all.' He quickly looked around, all his suspicions were confirmed; he was the morning's star turn.

The Station Master ran up the platform, breathing heavily (he wasn't a young man).

'What's going on, Dave? Get those girls back aboard. Come on maids, I've a job to do, come on?' He waited a moment, to catch his breath. 'This train's already more than ten minutes late?'

'We are not going anywhere until we've all had a good bye kiss from Brylcream,' Sonia the petty officer Wren said, taking hold of Weston's face in both her hands and kissing him full on the lips. 'Don't forget me

47

Brylcream, my name's Sonia, why don't you come on to Penzance with us?' The other girls followed, each trying to persuade him to go on with them.

'I'll come with he,' the porter shouted.

'I don't think you'd stand the pace somehow, granddad,' Sonia said. The Station Master ushered them back into the carriage and the porter looked questionably at Weston.

'What's this bloody hold you've got over women, boy? I think you must have pixilated them.'

'I've no hold over women. What do you mean pixilated?'

'That you be under the control of pixies, that's what I be thinking, boy.'

The Station Master managed to get the girls back on the train, leaving just petty officer Sonia standing on the platform outside the carriage door.

'Don't forget, Brylcream,' she shouted, 'you owe me a new pair of silk stockings, you've ruined these, look.' She lifted her skirt high, to show to all and sundry her stocking topped legs and non issue black French knickers. She waved something above her head. 'I've still got your underpants.' She was still waving them when the Station Master pushed her into the carriage.

The porter, a man of least sixty years of age took hold of Weston's shoulder in his hard sinewy hand.

'Bloody hell boy,' she be an made my legs weak; I be trembling inside. Enough to give a fully sexed man like me a heart attack. How did she get your underpants? Did they have your trousers off? I wish they'd done some of that loving and kissing around me. I'd have enjoyed that.' He sighed and looked skywards, fantasising. 'You're a fool boy, a bloody fool. I'd have gone on with them, if they'd asked me.'

The Station Master brought down his flag and the

train began to pull out, the Wrens went by waving frantically from their carriage window.

'Those girls didn't want you to go with them you old fool,' the Station Master said. 'She called you Granddad?'

The Station Master began to look strangely at Weston; it was as if he wasn't too sure of him.

'Funny things do seem to happen around you young man. Come on Dave. What made you think those girls wanted you, Dave?'

'It's their loss, they might have missed out on me, there's many a good tune played on an old fiddle.'

'Not when its strings are knackered and its bow's gone limp,' the Station Master said, laughing. 'Come on boy let's get you out of here. You must have had one hell of a good time with those girls, no wonder the bloody train was late.'

'You're not going to blame that on me?'

'I'm not so sure, come on I want to see the back of you boy, you've disrupted my station. That mess of lipstick's gone now, you're looking as handsome as ever. Your train's a waiting my lord.' He engulfed Weston's hand in his massive grip and pulled him to his feet. 'You and your lady friends have made one train late today. Don't make this one the same.'

'Listen to the old fart,' the porter whispered. 'This train is always late, I've never known it to go out on time yet. Half the passengers would miss it if it did.'

'Sure this is the right train?' Weston muttered. 'I want the one for Bravemouth.'

'We know, you be going to the holiday camp there.'

'No I'm not. I've to report to the RAF Marine Craft unit in Bravemouth.'

''Tis same place boy, 'tis same place,' they said, picking his kit up between them.

Weston sat on the slatted seat in the half empty

49

carriage and the train set out. The railway ran alongside the river and Weston sat there enchanted by the view, totally unaware of the dozen or so other passengers. I'm going to enjoy being in Cornwall, he thought. The tide was high, and the morning mist was only clinging to the more sheltered spots of the river. Swallows were swooping low across the still water and the herons were standing like sentinels in the shallows. The river scene that May morning was something that was going to remain etched into Weston's mind forever.

The tiny tank locomotive blew its whistle, to the obvious disgust of the dozens of seagulls screeching overhead, and the small train eased into Bravemouth's tiny one platform station.

Weston shuffled behind the other passengers down the platform and handed his ticket to the porter.

'Morning boy,' the porter said.

'Good morning. Could you tell me where the RAF Marine Craft Base is please?'

The porter stood back and pointed down the road. 'Just walk down 'ere my handsome, can't miss it, 'tis on the left and almost next door to the Riverbank inn.'

The RAF base in Bravemouth, much to Weston's surprise, was comprised of just two old cottages knocked into one. He dumped his backpacks and kit bag onto the narrow pavement outside the door and rang the bell.

The door opened slowly and a bleary-eyed airman peered out.

'Hello boyo. Just arrived have you?' He spoke in a distinctly Welsh accent. 'Come in. I'm William Mardey, better known as Taffy.' He offered Weston his hand.

'Paul Edward Weston,' Weston said, accepting his hand. 'I've been travelling for days, it's a long way from Northern Ireland. Call me Pew, everyone else

50

does.'

'Pew boyo, that's a bloody funny name?'

'It's my initials, my name is Paul Edward Weston.'

'Still a bloody funny name; anyhow, welcome to Bravemouth, Pew. Leave your kit there at the bottom of the stairs. The camp's fifteen hundred weight truck driver will take it up to the camp for you. We'll go up now for breakfast.'

Later that morning.

Warrant Officer Greenwith picked up all the papers he needed the C/O to sign and took them through to Squadron Leader Todmarsh-River's office.

'Ah, Mr Greenwith.' The C/O always called his W/O Mr. 'Did that airman, what was his name? Turn up?'

'AC1 Weston? Yes, sir, he arrived first thing this morning, everything was above board.'

'Did you read his file?' The C/O placed his hands behind his head, and leaned back in his chair.

'I just glanced through it, sir,' Mr Greenwith lied. 'Was there something you particularly wanted me to see?'

'No not really. It's just that I get the impression that he's a bit of a clever bugger, passed out 90% at the Marine Training School. That's an LAC pass. Do you know why he's not received his rank?'

'No, sir, would you like me to find out?'

'Yes, do that, and if there's no good reason, give him his new rank at once and backdate his wages. If we want to get rid of him, by the way, we can very easily lose him on that six month diving course with the navy. They said when they phoned me they wanted someone of LAC rank. What do you think, Mr Greenwith?'

The warrant officer wasn't a man to be rushed into making statements which would affect someone's life.

He answered cagily, 'Why not wait until this afternoon, sir, make up your mind after you've interviewed him.'

'Very well, Mr Greenwith, what time have you set the interviews for?'

'1300 hours, does that suit you, sir. Do you want to see them individually, sir?'

'No, I'll see them together as a group and don't let me forget that I've promised to send someone along to Mrs Ferrimins' home this afternoon.'

The C/O, looking very important, was sitting behind his desk when W/O Greenwith marched the four new arrivals into his office.

'Thank you, Mr Greenwith, close the door, I'll give you the word, when I'm ready for you to take them out.'

The office was hot and the C/O, who kept his eyes firmly focused on his finger tips, which he continually pressed together and released, went on and on, his voice droning into their ears. This took a heavy toll on Weston, who'd had no real sleep for several days; no matter how he fought it, his eyelids became heavier and heavier. Suddenly he was aware it had gone quiet, the C/O had stopped talking. Hell, I must have nodded off, he thought glancing at the C/O, who to Weston's chagrin was now looking directly at him.

'Your name, Airman?'

'AC1 Weston, sir.'

'Yes, of course, I should have known. Do you think I'm boring, Weston? I've not had anyone go to sleep on me before. It's not a very good start is it, AC1 Weston?'

'Yes, sir, I mean no, sir, I mean sorry, sir.'

'Make up your mind, Weston. It is hot today and perhaps I have gone on a little too long.' Thinking that's it my mind's made up, this bugger's going on that navy diving course in the morning, he picked up several pieces of paper from his desk and glanced through them.

He went through each of the men's appointments. Two of the new arrivals were joining the crew of the number one launch and the other one was joining the crew of the other launch which had only arrived at Bravemouth the week before and needed working up.

'Weston?'

'Yes, sir.'

'You will be receiving the LAC rank you earned at the training school and your pay will be backdated. However, you will not be staying on at Bravemouth. You are going on to a diving course with the navy; they have asked especially for someone of LAC rank.'

Rebecca heard this and she thought that's where you're wrong Mr Commanding Officer, my charge is here in Bravemouth and that's where he's going to stay.

'They are all yours, Mr Greenwith,' the C/O shouted. 'Take them out, and remember, I want LAC Weston to be sent to Rowanberry House.'

W/O Greenwith, showing how efficient he could be, brought them to attention and marched them out.

'Have you got Mrs Ferrimins' address there, Wittingham?' he said to the clerk.

'Yes, sir, it's here.'

'Then give it to LAC Weston.'

'You're a bloody lucky bugger, Weston,' Wittingham whispered, giving him the address. 'She's beautiful, she's the most fabulous woman in Bravemouth. I go to pieces every time I see her. She's got everything, looks, tits, legs and…'

'That's enough of that talk, Wittingham,' the W/O snapped. 'You've got the address, Weston, so get on your way.'

Chapter Twelve

Monday 14th May 1951 14:10pm.

Weston had no difficulty in finding Rowanberry House; Mrs Ferrimins' home in this small town. It was a large detached house situated between the end of Trafalgar terrace and the beginning of Waterloo terrace. Weston took this in as he walked up the road to the gate. The sign on the varnished hardwood gate read: Rowanberry House. His stomach churned as he apprehensively opened the gate. A short crazy paved stone path led down to a large porch with a hardwood door and hardwood leaded light windows. To the left of the property, and separating this house from the end house of Trafalgar terrace, was a strip of garden with a tall privet hedge. Rowanberry House's front garden was quite small; just a lawn with flowerbeds around the edges. The gable wall of the end house of Waterloo terrace made up the right-hand side of the property.

'Hello young man, you another of her admirers?' a disembodied voice said.

He looked up to see a white haired elderly lady's face peering over the tall hedge.

'I suppose you're her latest?' she said.

'I don't know what you mean? I've been sent here from the RAF base to do some jobs for Mrs Ferrimins.'

'Yes and we all know who one of the little jobs will be, don't we? I bet you're looking forward to it.'

'I don't know what you're talking about.'

'Young man, I'm beginning to think a lot of your lies aren't true.'

April Ferrimins awoke from her doze on the terrace and sat up on her lounger; she'd been waiting for David's little airman to arrive since twelve o'clock. She looked at her watch; it's ten minutes past two, she thought, where the hell is he? She glanced across to her long white wraparound skirt and the white silk shirt lying on a deck chair, which she had brought up especially to put on over her bikini. She wanted to look respectful when she opened the door to the airman. David's a rotten egg, he's let me down, she thought, and he promised; I shall have to go down and phone him. She slipped the clothes she'd brought over her bikini and ran to the hall. April had been brought up in the old school of serfs and masters; consequently, she thought she could have anything she wanted by just snapping her fingers. It was her friend Jemmy who suggested that she should live in Bravemouth when she told her she couldn't stand living in the hotel in London. So with her husband's blessing, she had purchased this house in Bravemouth. You must join us in Bravemouth darling, Jemima said, it's so upper class dear, if you must move out of London, Bravemouth's the place. Lucy and Judy our old boarding school friends are here. April's father had been in the diplomatic service in Africa and India; consequentially she and her one year older sister, Edwina, had spent their entire young life in boarding school. This had made her superior, haughty and hard. Although she had not been in Bravemouth for more than a few weeks, Jemima and her friends had introduced her into all the correct clubs: Bridge, Yacht, Tennis, Golf, Croquet and the Bravemouth Ladies' Luncheon club.

'I'll give him five minutes more,' she said to herself. 'If he's not here by then, I shall have to phone the base. She looked out of the hall window; to her astonishment, an Airman was standing in her garden talking to her hated neighbour.

That's got to be him, the horrid man, keeping me

waiting while he talks to that nasty old woman. She opened the hall door.

'Airman,' she screamed out, 'are you looking for the Ferrimins' household, if so, get in here at once.'

Weston looked around and saw her; good grief she's every bit as beautiful as Wittingham said, shot through his mind. April stepped forward to usher him into the house and her wraparound skirt snagged, exposing her long legs to the top of her thighs.

'There my boy have a good look, she's showing you all she's got on offer,' the old lady whispered, albeit loud enough for Mrs Ferrimins to hear.

'I heard that, you nosy old bat, come along airman, don't you dare keep me waiting a moment longer.'

Passing through the porch, Weston noticed the inscription on a ship's bell hanging by the door, it said H M S Rowanberry. Must have called the house after a ship, he thought.

She slammed the door shut behind him, she did this so hard the lock didn't catch and the door bounced back, still open.

Weston stood there feeling lost and in the way, holding his beret. The hall was quite cool and the fragrance of her expensive perfume wafted over him. I've got to get away from here, he thought. This woman terrifies me.

'You must have known I was waiting for you, yet you wasted my time talking with that old bat. I've a good mind to phone you're C/O and complain about you.'

Weston didn't answer; he stood there feeling like a naughty boy who'd been caught with his fingers in the biscuit barrel. The phone rang. She glared at it for a moment before picking it up.

'Yes, for goodness sake,' she shouted down the receiver. 'Oh it's you, Jemmy, can't possibly talk now, that bloody airman David promised to send over at one o'clock, he's just arrived, yes over an hour late.'

Weston took this unexpected opportunity to calm down a little and have a look around. It was definitely a wealthy person's home. The large porch and hall was panelled in oak from floor to ceiling. It had two large windows glazed in square leaded lights, one each side of the front door. Straight ahead from the front door and up two stairs there was a pair of varnished hardwood doors with large brass handles. I bet she calls that room her drawing, or sitting room he thought. To his left was another door, marked Study. To his right, the hall led onto a landing with a large round topped window at the end and a staircase going down. On the wall alongside to where he was standing was a framed photograph of a group of young girls in swimming suits.

'I must go, Jemmy, I must show this er, er, airman, what I want doing. Yes darling I will definitely ring and tell you all about it later.' She replaced the phone.

'Right airman,' she said in a voice so clipped and loud it resonated from the oak panelling. 'You've wasted enough of my time today and time's the bloody essence, never mind that picture. Come along.'

Weston followed her, wondering what he had done to deserve the attitude she was showing towards him. She took him down the stairs to the first landing; this appeared to run the whole width of the house, it had four doors opening from of it. She opened two of the doors and it was only then that it dawned upon Weston that she had never once looked at him or even cast a glance in his direction, or even asked his name.

'One of the jobs I need doing is in here, my dining room.' She stood in the centre of the floor with her hands on her hips, leaning slightly forward, allowing the tops of her breasts to show.

57

What on Earth am I doing here with this woman? went through Weston's mind. She might be beautiful, but why me? I don't know how to handle women, especially women of her type.

'You are not listening to me, are you airman? I shall tell you again and I don't like repeating myself. I want this carpet lifted and I want it putting away in the attic. Be extra careful with it, it's Chinese and very valuable, you will have to move the furniture out of course. You can place it all in here, the kitchen.' She pointed to the other open door. 'However, before you make a start in here, I've work for you to do in my cellar, follow me.' She took him down a second flight of stairs to the next landing; this one had five doors opening from it. She opened the first door and to Weston's surprise it led to yet another flight of stairs going down, however these were uncarpeted. 'This is my cellar.' He could see it wasn't really a cellar because it had windows overlooking the front garden. 'I want you to give this cellar a thorough cleaning and I want all those tins of oil and paint put away on the shelves. It's been like this ever since I moved in.'

Weston looked at it in dismay; the entire floor was covered in dust, dirt, sawdust, wood shavings and old leaves, as well as dozens of rusty tins of paint etc. There was also a fully inflated rubber dinghy in the centre of the floor. This place obviously hadn't been cleaned in years.

'Mrs Ferrimins,' Weston said, speaking for the first time. 'I'm sorry but I can't do this sort of work in my best blue uniform. I shall have to go back to the camp to get my denim overalls. The C/O sent me here directly from an interview.'

'You will not leave this house until these jobs are finished. I've waited far too long. Don't worry about you're uniform I shall find you something appropriate

58

to wear. What's your name?'

'LAC Weston.'

'Speak up. I can't hear you.'

'LAC WESTON.'

'I can't address you as LAC, you must have a first name, come along man.'

'It's Paul Edward Weston, my friends call me Pew.'

She thought about this for a moment or so.

'I see very clever, your initials I presume; very well, Pew, would you be prepared to wear something of my husband's?'

'Yes, I suppose so.'

She looked at him directly in the eye.

'My God. Oh my God. It's my Ernst, he's my, my Eagle,' she uttered, she felt faint. Oh my God, was all she could say or think, her heart began racing and her skin bristled with goose bumps. Her head spun and she keeled over in a faint.

Weston didn't know what to do; he was bending over her when she came around. She caught him completely off guard when without the slightest hint or warning she threw her arms around his neck, pulled him down, and kissed him. This is what she'd prayed and asked God for, for months. God had finally answered her prayers. Her long lost love Ernst, her Eagle, had been returned to her.

Feelings she hadn't experienced for years were once again surging through her body.

Jolly gosh, she thought, look at that long fair hair and those cold blue eyes, which I know can turn warm and loving. I want to feel his long fair hair, and his smooth pale skin in my hands. She attempted to roll over on top of Weston. Weston, taken back and flabbergasted by her behaviour, didn't know what to make of it. They must be men mad down here he thought, especially after his sexual morning with the

Wrens. He forcefully pushed her away and got to his feet. He looked down at her; she was showing most of her breasts, he didn't know what to say or do. She got to her feet looking embarrassed and smiled at him.

'Have I shocked you Ernst, sorry, Pew? I'm so sorry, but you look so like a very dear person that I once knew and loved many years ago. I'll go and find you something appropriate to wear Ernst, sorry, I mean Weston, sorry, sorry, I mean Pew, I'll get it right soon. I won't be long, wait here.' She ran up the stairs, two at a time, her eyes filled with tears, a cold shiver ran through her body despite the heat of the day. She wanted to shout from the rooftops, 'God's answered my prayers, he's returned my Eagle to me.' Yet at the back of her mind she knew Weston was a different man from Ernst, but was he? Only his performance in bed would really tell.

She ran into her bedroom and took out a bundle of letters and photographs tied in blue ribbon. On the top was a picture of a young man wearing only a pair of shorts and a pilot's helmet. She wiped her eyes, and whispered to herself, 'My lovely Ernst, my Eagle, God's given me a second chance with you.' She kissed the photograph and opened the first letter. Tears flowed down her cheeks as she read it through to the end, the letter finished with the words. *We'll be taking off shortly to drop bombs on your lovely country, April. I don't want to do it, this is wrong, I'm not only in love with you my darling, I also love your country. At least I know you'll not be there, I hate this war, April. We will get married as soon as it's over. Lots of love from your now fully fledged Eagle, yes I passed out as a pilot several weeks ago. I love you, April, Ernst. xxxxxxx.* She looked at the postmark, January 1946. Ernst had been dead for five years when she received that letter. She wiped the tears away, retied the letters neatly and put them away.

Right, April, get a hold of yourself, no more tears, she thought. I must find a pair of Michael's shorts and a pair of sandals for him to wear, it's so hot and humid today, he won't mind. I'd better phone Jemmy though first and tell her my good news.

'Oh it's you, April, I hope you're in a better humour,' a cool Jemima said.

'Never mind that, listen, Jemmy, you'll never guess but you know that airman David sent to do those jobs for me. Well he's Ernst's absolute double, I'm in love again, Jemmy, I'm going to take him to bed at once.'

'No, April, think, grow up, Ernst is dead. This man is just an erk, get him to do those jobs for you then let him leave, forget him.'

'No can't do that, Jemmy, I'm in love again, I've got to see if he makes love like he did before.'

'No, No, April, grow up for goodness sake. Even if you insist on making love with him, make sure he does those jobs first. David will punish him if you don't, he'll check up on him, I know he will.'

'Oh golly gosh, Jemmy, I suppose you're right, I'll phone you later.' The phone was replaced.

Weston was still unnerved from the fact that Mrs Ferrimins had kissed him, attacked would be a better word, he thought He just stood in the cellar wondering what other shocks were in store for him today, after all this was only his first day in Cornwall.

She shocked him again when she returned; she was wearing nothing but the tiniest white bikini.

He couldn't help but stare at her and he flushed with embarrassment when he realised he had lost control of his body and that she was looking at the bulge in his trousers.

Rebecca looked on, she wasn't in the least bothered about Weston, in fact she was feeling quite pleased at the way things were working out.

'Pew Weston,' April said, returning to her haughty voice. 'I have placed in the top bathroom, that's the one on the same landing as the dining room, a pair of my husband's shorts and sandals. Don't worry they've not been worn, what size shoes do you take?'

'Nines.'

'Good, so does my husband. Go now and change, you look so uncomfortable in that uniform. I shall now return to my sunbathing on the terrace, if you need me for anything at all, you will find me there, just walk across my drawing room and through the French windows.'

So she calls her living room her drawing room, went unnecessarily through his mind. He made his way up the stairs to the top landing and the bathroom.

She was right; it did feel good to be out of his woollen uniform. But why had she changed into that brief bikini, why is she bothering with me at all? She's such a beautiful woman, she's got everything. She said she's going back to her sunbathing. I hope she's there. I can't make love to a married woman. I wonder if she's teasing me. Perhaps it would be for the best if I leave my shirt and tie and socks on, I don't want to look naked.

He had a quick look round the refurbished bathroom. It had a larger than normal bath, a bidet, a hand basin and a lavatory all in a delicate shade of blue. There was also a glass door set into the far wall. Wondering where it led, he opened it, to see a cleverly made shower room. This is luxury, he thought, she must be loaded with money. No wonder that old lady asked if I was her latest. She must have dozens of men coming here. He returned to the cellar, he was feeling more trapped than when he was with the Wrens. Why me, he thought, of all the men in Cornwall, why me?

He found a hose pipe connected to a tap by the garden door and, after putting the assortment of rusty tins back on the shelves, he opened the door to the garden and hosed the place down. Later in the dining room he found by moving the furniture from one side to the other he could roll the carpet up with the furniture still there. He carried the carpet up to the hall and dropped it on the floor under the attic trap. It was just half past three; it had only taken him an hour and a half.

Feeling a little apprehensive, he walked up the steps into the drawing room, which he could see ran the whole length of the house. He could see the French windows in the centre of the room on the harbour-side. Her drawing room as she called it was very elegantly furnished with expensive antiques. In the left-hand corner there was even a baby grand piano with a beautiful flower arrangement on the top.

He peered through the open French windows and a cold chill ran through him; she was lying sunbathing on a lounger without her bikini top. Why the hell am I here? he thought; this woman's as beautiful as any film star, what does she want with me? I'd better make a noise, just to give her time to cover her body; however he didn't need to, she'd already heard him.

'Is that you, Pew,' she shouted. 'Do you need something, darling?'

Oh hell, why is she calling me darling? he thought, feeling sick.

'Pew Weston? Oh dear me, Pew Pew Pew, Weston?' She laughed out loud. 'You only need a handkerchief knotting over your head, you are a real Englishman. Don't you know it's not done darling, you can't wear shorts with a shirt and tie. Get those things off. Oh dear and no, no, no, my darling, not stockings with sandals, Pew darling, it's just not done.'

Oh hell she wants me naked, he thought.

63

'What do you want me to do with the carpet, Mrs Ferrimins?'

'Carpet, what carpet?' She sat up, holding a towel over her chest.

'The dining room carpet?'

'You've taken that big carpet up, so soon?' she said, turning her back to him while she replaced her bikini top.

'Yes, where do you want me to put it?'

'In the attic my darling I thought I'd told you, you will find the trapdoor in the hall ceiling, there's a bamboo cane with a hook on its end in the study, use it to pull the trapdoor down and you'll find there's a ladder attached. Did you check the state of the dining room floor when you lifted the carpet, is it in good condition? I must see it. Oh bloody hell, for crying out loud, Pew, Pew, Pew Weston, take that bloody shirt off. Come here.' She undid his shirt, slipped it from his shoulders and ran her hands seductively over his hairless chest.

To Weston at the receiving end, it felt as if electric shocks were emanating from the ends of her fingers.

'I like a man with a smooth hairless chest,' she said, smiling. 'May I?' She looked deep into his eyes. Wondering what she meant, and before he could answer, she undid the top button of his shorts.

'No, no stop it, don't do that.' Weston uttered.

'Don't worry, I'm not going to compromise you, you prude I only want to see if you've got the same birthmark shaped like a bird, like my dear friend Ernst had? I've got to know, please.'

Weston allowed her to ease his shorts down until the bird shaped birthmark came into view. While she silently stared at the mark, the colour drained from her face, despite her tan. She stood.

'Come along, show me this floor.'

Weston followed her down the stairs, his eyes glued to her pert boyish bottom, which moved seductively from side to side as she went down each stair. She opened the door wide and walked into the dining room where she stood in the centre of the floor with her hands on hips.

'This floor's absolutely wonderful.' She dropped to her knees, obviously fully aware that her breasts had fallen from the bikini cups and that he was staring at them. She ran her hands lovingly over the parquet blocks. 'You've worked jolly hard, well done. This floor is exactly how I hoped it would be.' She stood up, replaced her breasts into the bikini and again shocked Weston by kissing him and pressing her body hard against his.

'I thought so; you're Jiminy Cricket's as hard as iron. Have I done that to you?' She laughed. 'You deserve a drink my Ernst, sorry, Pew, darling.' She went to kiss him again but Weston pulled away.

'Don't you like me kissing you? Never mind, help yourself to a bottle of my husband's Indian light ale, there are several in the fridge. You can also make me a dry Martini while you're about it; I like lots of Gordon's with ice and lemon, but only a briefest drop of Vermouth.' She turned quickly, caught him off guard and again she kissed him full on the lips. 'Do you know you have the very same birthmark in the very same place as my old friend Ernst? It looks to me that God has used the same mould for both of you.' But he didn't put in the same attitudes, she thought. However, her heart fluttered at the thought of taking this replica of her old heart throb to bed. He opened the kitchen door.

'Where do you keep the drinks, Mrs Ferrimins?'

'The drinks are in the cabinet at the end and the beer is in the fridge. I'll return to my sunbathing, bring the drinks up to the veranda. By the way I'd like you to call me April while you are here, please do so.' She smiled broadly. 'Don't forget to wash your hands before you make the drinks, that carpet wasn't very clean.' She ran her hand around and felt his erect.........through the shorts fabric. Weston jumped back.

Why couldn't this Pew be more like my sexy Ernst? she thought. If Ernst were here now, I'd definitely be in bed with him...

She was again lying on her stomach when he brought the drinks out. He noticed her top was left undone when he placed the Martini on the table beside her.

'Sit here,' she said, patting a deck chair.

He sat where she told him and drank the ice-cold beer.

'You did wash your hands before you put the ice into my glass darling?'

'Yes of course I did, Mrs Ferrimins. Doesn't it taste right?'

'Yes the drink's fine, you make a wonderful Martini. However, I've another job for you. What exactly did David tell you to do today?'

'I was to do whatever you wanted.'

'Jolly good, he might not have intended for you to go quite so far as this, but what the hell. I want you to rub some of this sun lotion over my back, it's so hot today.'

'I couldn't do that,' Weston said, leaping to his feet. 'I couldn't possibly touch you, Mrs Ferrimins.'

Good grief, Ernst wouldn't have acted this way, she thought.

The idea of touching her soft sensual skin made Weston cringe; he knew he'd already lost control of his body; his penis was so erect he thought it would explode if he did as she asked.

'I'll put the carpet away, if you don't mind, Mrs Ferrimins.'

'Don't be a silly boy I only want you to spread a little of this sun lotion over my skin.'

'Sorry, Mrs Ferrimins. I can't do that, you're a married woman.'

'Married woman, of course I'm a married woman. What's that got to do with it? Don't be so bloody prudish.'

'No, Mrs Ferrimins, I can't, this is wrong, you're making me a guilty party and I've done nothing wrong. I wasn't sent here to do anything like that. No, sorry, I'm not going to do it.'

How can he hold out against me, she thought. It's plain from his bulging erection, his body's screaming out for me.

'Pew Weston, do you want me to complain about you to your C/O? I will do so if you don't obey me and do as I say, I will give you one more chance.'

That word "obey" was the breaking point for Weston. He thought, I'm not taking orders and obeying her. Look at the state she's got me in, I'm trembling. I've got to get away from here.

'Mrs Ferrimins, if you want to phone and complain about me to my C/O, do so. Because I will not be obeying you. I'm going to put that carpet away and then I'm leaving this house.' He walked towards the French windows.

'Don't you dare walk out on me,' she hissed, her voice tinged with temper.

'Put your own sun lotion on, Mrs Ferrimins. I'll tell you again I'm going to put that carpet away and then I'm leaving this mad house.'

'If you leave now I'll scream and I'll scream so loud, everyone will hear me. I will tell them you raped me. They'll believe anything I tell them.'

67

Weston hesitated in mid stride.

'Good.' She sighed. 'The jar's over there, now obey me and get on with it.' She stretched herself out on her stomach again.

I'm sure she wants me to rape her, he thought. I'll show this bitch, she might be beautiful, but there are limits. He cast a glance at her tight boyish bottom covered only by the fine fabric of her bikini bottom. Well this is it, I might as well be hung for a sheep as a lamb; I don't give a damn or care anymore. To hell with her, she can scream her head off.

He took her completely by surprise by grabbing her hair and twisting it tight in his left hand, she screamed with pain. However, Weston, now thinking calmly, ignored her protestations and pushed her face hard down onto the lounger and held it there.

'Let me go you monster,' she somehow managed to get out. 'Don't you dare lay one finger on me you big big bully.'

'Don't worry about one finger, I'm going to use all five of mine on your tight little bum,' he whispered close to her ear. He brought his hand down hard on her tight bottom, time after time. She howled and screamed, but to no avail. He finished her off by pouring the entire contents of the jar of sun cream onto her back.

'Right, Mrs Ferrimins, there you are, you can do what the hell you want to now. Phone my C/O, phone everybody including the police if you want. I'm going to put that carpet away, then I'm leaving this stupid house. I'm only human.' He let go of her hair and she shot to her feet, holding her undone top in place.

'You, you, you are nothing but a great big bully, you won't get away with this, Pew, Pew bloody Weston.'

'Oh shut up, go and get yourself sunburnt.'

He disdainfully threw a towel to her to wipe her back and walked through the French windows. She sighed as she wiped herself dry of the cream and rubbed her bottom. What a bloody man. If God hadn't sent her her old Ernst, he had definitely sent her another Eagle.

She thought, that's the first time, but it will be the only time I shall ever be spanked in my life. Hell I'm angry and my botty's sore. She eased the bikini down and looked at her bottom; it was bright red, she could even see his finger marks on her skin.

'He won't, no I can't let him get away with this, if he does do, I'll be the laughing stock of the town,' she said out loud to herself. She put on her skirt and shirt and crept into the drawing room. Weston had left the double doors to the hall wide open. April knelt on the floor out of sight behind the left-hand door, to wait her chance.

Weston had found the trapdoor cane in the study and he used it to pull the trapdoor and ladder down. He then dropped the cane on the floor. He was so engrossed in rolling the carpet up tight that he didn't hear her creeping up behind him.

She quietly picked up the discarded cane and brought it down as hard as she could across his bottom; she somehow managed to do it twice before he snatched it from her hand. 'That wasn't funny, Mrs Ferrimins; you've probably marked me for life.'

'Jolly good. I am glad it hurt. You don't get away with doing anything to April Ferrimins without suffering retribution. Now, if you want to talk around Bravemouth about spanking me, I shall tell everyone I put you across me knee and caned you.'

Weston, shaken by the severity of her attack and not trusting her future intentions, stepped back from her and tripped backwards over the rolled up carpet. His head hit the floor and he actually saw stars before briefly passing out.

Seeing Weston dazed, April ran over and whipped his shorts off; she was standing looking at his nakedness when she felt someone alongside her…

'I love naked men, may I join you, April?' Lucy said, smirking. 'What about us having a threesome, April?'

'Where the hell have you come from, Lucy? How did you get in here? I didn't hear you ring the door bell, have you a key, Lucy?'

'No, the door was open, but I did ring the bell several times, there was no answer, so seeing the door was open I walked in, just in time to join you in your private striptease show.'

Weston opened his eyes to see April and another woman looking at him. This other lady was dressed in a green sundress. They were both laughing. That was when he realised they were laughing at him; he was naked. He leapt to his feet and ran into the study.

'Your friend can certainly move fast, why didn't you take him to bed, April? It's far more comfortable; however, if you do want to use the hall floor, make sure the front door is on the latch.' She laughed. 'What about introducing me to your ere friend, April darling.'

'What the hell are you doing here, Lucy?' April said angrily. 'I despair at times, nothing ever works out for me.'

'Sorry, April, I didn't know you were having a romp. Who is this man, he's very handsome and yes he's been circumcised. It's not very often I see a naked man who's been circumcised. Must say he's got a lovely body. I do love naked men.' April was about to say something when Weston came out from the study holding a small rug around his waist to cover his embarrassment.

Pity she came in, that would have been a perfect opportunity for them to make love, Rebecca thought.

'Well, Lucy, now you are here you might as well come out onto the terrace for a Martini. How did you open that door? I distinctly remember banging it shut.'

'I did ring the bell, April. I can assure you of that, but the door was open, honest. Better make sure it's locked in the future, especially if you plan to make love on the hall floor.'

'We weren't making love, we were having a private fight and you were not invited, Lucy.'

Weston saw his shorts lying where April had thrown them and moved over to pick them up, but Lucy beat him to them.

'What are those nasty red wheals across your bottom darling?' Lucy said laughing. 'Not into S&M are you, April?'

'How dare you, Lucy, I'm not queer.'

'It takes all sorts, April darling,' she tittered. 'I didn't expect to see you with your latest in the altogether, what a sight. Oh, I do love naked men. They set my senses reeling. What's your name, darling?'

Weston didn't answer.

She was so tiny she didn't reach Weston's shoulder, yet everything about her was in proportion. She had an impish face, rich brown velvety eyes and very short dark hair parted across the forehead like a boy. Weston thought, she's like a female Peter Pan. She turned and ran her hand up and down his body.

'I like to feel a man's naked chest. When are you going to introduce me to this, this young man, April?'

'Lucinda, stop it at once, give him his shorts and behave yourself, leave him alone, you've embarrassed him. You will never change, Lucy; all men are fair game to you.'

'You're right, I think I have embarrassed the poor

71

thing, here boy put your shorts on. Please introduce me April?' She looked directly into Weston's eyes; however, Weston didn't need his new powers to win her over. Why does April always find the men first, she thought. Well April or no April, I'm having this young man in my bed and it will be very soon.

'Lucy, for goodness sake, leave the boy alone, he's got work to do.'

'Yes I saw him at work with you when I came in, would you like to do some little jobs for me? I live quite nearby, where do you live?'

'Lucy, for goodness sake. This is "Weston". He's come over to do those jobs I need doing.'

'Hello my handsome do I call you "Weston". I had better introduce myself; I'm Lucinda Carrington-Townley. However you can call me Lucy.'

'Lucy, for goodness sake leave the lad alone. Come along we'll go and sit on the terrace. Weston make yourself useful, make two large Martinis and bring them out to the terrace.' She took Lucy by the hand and led her from the hall.

'So I'm her bloody wine waiter now,' Weston said out loud to himself, having another quick rub on his bottom. He took the Martinis out on to the terrace, conscious of their eyes burning into him while he placed the tray on the table. Lucy gave him a huge provocative smile.

'Thank you, that will do, Weston, there are several small boxes of bric-a-brac in the study. I want you to put those away in the attic while you're about it, back to your duties.'

'Yes memsahib,' said Weston, touching his forelock. Dow yow wants the cotton picking as well before Iss goes?'

'Don't be so mean, April, let him stay; I'd like to talk to him. Here sit by me, Weston.'

72

'Indeed he will not stay, memsahib indeed, just remember who you're talking to, Weston. Go now, and put that carpet and those boxes away.'

Weston smiled and walked out.

'April darling this is a lovely Martini. I've not had one like this for years. I love lots of gin in the vermouth.'

'Yes, he's very good.'

Lucy's mind was in overdrive, desperately trying to work out how she could get hold of April's latest boyfriend.

'Tell me, April, where did you find Weston, I need lots of jobs doing around the house. Could you give me his address?'

'No, Lucy, I will not help you and don't bother asking me again, keep your hands off Weston. I found him and I'm keeping him. You have your husband at home.'

'What? You mean George? What bloody good is he with a soft five inches in the middle?'

'Yes, I heard you telling Edwina about that.'

They laughed and talked on for a further half-hour or so. Eventually Lucy stood and took in the view across the harbour.

'So I can't change your mind regarding your latest heartthrob? Must say I enjoyed the Martini he made. May I thank him personally?'

'Sorry darling, he's out of bounds to you and at this moment he's busy putting things away in the attic.'

'He could put his circumcised todger away in me any time; don't you think men with circumcised ones are much cleaner than those with, ugh, foreskins, April?' She stood and held her hands on her groin 'It's been years since I really enjoyed a fulfilling orgasm.'

'Well you can forget about having sex or for that matter anything else with my friend Weston. Come along, Lucy, it's time you went home, I'll show you out, I can't say it's been a great pleasure seeing you today.'

'Put my mind at ease, April, if I hadn't disturbed you, would you have had sex with Weston there and then?'

'Yes I suppose I would and why not? You wouldn't have missed an opportunity like that.'

'I thought so, tell me where I can find him, I need lots of jobs doing around the house. Please, I'm begging you, April? Please?'

'No way, Lucy, and don't you try to appeal to my better nature, I haven't got one, Weston's all mine, and I'm keeping it that way.'

Weston could be heard moving about in the attic while April was showing Lucy out.

Giving each other the usual patronising hugs and kisses, Lucy left.

Chapter Thirteen

Monday 14th May 1951.

Weston could still be heard moving around in the attic when April passed back through the hall; she glanced to the open trap door and thought, typical of my luck. Why the hell did Lucy have to turn up at that moment? This is terrible, I didn't want either her or Judy Wendover to learn about Weston being in town. Well my new Eagle, whether you want to or not, you are taking me to bed before you leave today.

The temperature in the attic was hot, it must have been well over a hundred degrees, and by the time Weston had finished he was covered in sweat and grime. He pushed the ladder back and closed the trap door and looked at his watch, it was four thirty.

April heard him come down the ladder and ran into the hall; she was dressed again in her silk shirt and skirt.

'Good grief, Weston; you're dirty, you're absolutely filthy.' She ran her finger across his back. 'Ugh you're horrid, you're even sticky.'

'I'm not surprised,' Weston uttered. 'There's years of dirt and grime up there and I've been sweating a little you know.'

'Don't use your gutter language here, Weston, people don't sweat.' She smiled. 'They perspire, only horses sweat.'

'The way I've worked this afternoon, perhaps I thought I was a horse.'

'Don't try to be clever.' She rubbed her bottom and saw Weston was watching. 'Yes, yes you clever bugger, Pew Weston, my bottom's bloody sore. How's your little botty darling? Would you like me to kiss it

75

better? It looked rather nasty when we saw you run into the study.' She laughed. 'I couldn't resist getting my own back, especially when I saw the cane.'

'I'm going to get dressed now and then I shall leave, if that's alright by you, Mrs Ferrimins.'

'Don't be ridiculous, you can't put your uniform on over that filth. You must take a shower. Come along this way, I'll show you the shower room.' She took him to the large bathroom, opened the shower room door and turned on the water. 'Use the levers to get the right temperature. Come along, I'll wash your back?'

'No thank you, no and I mean it, no,' he emphasized. 'Please, leave, you've done enough for me today, leave me alone, I'll manage quite well without your help, Mrs Ferrimins.'

'Did I not tell you to address me as April, and what's the score now, I've already seen everything you've got. Oh very well prude if that's what you want, I'll get you some large towels, wait by the door.' She returned within a minute and handed the towels through the half-closed door.

Checking twice, making doubly sure the door was locked, Weston stripped off the shorts and hung them on the coat-hooks next to where he'd hung his uniform. He then placed his watch on the window ledge above. He found a bottle of shampoo and a tablet of soap and climbed into the shower. It was a wonderful shower with loads of hot water; he luxuriated in it for a while.

April could hear the shower running when she opened the safety release on the bathroom door lock and walked in. Weston could be seen quite plainly through the obscure glass of the shower door. Smiling to herself, she removed his clothes and towels and took them out.

Weston, rubbing his eyes, came out of the shower; he felt around for a towel. They weren't there where

76

he'd placed them; his eyes were just about beginning to burn when a towel was placed in his hand. He wiped his streaming eyes and saw April standing there; she was naked.

Weston was startled, but he still took in her well-shaped breasts and small boyish bottom; he also noticed she had little to no pubic hair.

'There's no point in covering yourself, Pew Weston. I've been watching you through the glass door for the last five minutes.' She placed her leg behind his and pushed. Weston fell back on the floor and she dropped on top of him. 'I've waited for so many years to do this my darling.' She took his erect penis and placed it into her receptive body. Within seconds they were making frantic love.

She kissed his face, neck and nipples, all the time working her back in a wild animal manner. After about ten minutes she suddenly stiffened, arched her back and, moaning loudly, she dropped alongside him, breathing heavily.

'That was the most heavenly fantastic sex I've had for years Ernst, it's so good to have you back,' she uttered. 'Did you enjoy it? Ernst. Oh I'm sorry, Pew, you are so alike. Good grief look at you, you've not come have you? Why didn't you come at the same time as me?'

'I didn't know you'd come, it was over in a blink of an eyelid, it didn't last long enough for me. I'm going now to get dressed.'

'You will not leave me; I'm not wasting this bountiful treat of an erect penis. We're going to do it again my Eagle lover.' She smiled broadly. 'However this time we will do it in bed.'

She kissed him and, taking him by his penis, she led him out from the bathroom into the bedroom.

'No, Mrs Ferrimins. We shouldn't have done what

we've done, I must leave, this is wrong, you're married.'

'Don't go shy on me now, Pew. What we just did was wonderful and look at you, you are ready to go again. Come along darling please, please darling.'

'Mrs Ferrimins, I can't go to bed with you, you caught me off guard in the bathroom, you are a married woman you're not free. My family are strict Methodists, they would never forgive me if they discovered I'd had sex with a married woman. Then again what would your husband say if he found out? He'd probably kill me.'

'Forget my husband, he's old, and forget your bloody family, they're not here.' She kissed him and taking his hands she placed them on her full breasts. 'Pew Weston, I've prayed and prayed for this moment, don't spoil it for me or disappoint me.'

'I can't do it, sorry.'

April decided that if it was going to happen with this prude, she had to take the bull by the horns. She took his hand and placed it on her clitoris. 'Play with me down here for awhile please.' After a few minutes she kissed his lips and slowly pushed him back until they both fell on the bed. Once there she commenced to kiss him all over his body until she finally kissed his penis.

Within a second or two she moved over and inserted it into her body and they were at it again. How long this session of heavenly love lasted they had no idea, they however will not forget in a hurry the final climax they shared together; it could only be likened to one huge explosion. They lay together out of breath, holding each other.

Rebecca was thrilled to think April and Weston had got together.

Mr Greenwith was taking his dog for a walk when he saw the C/O stride briskly by him.

'Good evening, sir,' he said saluting. 'Did you call at the Ferrimins' household, how is Weston getting on?'

'No, bloody hell I didn't, that's funny, Mr Greenwith, I set out to see him. I don't know why I didn't go, it's so hot today I seem to be forgetting everything. I'd better get back to Rowanberry House now.'

'Well goodbye, sir,' Mr Greenwith said; smiling broadly, he resumed his walk.

April Ferrimins was lying fully contented for the first time in years alongside Weston.

'That was sheer heaven Weston, I mean, Pew, would you like a cigarette?' She held a cigarette case out to him.

'No thank you, I don't smoke.' She closed the case with a click.

'Weston you told me you had no experience with women, if you were telling me the truth then I've had no real experience with men.'

Weston slipped out of the bed and looked out of the window.

'Hell fire, the C/O's here,' he yelled. 'He's opening your gate. Where are my clothes? He'll want to see me.'

'They're on the floor outside the bathroom,' April said, picking up her shirt and skirt. 'I'll keep him talking while you dress. When are we going to do this again, Pew?'

'I don't know, probably never, the C/O is sending me on a three month diving course with the navy tomorrow.'

'No, oh no I can't allow that, now that I've found you I can't let you go.'

Weston was almost dressed by the time the C/O came into the bathroom.

'Ah, Weston, Mrs Ferrimins tells me she's very pleased with your work. Well done, but you've missed dinner. What on Earth have you been doing until now?'

'I had a lot of work to do, sir, and it was so dirty in the attic I had to take a shower afterwards, sir.'

'Very well, well done, but don't be long, get along to the camp.' Without uttering another word, he walked out.

Rebecca, feeling very pleased with her day's work, decided to leave Weston for a while and return to the Earth Department to report on her progress.

Weston was about to leave when he thought he should say goodbye to Mrs Ferrimins. Through the open French windows he could see the C/O sitting on the handrail.

'Yes, Weston, what do you want?' he said, sounding irritated.

'I came to say goodbye to Mrs Ferrimins, sir.'

'Thank you, Weston, that was very thoughtful of you,' Mrs Ferrimins said, getting to her feet. 'Come along, LAC Weston, I will show you out. I won't be long, David.'

'Let him see himself out, April.'

'No, not from my home, I see everyone out, come along, Weston, could I possibly see you again this week?'

'I don't think so, the C/O is sending me away on a twelve week course with the navy tomorrow.'

She pushed something into his tunic top pocket.

'This is for you, it's five pounds, it's for working so hard. I must see you again, Pew. Is that an Eagle I can see on your shoulder?'

'Yes, that's the RAF Eagle, all erks wear one on their shoulders.'

'Would it be alright if I call you my Eagle?'

'Eagle? Me, why your Eagle? You called me your

Eagle when we were in the bathroom, why?'

She shivered; they were the very same words Ernst had used when she first called him that name.

'Please, may I call you my Eagle? You do have the birthmark, why is David sending you away? I must see you again, Pew, now I've found you, I don't want you to spread your wings like Ernst and fly away.'

She stood and waved until Weston closed the garden gate. She heard a movement behind her and turned to see the C/O.

'Goodbye, April, I must go,' he said. 'I'm pleased Weston did well for you.'

April dropped onto one of her un-upholstered hall chairs thinking, why did God send me the man of my dreams and prayers, only to take him away again? She knelt and prayed, first demanding, then asking God, to keep her newly found Eagle in Bravemouth.

Chapter Fourteen

Monday 14th May 1951.

Weston walked through the town looking for somewhere to eat. His mind was spinning like a Maelstrom; he couldn't believe what had happened to him in less than a day. What was this place where all the women appeared sex mad? In those few hours he'd been ravaged by the Wrens and he actually made love, not once but twice, to that beautiful creature Mrs Ferrimins. Something had changed in his life and Weston didn't know whether he liked his new life or not. Why me? he pondered. A woman like Mrs Ferrimins shouldn't be bothered with a person like me; she could have any man she desired.

'Pew, over here,' he heard someone shout. He looked across to see Taffy, the first man he'd met at the base, on the other side of the road; he had a large boxer dog with him on a long lead.

'How did you get on with the beautiful Mrs Ferrimins?'

'Why, who told you I'd been sent there?'

'Everyone in the camp knows about you. The other two lads who arrived today said something very strange about you. They said the porter on Polcastle station told them when you arrived you fell out of the carriage hardly dressed onto the platform. He also said you'd been alone in that carriage with six Wrens and they were all beautiful girls.' Weston laughed.

'He's been pulling their legs.'

'I don't know about that, because he also told them you've got some kind of hold over women. That must be true; he couldn't have made that up could he.'

'Bollocks Taffy, I've got no hold over women, I

only wish I had.'

Taffy walked on smiling, still unconvinced by Weston's argument.

Weston found a café and bought himself a large Cornish steak pasty which he ate while walking up to the camp. The church clock was striking eight o'clock as he strode up to the camp gates. Standing outside the camp's open gates were two extremely large men and a woman.

'That's the one, that's the bastard,' he heard the woman say. 'He's the only one with brass buttons on his uniform. The next moment the two men just grabbed Weston and punched him so hard that he staggered backwards until his heels caught on the kerb around the camp garden. He fell hard on his back; luckily for him he was on the lawn. They followed and commenced kicking him while he lay there. However, Corporal Geordie, the camp cook, had seen what was going on and he told one of the mess lads to phone for an ambulance. He then gathered a group of lads and they ran across and the two men were quickly subdued and taken into the mess. Corporal Geordie waited with Weston until the ambulance arrived.

Rebecca returned to find Weston had been attacked and was now in the hospital.

'You're very badly bruised, that's all,' the doctor said after examining him. 'You've not broken anything. I think you may have pulled a muscle or two; those bruises will soon go. I really don't think there's anything seriously wrong with you. How do you feel?'

'I'm alright, doctor, I feel fine now, can I go, doctor.'

'No not yet, perhaps later, a little physiotherapy may help, is Dr Wendover on duty tonight, Sister?'

Rebecca was thrilled to hear this; Dr Wendover – Dr Judith Wendover –was yet another of the Five Clover

83

Group ladies. So perhaps I did a little good leaving Weston unattended for those few minutes, she thought.

'Yes, doctor, her private clinics are on Monday and Tuesday evenings,' the Sister said.

'See if she can spare me a few moments Sister.' The Sister left and returned a few minutes later with a tall, fair haired strikingly good-looking woman.

'Dr Wendover, thank you for attending so promptly. This is LAC Weston and he's been the victim of an assault. Would you check him over please, just to see if there's any lasting damage?'

Dr Wendover smiled; this was an opportunity indeed for her, she rarely had a young man on her couch.

'Those bruises look nasty, what's his other side like? Turn over,' she said, looking directly into Weston's eyes.' Weston obliged and she leaned over and took his underpants down. She looked him over. 'I don't like the look of those marks,' she said, pointing to the bruises left by April's cane. 'Yes this is quite nasty. Would you like me to give him a good going over, doctor?'

'Yes if you don't mind, Dr Wendover. I think most of the damage is superficial, but I can't be sure.'

'Give him a towel to wear sister, then bring his clothes to my room, it's not worth him dressing.'

Weston was placed in a wheelchair and taken to a room marked Physiotherapy.

'Put his clothes in the cubical sister and LAC Weston, you can lose those underpants and I would like you on your back on the couch. Weston did as he was told but he held on to the towel the sister had given him. The doctor snatched the towel out of his hand. 'There's no place for shyness in this room, LAC Weston. I see at least a dozen naked men every day and you're made no different.' She washed her hands.

Weston lay thinking, what would he do if his.........was to rise to the occasion?

'Just a few particulars first. Name and address?'

'Weston. Paul Edward Weston. You know the address.'

'It's not often that I get a young man on my couch. I only get the old and infirm.' She stood looking at him for a moment before she began to massage him, beginning at his neck.

Without a knock on the door or any warning, the door opened and Squad Leader Todmarsh-Rivers, W/O Greenwith and a Police Sergeant walked in.

'Get out of here, and close the bloody door, can't you see I'm treating a patient?' Dr Wendover screamed, kicking the door shut in their faces.

'Are they your officers?' she asked.

Weston nodded.

'Perhaps I'd better have a word with them.' She threw a towel to him and went out.

'Yes gentlemen? I would have thought officers in your position, especially you, David Todmarsh-Rivers, would have respected a door marked private.'

'Sorry, Judy,' Weston heard the C/O say. 'Must apologise, bad behaviour. What? We were only informed of the assault a short time ago. How is he?'

'Extremely bruised, but he's young and strong.'

'Could we have a few moments with him, it's most important; it's about bringing charges against the men who assaulted him.'

'Very well but don't waste time, I've work to do.'

They trooped in and stood around the couch, looking a little crestfallen.

'How are you boy?' W/O Greenwith said.

'Alright, sir, do you know why those men attacked me, sir?'

'It was nothing to do with you boy, they mistakenly

85

thought you were someone else. They thought you were the airman who had been sleeping with their wives,' the Police Sergeant said, taking out his notebook. 'Tell me in your own words what happened?'

Weston thought, I'm not telling him anything. I'm not going to get involved in a court case.

'Sorry Sergeant I can only remember the men running towards me. The next thing I knew, I was in the hospital.'

'Very well, but we have to know, do you wish to bring charges against these men?' W/O Greenwith said.

'I don't think so, sir, especially if it was a case of mistaken identity. I don't want to go to court.'

'It's probably for the best I suppose,' the C/O said. 'We won't need to bring LAC Broughly back if there's no case to answer. LAC Broughly was the man you were mistaken for, by the way, Weston.'

'You are sure you don't want to press charges, LAC Weston?' the Sergeant said.

'Yes, sir.'

'Very good, so I can close the book on this case.'

'Right gentlemen you've had your two minutes,' Dr Wendover said. 'Perhaps you will now let me get on with my work.'

'Enjoy your massage, Weston,' said W/O Greenwith. 'I've seen a lot worse looking nurses.'

'I can assure you, sir, I am not a nurse, sir, I am Doctor Wendover.'

'Sorry, doctor,' Mr Greenwith murmured, his face turning red.

Squadron Leader Todmarsh-Rivers's wife waited for around ten minutes, hoping her husband would be well on his way to the hospital before she phoned April.

'April darling, I thought I'd better let you know, your little man, LAC Weston, has been assaulted by two thugs just outside the camp. David and Mr

86

Greenwith are on their way now to the hospital. I'll find out what I can and I'll phone you back.'

'Who did it? He couldn't possibly have enemies here; he only arrived in Bravemouth this morning.'

'Some irate husband and his friend, they apparently wrongly thought Weston had been sleeping with their wives.'

'Thank you, Jemmy, I'm going to the hospital to see him, the poor sweet darling, he's so shy he wouldn't hurt a fly.'

'April you shouldn't be seen in the Bravemouth hospital visiting a lowly airman.'

'I don't care what rank he is, Jemmy, he's my Eagle.'

'Eagle my foot, he's a national service erk, he's a nobody, he'll be gone from Bravemouth tomorrow, forget him, April.'

'I will not forget him, Jemmy.'

'April, this man is not Ernst, Ernst is dead. He died a long time ago. You're my best friend and I can't stand by and watch you make a fool of yourself.'

'You will not talk me out of going to see him in the hospital.'

'Very well if I can't stop you I shall go with you. I can't wait to see this Eagle of yours.'

The C/O and Mr Greenwith were leaving the hospital just as April and Jemima arrived.

'What on Earth are you and April doing here, darling?'

'I told April about that airman darling and apparently he's the same man you sent to do that work for her this afternoon. She's quite concerned about him and wants to see him. I came up with her.'

'How is he, David?' April asked.

'He's fine, just a little bruised. You've had a wasted journey.'

'No, now I'm here, I shall pop in to see him,' April said.

'Do you mind if I go back with David, April darling?'

'Of course not, Jemmy, what could happen to me in Bravemouth?'

'That's what LAC Weston thought,' Jemima said.

'You don't need to worry,' the C/O said. 'The police have arrested the two men involved; they thought Weston had been sleeping with their wives.'

'I'll give you a bell tomorrow darling,' Jemima said.

The Physiotherapy room door was open, and April, ignoring the nurse sitting at her desk outside the treatment room door, barged right in, the nurse following her.

'Sorry, Dr Wendover, I couldn't stop her,' the nurse said.

'April, you should know better, get out, can't you see I've a patient on my couch in a state of undress.'

'Sorry, Judy, I wanted to see how Pew Weston was.' She looked at Weston. 'How are you my poor darling?' she whispered, kissing Weston on his forehead.

'I'm sorry, April. I can't have you in here while I'm working,' Dr Wendover said. 'You must leave. Nurse show Mrs Ferrimins out and make sure she stays in the waiting room.'

April sighed, but she allowed the nurse to take her out.

'If you're good, April, you can come in when I've finished,' Dr Wendover shouted.

Fifteen minutes later she stood back from the couch and wiped her hands. 'There you are, LAC Weston, do you feel any better?' She threw him a towel and opened the door.

'He's still undressed, April, but if you promise to behave yourself, you can come in.'

'My poor darling Pew,' April said, walking in. 'Oh dear look at those nasty bruises.'

'Those marks are nothing,' Dr Wendover said. 'You should see the ones on his bottom. Come along LAC, turn over.' She pulled Weston over onto his stomach.

April saw the welts she'd made with the cane and began laughing.

This was enough for Weston, who knew exactly what she was laughing at; he slipped from the couch and did a dash into the cubical to dress.

'What was so funny, April?'

'Sorry darling can't tell you, it's a private joke between me and Pew Weston.'

Weston came out fastening his tunic.

'So you decided to dress have you? Good. Come into the waiting room and sit down while I make your report out,' Doctor Wendover said. 'You can wait in here; sit on the couch, April,' the doctor said, sitting at the nurse's desk. She scribbled something on several pieces of paper and sealed them in envelopes. She gave one to Weston. 'Give this to your commanding officer, tell him I must see you again at eight thirty tomorrow evening. I'm afraid I can't sign you out of the hospital, LAC Weston, only Sister or the doctor who first treated you can do that.' The nurse came in. 'Nurse, will you try to find Sister,' she said walking back into the treatment room.

'I'm free now for the evening, April, thank goodness, would you like to join me in a coffee in town? Must say I enjoyed that spiffing cocktail party on the Yacht last week, thank you for inviting me.' They walked through the town to the anchorage Café and sat at a vacant table.

'Will Pew Weston get over this, Judy?'

'Of course he will, there's very little wrong with him, he'll be fine. But tell me, before I explode with curiosity, what is your connection with this LAC Weston. Why do you call him Pew?'

'Why do you want to know?' April said cagily. 'I'll tell you this for nothing, Judy Wendover, keep away from him he's mine. I even had to warn Lucy off this afternoon.'

'I see, so you've already had that little boy in your bed, April. You're nothing but a cradle snatcher.' She gave April a huge smile. 'How does he perform in bed?'

'Mind your own bloody business, Judy, be happy that you've your husband at home.'

'What my queer Monte? He's going worse; if he's not whipping someone or tying them up he doesn't want to know. He's going worse with age, he's as queer as a nine shilling note. If it wasn't for our lovely naturist farm and my horses I'd leave him this very minute.'

'I always thought you and Monte were made for each other,' April said. 'I must say, I didn't know Monte was like that. However, I do know you're not queer, you're like me and the others in Five Leaf Clovers, short of satisfactory sex and young man mad.'

Judy thought, I'd better not let her know her new boyfriend will be visiting me again tomorrow. I really must be slipping, having the town's latest stud on my couch and not taking advantage of him. Still, never mind, I shall have him all to myself tomorrow evening.

The duty nurse returned, she told Weston he would have to wait because both Sister and the doctor were busy.

The door to the waiting room opened. Weston looked around, a young man and two young ladies were walking in.

'Hello, Pew, will it be alright if we come in? I'm Corporal Geordie, the camp cook. I phoned for the

90

police and ambulance for you this evening. This is my girlfriend, Barbara, and this is her cousin Tamsin.'

Weston looked askance at the nurse.

'Yes, you can come in but you can't stay long,' she said.

'Thank you nurse, I know it's after visiting hours,' Geordie said. 'How are you feeling, Pew?'

'I feel fine now, they've told me I can leave as soon as I'm signed out.'

'This is Barbara my girlfriend, Pew.' Weston stood and offered his hand. She was a tall attractive girl with brown eyes and long dark hair, dressed in a short white cotton dress. Weston thought she was very pretty but for his taste she was wearing far too much makeup. Geordie took the other young lady's hand.

'This is Tamsin, Barbara's cousin, Pew.'

Weston had been glancing cautiously at Tamsin ever since they'd walked in. She was Weston's sort of girl, good-looking with short ash-blonde hair and alluring blue eyes. She was dressed in a tight white polo necked sleeveless top, which left nothing to the imagination. She flushed when Weston shook her hand and looked into her eyes. Unlike her cousin she wore just a light coating of lipstick. Weston made up his mind there and then that if he stopped in Bravemouth he would try to see her again. Sister came in and signed him out, and Weston and his new friends left.

Back in the billet, Weston was subjected to a lot of friendly leg pulling regarding his afternoon with Mrs Ferrimins. They also said he deserved the beating he got from the irate husbands. Weston let it all go over his head and eventually he slipped between the cool sheets of his bed, his mind once again full of thoughts about his first day in Cornwall. First the Wrens, then the delectable Mrs Ferrimins, hell what a woman, then the assault followed by receiving treatment from the

91

beautiful Dr Wendover. Why me? I can't understand what's happening to me, he thought. Then again he thought about his out of the blue meeting with Tamsin, she was the sort of girl he'd always wanted to meet. The words from a song in the film "State Fair" went through his mind –"I keep wishing I was somewhere else, walking down a strange new street, hearing words I have never heard, from a girl, I've yet to meet." My street is in Bravemouth and the girl is Tamsin. I'm going to marry that young lady one day. I hope I stay on in Bravemouth. I don't want to go on that diving course. Within a minute he was fast asleep.

Chapter Fifteen

Tuesday 15th May 1951.

April heard someone knocking on the front door; she ran up the stairs and opened her front door to her friend Jemima.

'Hello, Jemmy, you're early this morning. How's my lovely Eagle, or should I say, LAC Weston, this morning? I phoned the hospital, but they wouldn't tell me anything.'

'Oh him, he's fine, David phoned this morning and they told him LAC Weston had been discharged last night. Come along darling tell me about this so-called Ernst look alike of yours. Did you really get him into bed?'

'Of course I did, but let's not talk about that, I'm upset; Pew Weston told me yesterday that David is sending him away on some course with the navy.'

The daily help brought the coffee.

'Thank you, Kathleen, carry on with your duties.'

Kathleen scowled as per usual behind her employer's back and left.

'Will you please ask David to keep my Eagle in Bravemouth, Jemmy?'

'Sorry, April, I can't interfere with the way David runs his unit.'

'I'm a hundred percent sure God's sent my Ernst back to me, he's even got the same Eagle birthmark and he wears an Eagle on his uniform shoulder. You know how I always called Ernst my Eagle.'

'April grow up for goodness sake grow up, I don't know about the birthmark, but I do know Ernst is dead and he can never come back. Every airman wears the RAF Eagle on their shoulders. You can't possibly be in love with an erk, April. Perhaps it would be for the best if he did leave Bravemouth for good. You're my best friend, April, I can't have you falling in love with an erk, not while I'm the wife of the commanding officer. I can imagine what fun it would be if we went out as a foursome. Then there's his age, he can't be more than twenty. You've got to be at least twelve years older.'

'I only feel twenty when I'm with him.'

'Sorry, darling I'd love to help. But I couldn't ask David to keep him here. It would be a waste of time anyway, David was adamant last night that he was going to send Weston away. Come along darling, I'm still curious, tell me about him.'

'What do you want to know?'

'How you made out with him in bed?'

'He's so shy, Jemmy, he even locked my bathroom door, but I opened it with the safety release and after a few words, we got together. By the way, Jemmy, guess who called upon me yesterday afternoon?'

'I've no idea.'

'Lucy of all people, I think she's psychic, she knew I had someone new here. Weston was doing those jobs for me when she arrived and he was only wearing a pair of Michael's shorts. Jemmy, you should have seen her, it was nauseating the way she ran her hands over him. "You must call me Lucy, Weston,"' she said.

'Oh I bet he enjoyed that.'

'No, I don't think he particularly did, but she enjoyed doing it. I really wish I knew why David's sending Weston away, Jemmy. Have you any idea why?'

'Well all I know, if it will help, is that David said last night that this new man LAC Weston is nothing but a load of trouble with a big T and he wants to get him out of his hair. That's all I know darling, forget LAC Weston, he's only an erk. This is your happiness

94

darling.' Jemmy pointed to April's wedding ring. 'Don't jeopardise everything for a quick romp in bed. There are thousands of men like Weston around. I'd love to help you darling, but like I told you before, I can't interfere with the way David runs his unit. Plus, and I mean this, I won't be part and parcel to you ruining your marriage.'

Meanwhile back at home, Lucy had been on the phone all the morning trying her utmost to discover Weston's address. Not one person she knew had even heard of him. How and why did April always find the new men in town first?

'Lucy my darling, are you on the phone?' Lucy's husband said, walking into the hall.

'No darling, I have now finished with the phone. Was there something?'

'Yes darling, Jeremy and I have been invited as late entrants into the Plymouth Guernsey race on Saturday. Don't mind if I go, do you? We'll have to leave for Plymouth on Wednesday morning. Give us a bit of time for knees up, what?'

This was wonderful news for Lucy. It meant she would have almost a week to herself. I've got to find the whereabouts of April's Weston now, she thought, I've got to get that man in my bed.

'Yes my darling I don't mind, you go and enjoy yourself, it will do you good, don't worry about me, I'll be fine.'

'Are you quite sure, darling?'

'Yes of course I am, you go and enjoy yourself.'

Lucy was shaking in fact she was agitated to the point of screaming with frustration at not being able to find Weston's whereabouts. She finally gave up and decided to improve her tan by sunbathing naked in her yard which over looked the harbour.

Chapter Sixteen

Weston was officially informed by the C/O on the Tuesday morning parade that he would not be going on the naval course. He would be staying on in Bravemouth, and was now a member of High Speed Launch 7412's crew. The C/O only grunted when Weston gave him Dr Wendover's letter.

That evening Weston, after having spent the entire day at sea on the launch, was absolutely knackered. He still hadn't caught up with his lost sleep, so he decided to turn in early. He was about to go for a shower when he remembered his appointment with Dr Wendover.

Trying to make up for lost time, he ran all the way to the hospital.

Doctor Wendover was waiting outside when he arrived.

'Your late, LAC Weston, how do you feel today?'

Weston stood catching his breath, he'd run more than a half a mile.

'I feel-I feel alright, Dr Wendover.'

'Good, there can't be much wrong with you, running like that. Still I'd better have a look at you now you're here.' The hospital door opened and the nursing Sister who had attended to Weston the previous evening came out.

'Dr Wendover? Thank goodness, I thought you'd gone, it's Mr Whiston, his back's gone again, we can't straighten him. Could you have a look at him?' Dr Wendover looked longingly at Weston and sighed.

'Sorry about this, LAC Weston,' she uttered. 'You know where my room is, go through and prepare yourself, I shall not be long.'

She returned ten minutes later to find Weston waiting, covered by a towel.

'We can't stay here, Weston, the staff will give me no peace; we'll go to my private clinic in town.' She threw him a dressing gown and a pair of slippers. 'Put these on, there will be no need for you to dress. I'll put your clothes into my holdall and we'll drive down to the clinic in my shooting brake.'

Weston put the dressing gown on; it was so short it didn't reach his knees.

'This dressing gown's a bit short, Dr Wendover.'

'Covers your friendly bits, does it not, what more could you ask?'

'These slippers too, they're about a size twelve, I only take nines.'

'Oh shut up, stop moaning.'

Wondering what the hospital staff were thinking, seeing him in that short dressing gown, he climbed into her half-timbered Humber estate car. She drove in a very superior manner around the top of the town, expecting every car she met in the narrow streets to reverse out of her way. She eventually turned into a parking space outside a large terraced house; Weston noticed it was quite close to Rowanberry House.

'This is "Top Sails" my private clinic, Weston,' she said, inserting the key and opening the door. 'Go through the hall and down three flights of stairs, my treatment rooms are on the bottom floor.' He could see as he descended the stairs that this house, even though it was in a terrace, had been built to the same design as April's. The treatment rooms looked over the front garden which, like April's, ran down to the harbour. They were in what in April's house she called her cellar. However, these cellar rooms had been made into two large comfortably furnished bedrooms, each with en suite bathrooms. Weston eyed these rooms with trepidation; these were definitely not treatment rooms by any stretch of the imagination.

She pushed him into the first room and locked the door.

'This is just a bedroom, Dr Wendover, not a treatment room.'

'I hope to hell I'm not going to have trouble with you, LAC Weston. By the way I'm intrigued, why does April call you Pew?'

'It's my nickname, everyone calls me Pew. Look, Dr Wendover, I'm fine I don't need any further treatment.'

'I'm the doctor, I'll be the judge of how you are, let me have a good look at you, take that dressing gown off.'

'No, sorry, doctor, first I don't need any treatment and secondly I don't want you to treat me here, this place is a bedroom.' Rebecca thought, what on Earth's the matter with him, he's being obstinate again, I'd better help her out; she slipped into Weston's mind.

Weston came round from his momentary loss of willpower and found himself lying naked on the bed.

'You're quite right, LAC Weston, this isn't my clinic. This is my husband's bondage room. He and his queer male friends play their strange sex games in here. It's come in very handy for me today though. Would you like me to whip you or tie you up so you can't move?'

'No I would not, I'm not like that.'

'Do you know I could be struck off for what I am going to do to you this evening? Because I'm going to enjoy forcing myself on you. In fact you are going to be raped, young man.' She laughed. 'But no one would believe you if you told them. Actually Pewsy, do you know I like that name, I'm going to call you Pewsy. She took hold of his erect penis. Weston squirmed; she was evoking new feelings in him by the minute.

'This will be the first time I've ever seduced anyone

in my life, I prefer the word seduce to rape don't you. You're making history, Pewsy.'

She ran her hands seductively, slowly up down and around his naked skin, feeling teasingly around then taking hold of his nipples, which she playfully squeezed. She removed her overalls to show she was wearing nothing whatsoever underneath. Her large breasts caressed his now goose pimply body.

'Good grief I wouldn't have believed it,' she uttered. 'If I hadn't seen it for myself, there is not a single blemish on your skin, Pewsy. You have a fantastic healing body. You don't mind me calling you that do you?'

'Call me what you like, but I'm not having sex with you. How you got me on this bed is a mystery to me. I think you and your husband are perverts.' The expression on her face changed.

'Don't say that, Pewsy, I can assure you I'm not a pervert; however I am a Naturist and I'm proud of it. Monte, my husband, well he's a different kettle of fish altogether, he's all things to all men. Still, let's not talk about him.'

'Dr Wendover, sorry I can't have sex with you, you're a married woman.'

'What about April Ferrimins and Lucy, they are both married?'

'Well, yes it's true and I have had sex, albeit under protest, with Mrs Ferrimins, but I've not had sex with Mrs Carrington-Townley.'

She frowned as she thought about his answer; the next moment, as if to say to hell with it, she kissed him full on the mouth before slowly kissing him down his body. He squirmed and moaned, his body bursting and alive with the fantastic sensations she was giving him. 'If you thought that was nice, Pewsy, you're certainly going to enjoy this; if God invented anything better, he kept it to himself.' She took his massively erect penis and carefully guided it into her receptive body.

Rebecca watched, she was feeling quite pleased with herself. Dr Wendover was the second of the four women he'd been sent to satisfy. Two hours later Dr Wendover, who had not held back in using her huge knowledge of sex, suddenly went into an Earth-quaking volcano-erupting, scratching and biting orgasm; its effect on Weston was devastating and he literally burst inside her. Afterwards they lay together panting for breath like a couple of newly landed salmon, listening to the church clock chiming eleven o'clock.

'This weapon of yours my boy,' she said taking his penis into her hand. 'Is not the dick of a sexual beginner, that was fantastic, in fact it was an out of this world experience for me. How was it for you?' She again kissed him. 'That definitely wasn't the performance of a virgin, my boy. I've had lots of sex in my life, no wonder April wants to keep you to herself. I've never enjoyed sex like that before.' She sighed as if to emphasize her thoughts. The sound of the front door being opened brought them back to reality.

'It can only be my bloody husband, what the hell does he want? Yes it's got to be him, no one else has a key.'

'Saw the shooting brake darling,' a man's voice shouted. 'I'll leave my car here, we can go home in the brake together, what.'

'It's Monte my husband, quick get in here.' She pushed Weston out of the bed and into the en suite bathroom and closed the door. She hurriedly straightened her hair and replaced her overalls; she bungled Weston's dressing gown and slippers on the top of his other clothes in her large holdall and awaited her husband.

Weston heard the door open and someone walk into

the room.

'What are you doing here, Judy? I couldn't believe my eyes when I saw the shooting brake,' he said this, speaking in cut glass clipped English.

'Just enjoying a drink of your brandy darling, I wanted to be on my own for a while. What are you doing here, surely not more of your weird practices tonight?'

'Yacht club committee meeting, darling, you forgotten darling, come along, best foot what, I'll drive?'

Weston heard them climb the stairs and the door being banged shut. He looked at his watch, it was ten past eleven, he waited for another minute before he came out.

To his dismay, her holdall containing all his clothes had gone. He searched the house from top to bottom but couldn't find a thing to wear. The enormity of his situation was quite plain; he was a mile from the camp, without a stitch to wear. Why on Earth did she put his clothes into her holdall? He saw the phone on the hall table and considered phoning the camp to ask one of the lads to bring his uniform down. He quickly changed his mind; if any of the lads saw him like this, he'd never hear the last of it. There had to be another way.

The phone rang and he thought he'd answer it. Only Dr Wendover knows I'm here, he thought. It was Dr Wendover.

'Pewsy, have you found anything to wear? Stupid bloody hubby, he put my holdall into the brake. Whatever you do, don't put any of the lights on, I will deny all knowledge of you, if you are found there.'

'What are you going to do? Are you going to bring my clothes back? I can't go through the town like this.'

'Sorry, Pewsy. Can't help you; Treroscoe Farm's miles out of town and I've no one to send.'

101

'Can't you phone someone?'

'I shall have to go; I can hear Monte coming back.'

'Who on Earth was that on the phone at this time of night darling?' Weston heard her husband say.

'It's only Lucy, darling.'

Rebecca looked on; for once she felt helpless. Weston would have to get himself out of this predicament.

Chapter Seventeen

Weston was in a real dilemma; he was over a mile from the camp without a stitch of clothing to wear. Perspiration was streaming down his face, despite being naked. However, he was just about to phone the camp when he pulled back the curtain and looked out of the window. He saw his salvation; there was a small dinghy lying to a mooring just a few yards out from the end of the garden. If he could get aboard the dinghy without being seen, he could quite easily make his way up the harbour to the RAF base, where he knew there were denim overalls hanging in the base shed. He could wear a pair of those to get back to the camp and no one would be any the wiser.

The moon was bright and Weston had to wait for a dark cloud he could see moving across the sky to obscure it. He opened the door to the garden and quickly ran to the water's edge. It felt strange, feeling the warm breeze on his naked skin. He kept as low as he could and he slipped down to the water's edge. The tide had turned; it was now flooding. Lowering himself carefully, he tried not to splash into the surprisingly warm water. He swam out to the dinghy and scrambled into it by climbing over its transom. Luckily for Weston the oars and rowlocks had been left aboard. Casting the dinghy's mooring over and using one of the oars over the stern to scull and steer, he allowed the flood tide to take her upstream. He didn't secure the dinghy to the RAF jetty, because he knew it would be reported as stolen in the morning. Instead he tied it alongside a small motorboat moored directly across from the RAF base. Under a single gas light on a slipway close to the RAF base jetty, he could make out three men angling. Hoping they wouldn't see him, he slipped over the side and, using breast stroke to avoid splashes, which caused flashes of luminance, in the warm water, he swam across to the RAF base jetty. Now the most challenging part had arrived. No way could he avoid it; he had to climb the vertical iron ladder that ran up the end of the jetty. He began the climb and, feeling more exposed than any performer on the stage, he eased himself up rung by rung, hoping the airman on duty at the base and the anglers who were fishing a few yards away wouldn't see him. Fortunately, the duty airman had turned in, and the light under which the anglers were standing was too bright for them to see him. Once he'd got to the top and was in the base yard, he eased the shed door open, hoping it wouldn't make a noise. He thankfully helped himself to a pair of overalls, put them on and, still barefoot, he ran up the steps to the street. There he found a Godsend; someone had left a bicycle leaning against the base wall. He leapt on it without switching on its lights and pedalled as hard as he could until he reached the camp. He pushed the bicycle out of sight through a gap in the field hedge opposite the camp gates and ran across the lawn to his billet.

Rebecca was pleased to see Weston had surmounted his problems without her help. However, she frowned when she saw the bully Flight Sergeant Fenship. He was standing on the edge of the lawn relieving himself; no way could he have missed seeing Weston.

Weston opened the billet door as quietly as he could; everyone was asleep, he tiptoed down between the beds without waking anyone, removed the overalls and, rolling them into a ball, he placed them under Wittingham the base clerk's bed. Feeling pleased at the way things had worked out and wondering what Wittingham would say when he looked under his bed, he eased himself between the sheets.

Flight Sergeant Fenship had seen Weston and, being in his usual inebriated state, decided that now was time to give Weston a good hiding.

Rebecca, forever watchful and realising what the Flight Sergeant had in mind, guided him away from Airman's quarters No 3, Weston's billet, to the next one, which was Airman's quarters No 2.

'I warned you to keep away from Mrs Ferrimins, didn't I? Now I'm going to cripple you, Weston, you bastard.' He shouted, grabbing LAC Stringfellow by the throat and throwing him on the floor. The uproar he created woke the entire billet, followed shortly by all the camp. That is with the exception of Weston who slept soundly through it all.

The next morning the camp was alive with rumours. Someone said all the officers were coming up to the camp for the morning's parade.

Whispers abounded about Flight Sergeant Fenship; some said he was being posted out of Bravemouth. Someone else said that Gabley the camp lorry driver was at this very moment driving him to the station at Plymouth. It was also said that the police had been up to the camp because someone had stolen the Police Sergeant's bike from outside the RAF base. The Sergeant had only gone to talk to some anglers for a few minutes; when he returned his bike had gone.

'Hope you've not given me bad advice, Mr Greenwith, regarding LAC Weston?' the C/O said. 'I'm still not convinced about that clever bugger. This is the second good man I've lost since he arrived. Don't argue; you know he was implicated with both of them.'

Chapter Eighteen

Lucinda Carrington-Townley's life hadn't been the bed of roses she'd imagined it was going to be when she married George, her much older but extremely wealthy husband. There were many aspects of her married life that she wasn't happy about. However, her main bone of contention was the fact that although she wasn't a one hundred percent nymphomaniac, she certainly enjoyed her sex, and her husband had been impotent for years.

Ever since she'd made the acquaintance of Weston at April's home, Lucy had done nothing but fantasise about him. Why was it April always got her hands on the new young men first? It didn't seem fair.

She'd spent the whole of Tuesday phoning around, trying to find out where Weston lived. The only person who knew of his whereabouts was April Ferrimins, and no way could she ask her.

However, fate took a hand when Jemima told her about April visiting an RAF boy called Weston in the hospital on Monday evening. She now had the answer to her problem. Weston was in the air force; she should have guessed, she'd had quite a lot of fun in the past with the Royal Air Force boys.

She knew Wednesday afternoon was sports day in the air force, and she wondered whether Weston would be taking part in some sport. To that end, she parked her large Ford V8 pilot close to the camp gates so she might catch sight of him.

Her plan, if she could possibly get her hands on him, was to take him out to her holiday cottage in the nearby village of Kings Landing. Once there, she could seduce him. Now her husband was away for a few days, she was a free agent.

Wednesday proved to be another hot day, although the weather forecast said thunder and rain later.

Weston had only been in Bravemouth for a few days, therefore he hadn't been picked for the cricket team; consequently he had whole afternoon free. He set out to see the highlights of Bravemouth, wearing his brand new white shorts and pale blue sports shirt. He'd made arrangements to meet his friends Tom and Richard on the town quay later.

Lucy Carrington-Townley's body actually trembled with anticipation of what was to come when she saw Weston striding through the gates. Now for it, she thought, moving in for the kill.

Weston stood to the side of the narrow road upon hearing a car approaching. The car stopped and the beautiful diminutive Mrs Carrington-Townley got out.

'Weston I thought it was you. I must say you look incredibly sexy in those shorts, you've gorgeous legs. I'm on my way to the cottage, in the village of Kings Landing, would you like to come?'

Weston's first thought was to say no. However, he thought it might be fun, so throwing caution to the wind he climbed into her car. He sat alongside this beautiful albeit tiny woman who he hardly knew while she drove him out of town.

'I'm so glad you decided to come along, Weston,' she said, laughing. 'That sounds rude doesn't it?' She pulled her dress high up her legs. 'Sorry about that, but this dress is a little tight and I need the freedom for the controls. Your shorts aren't tight though are they?' Without a hint of warning, she shot her hand up his shorts leg and took a hold of his penis. This was something Weston hadn't been prepared for, and he involuntary jerked upward with the shock, hitting his head on the car roof.

'Whoops, whatever must you think? I don't know

what came over me,' she said giggling.

'That's enough of that, stop the car,' Weston shouted, taking a hold of her wrist and pulling her hand out, his face bright red with embarrassment.

He placed her hand on the wheel.

'What do you call your penis? You must have a name for it; my husband calls his his todger.'

'Mrs Carrington-Townley, if you're going to carry on like this I'm getting out,' Weston said firmly.

'I'm so sorry, am I embarrassing you, Weston? So sorry.' She gave him a peck of a kiss. He looked at her and although quite small, she was a very handsome woman. She was wearing a low cut white sundress that showed quite lot of her suntanned breasts. Like April, she wore just the briefest touch of light pink lipstick just to emphasise her impish face.

She looks just like Peter Pan in a dress, he thought.

'Do you think I look nice today, Weston?'

'Yes of course I do, you look lovely, Mrs Carrington Townley.'

'Weston may I have a real feel of your penis? I've not felt a circumcised one before and don't call me Mrs Carrington-Townley. It's Lucy to you, Weston. You're not Jewish though by the way are you?'

'No of course not, I'm like the rest of my family, a Methodist, now keep your hands on the wheel and leave me alone please.'

'But, but, but, Weston,' she pouted.'I've wanted to play with your penis ever since I saw you were circumcised, when you were romping naked with April on Monday. Do you really think I look nice today?'

'Yes, I told you so, you could quite easily play the lead in Peter Pan.'

'Oh and who might you be, Captain Hook? Judy calls you Pewsy, why?'

'It's not Pewsy. My name is Paul Edward Weston.

I'm known as Pew, because of my initials. Only one person calls me Pewsy, that's Dr Wendover. Is the doctor's name Judy?'

'Yes it is, but tell me, why did April introduce you to me as Weston?'

'Mrs Ferrimins and I weren't on very friendly terms when you gatecrashed in on us; we'd had a disagreement.'

'Well it didn't look like a disagreement to me. I don't want to call you Pew, I don't like that name, it doesn't suit you, would you be upset if I called you Weston?'

'If that's what you want, I don't mind.'

She didn't answer, but he could see she was smiling. She turned the car off the main road into a narrow lane and she drove down this for about a mile. At the bottom of the lane she turned sharply to the right and passed through a pair of open wooden gates into the drive of a large white painted house. Weston thought, so this is what she calls her country cottage.

'Typical holiday makers,' she said. 'They never close the gates when they leave, will you close them for me, Weston?'

Weston climbed out, taking in the spectacular view of the River Bravy spread out below. The tide was out and there were yachts and small boats lying dried out on the mud. A small creek with high wooded slopes meandered down to join the river on the opposite side; it was a breathtaking view.

Weston closed the two five-foot high wooden gates. On one was a sign written in old English writing, which said, "Peter Pan's Cottage, Kings Landing". A high well-trimmed hawthorn hedge coming into blossom surrounded the whole place. Once the gates were closed, he could see the property was very private.

He walked through the small front garden to the

front door. The borders of the immaculate small front lawn were full of colourful spring flowers.

'Hurry, Weston, I've something to show you,' Lucy shouted from the open front door.

Weston, wondering what on Earth she had to show him, looked through the white painted studded front door into a small black and white tiled hall. Straight ahead across the tiled floor was a lovely old oak door, which obviously led into the drawing room. To the right through another open door he could see the kitchen.

'Up here, darling.'

Weston heard her, but he wanted to see the cottage before he joined her. He walked into the large Cornish slate-floored drawing room. This room boasted a long low granite fireplace which was covered in horse brasses. Either side of the fireplace were two oil paintings, one of the view of the river from the cottage window and the other a picture of Bravemouth, painted from the East Bravy side of the river. Directly above the fireplace was a large oil painting of an elfin-faced young ballet dancer. That must be Lucy when she was a young girl, he thought. A grandfather clock, a five-piece suite with two sofas covered in deep red Chintz and a coffee table furnished this end of the room. At the far end was a large oak refectory table with twelve upright chairs and an oak dresser. The cold slate floor was covered with scattered rugs. Weston thought, this is some country cottage, it's more like a manor house.

'Weston, come along hurry, up here,' she shouted. She listened and listened but there was no sound from downstairs. She leapt from the bed and, undoing the shoulder straps to her dress, she let it drop to the floor, revealing she was wearing not a stitch underneath. She ran down the stairs naked.

Weston was shocked to see her naked, but he

thought, nothing surprises me about the ladies of Bravemouth. He took in the view of her tiny perfectly shaped suntanned body with not one white mark to show where her bikini had been; she ran over to him and placed his hands on her breasts and, standing on tiptoes, she kissed him full on the lips.

'I've been waiting to be fucked by you ever since I saw you with April on Monday afternoon, Weston.'

'Don't use that language with me, Lucy, I don't like it.'

'Sorry, but please come along, Weston; don't waste time the bed's waiting.'

'No, Mrs Carrington-Townley, stop it, who the hell do you think I am?'

'Don't you want to have sex with me? I suppose I'm not good enough for you? You were going to have sex with April.'

'Do you mean that debacle you saw in the hall? We had nothing like sex planned that day; I fell backward over the rolled up carpet and she snatched my shorts off, that's all.'

'I'll pay you whatever April pays you, in fact I'll pay more.'

'I'm not a gigolo, Lucy.'

'What's a gigolo, Weston?'

'I'm not really sure, but I think it's a man who does sex for money. Whatever made you think I did sex for money? I think I should leave, before I find myself in trouble.'

She threw her arms around his neck and kissed him again.

'I'm so sorry for upsetting you, Weston, I don't know what to say, I certainly had you wrong. Forgive me please. I just wanted to have sex with you, nothing else. I'm sorry I said those things about April. Come along let's go upstairs now, please.'

111

'Well I can't think of anything better to do at the moment.'

In the bedroom Lucy played with his erect penis at the same time holding his hand on her clitoris, or cherry as she called it. This went on for several minutes; she then climbed on top and eased his more than ready penis into her tiny body. Within less than five minutes, to Weston's disappointment, she went into an uncontrolled wild back-arching orgasm. Weston was upset; unlike the previous evening with Judy, there'd been nothing in it for him.

Lucy lay alongside, breathing deeply, her tiny body glistening with sweat.

'I couldn't wait, Weston, my body was screaming out for it. You're a wonderful lover, I feel much better now.'

Weston glanced down at his still fully primed weapon.

'So that's sex according to Lucy Carrington-Townley, is it?' he said, critically. 'The whole lot done and dusted in the blink of an eyelid.' Lucy rolled onto her stomach and, looking up at him, she sighed.

'It was fantastic for me.' She took in a deep breath. 'How long do you usually take? Does April take longer?'

'I'm not discussing Mrs Ferrimins with you.'

'You're still rearing to go, Weston, aren't you? You're sulking because you didn't come. I'm so sorry, Weston I've been very selfish. Never mind my darling, you're still hard, so that is something we can't waste can we? Come along, let's do it again.'

Two hours later they rolled away from each other, this time both contented and exhausted.

Lucy sat up and lit a cigarette and offered one to Weston, who declined. 'That was fantastic, Weston. We did actually come together didn't we? You're incredible, where did you learn to perform like that? That's the best fucking, I've ever had, Weston; sorry prude but no other word can describe how I feel at this moment.'

'By the way, Lucy, how long have you been a widow?'

'Widow, I'm not a widow; my George is very fit for his age, even if his todger won't stand up for itself.' She laughed. 'My husband was very ill when we were in East Africa, we thought he was going to die; however he's alright now, although he's not been able to perform since. He's turned sixty-eight, more than twenty five years older than me.'

'I didn't know you were married. I wouldn't have had sex with you if I had known.'

'Forget my George and his floppy todger. He sailed to Plymouth this morning; he's taking part in a yacht race to Guernsey on Saturday. I won't see him until Tuesday at the earliest.' She pushed Weston's hair back from his face and sighed. 'No wonder April wants to keep you to herself. You're brilliant in bed.'

'I'm no different than any other man.'

'Yes you are, you're very very special, you're fantastic.'

She bent over and fondled his.........again. 'I love this of yours, I could play with it all day. Do you know when it goes in, it fills me completely and leaves me glowing inside.' She took a long draw on the cigarette and let the smoke trickle out. 'I've got to see you again, are you free every Wednesday afternoon? We can always use our Yacht, it's well equipped with bunks?'

Weston slipped from the bed, self-conscious of being naked. He looked out of the window; it had started to rain.

'You were right about the weather, Lucy; it's already started to...' He didn't finish his sentence; the

113

bedroom door shot open so hard that it hit the wall and a tall well-built young man dressed in a marine's uniform walked into the room. He had Weston's shorts and shirt in his hand.

'I thought you'd be up here in bed with some shit when I found these lying on the floor. You told me when I phoned that you couldn't make it this afternoon. Who the hell's this effeminate excuse for a man?' Without giving Weston the slightest warning, he swung his huge fist and struck Weston under the chin. Weston actually did momentarily see stars, before his legs crumbled under him; for the first time in his life he'd been knocked out.

'You might have killed him, you brute, get out of here,' Lucy screamed. 'Get out before I phone the police.'

'He's not dead, but he'll wish he was after I've kicked his balls off.'

'Get out, get out, get out,' she yelled. 'I've finished with you.' She threw the bedside clock at him. He caught it, and laughed.

'So he's warmed you up for me? You'll be able to compare notes later.'

Lucy threw a vase of artificial flowers at him, he ducked and it smashed against the wall. He laughed.

'He's certainly put you in the mood my little bare breasted vixen.'

'My breasts, oh.' She quickly covered herself with the eiderdown.

'I've only come here to collect what you promised me.'

Weston came around slowly, his head hurting like hell, but he thought it prudent to lie quietly on the floor. He could feel the back of his head resting on the hearth of the cast iron fireplace. He felt around and discovered the hearth had given him a large gash; it ran down from

114

his crown to his neck.

'I say, I say you bounder, who are you and what are you doing here? Lucy darling, what's going on?' Weston strained his neck round to see who was speaking. There was a distinguished looking elderly man now in the room; he was wearing a yachting cap.

'George, George,' Lucy shouted. 'This bounder was going to rape me.' She leapt out of the bed holding a sheet around herself, making sure the other bed covers dropped over and covered Weston's stationary body.

'I wasn't raping her,' the young man said. 'Honest. I'm not like...' He stopped talking and decided to make a quick exit.

Rebecca was upset; every time she turned her back for a minute or so, something inappropriate happened to Weston. She consoled herself this time by thinking, if it hadn't happened, Lucy's husband could have caught Lucy and Weston in flagrante delicto. I just hope the Head of the Earth Department sees it that way.

Weston lay on the floor hardly daring to breathe. He could feel the hot blood running down his neck, but there was nothing he could do about it.

Lucy ran into her husband's arms.

'George, I'm so glad you came back, hug me close darling. You were very brave you know. That brute could have killed you. What on Earth are you doing here? I thought you were on your way to the Channel Islands?'

'No choice, darling, had to turn back, what? Jeremy, selfish bastard, decided to get himself a little food poisoning. I was on a loose end. So thought, seeing the tide was flooding, I'd come up the river in the dinghy and give you a hand with the cottage. Jolly good job I did, what? Why on Earth are you naked, darling?'

'You know I always strip off when it's hot, sweetheart.'

115

'Sure you're alright, my little sparrow? Think I should phone for the police, what?'

'No, darling, definitely no, I don't want my name spread all over the local newspaper. Tell you what, now you're here you can drive me home.'

'Sure you don't want me to phone for the police?'

'Positive, darling. I don't want the locals gossiping. You know what they are like. It would be a waste of time anyway, I couldn't describe the blighter, could you?'

'Well for starters I think he was wearing a marine's uniform.'

'Let's forget it, darling, pretend it never happened, come along we'll go downstairs.'

Lucy picked up her dress from the bed and took her husband down into the drawing room.

Weston's shirt and shorts had gone; she remembered seeing the marine had them in his hand.

'Did you get a good look at the rapist, George darling?'

'No, other than the uniform, I'm afraid not, dashed, poor show what, frightfully bad form on my part, darling.'

Weston lay under the covers wondering how he'd ever got himself mixed up with these women, this was the second time in less than a week that he'd had to hide from a husband.

He heard a car engine start and he waited for a few moments before he threw the covers back and ran down the stairs to find once again he'd been abandoned in a strange house without his clothes.

Back in Bravemouth, Lucy waited until her husband was out of the way before phoning Dr Wendover to ask her to check on her boyfriend's head, omitting to tell her it was Weston.

Weston searched the place from top to bottom, but

116

could find nothing to wear; he felt a little better after he'd wrapped a towel around his waist. The phone rang; it can only be Lucy, he thought. He picked up the receiver.

'Weston, I've only got a few moments before George comes back. I've phoned for the doctor to come to see you; she'll be there in about half an hour.'

'She? Not another woman doctor? I'm naked, I can't find my clothes?'

'That brute who punched you had them in his hand, he must have taken them with him. Oh, darling. I wish I was there with you, I love to see you naked. I've got to go, he's coming back.' The phone went dead.

Half an hour later, Dr Wendover arrived.

She thought it extremely funny when she saw Lucy's new boyfriend was Pewsy Weston.

'I don't believe it. Don't tell me Lucy's also had you in bed? Wonder why she didn't tell me it was you? Don't you think you should stop these stupid capers, before you get really hurt? I think it must be a record, being beaten up twice in three days, never mind being abandoned yet again in a strange house without clothes. Tell me, Pewsy, how did you get out of that situation I left you in?'

'You will have to find out for yourself. I won't tell you. It wasn't very nice, that game you played on me. You could have brought my clothes back.'

'I would have done so if I could; however, I just couldn't, sorry, Pewsy. Now then let me have look at your head, at least the bleeding stopped, it is quite nasty a wound, I'm afraid it is going to need stitching. This is a hospital job, the wound should be injected with a painkiller first.'

'No, I'm not going to the hospital, do it here. I don't want everyone in Bravemouth knowing I've been assaulted again.'

117

'Think about it, Pewsy, it's going to hurt like hell.'

'Did you bring those clothes of mine back, you took last night?'

'Yes, don't worry my holdall is in the brake.' Twenty minutes later, she put the last stitch in and straightened her back.

'You were very good, Pewsy.' She kissed him. 'That's for being brave. I'll get your things from the brake.' She snatched the towel away. 'Well I wouldn't have believed it, and I've made that statement quite a lot since I made your acquaintance, Pewsy.'

'What, what don't you believe?'

'That you're ready for sex again, especially after romping all the afternoon with Lucy.'

'I think I'm always ready for sex, don't you think all men are?'

'I'll have to think about that one, but we can't waste that beautiful erection.' She took it to her mouth. Weston squirmed so much with the sensations she was evoking in him that he forgot all about the wound in his head. She came up for air and smiled. 'Come along, Pewsy, we've the whole of Lucy's cottage at our disposal.'

'What about my clothes?'

'There'll be plenty of time to get those; you won't need clothes in Lucy's double bed.'

Two hours later, Weston and Judy, worn out with the exertion of their frantic love making, climbed out of the bed.

'I'm so hungry,' Weston said. 'I've not eaten since lunch time. What time is it?' Judy looked at her watch.

'It's seven thirty. Come along I'll buy you a meal in the local inn. You're a wonderful lover, Pewsy. In fact you're wonderful in more ways than one. That nasty cut in your head's healing already.' She put her overalls on. 'I'll get your clothes.' A few minutes later she came

118

back, laughing.

'Sorry, Pewsy, Monte must have taken my holdall out.' Weston lay back on the bed.

'Well if that's the way you feel, Pewsy, I'll join you.' She dropped her overalls and within a minute they were at it again.

Much, much later that evening, Dr Wendover dropped a drained and still hungry Weston outside the camp; he was wearing one of the doctor's white overalls. Luckily there was no one awake in the billet when he crept down to his bed.

Chapter Nineteen

With a look of triumph on her face, April Ferrimins threw down her last card.

'Well played, Jemmy, I make that game and oh yes a seven hundred rubber.'

'You had the cards,' one of the other ladies said peevishly, looking at her watch. 'Good grief is that the time? I must go. School governors meeting at four o'clock. Thank you for a pleasant afternoon, April, my place next week. Bye bye, Jemmy.' With the usual hugs and kisses, April and Jemima saw their friends out.

'Jemmy, it's only quarter to four? What do you say to a Martini on the terrace? The weather's simply gorgeous at the moment.'

'Only if you let me make them, your Martinis are nothing but gin; they have very little vermouth.'

'Do you know who made the finest Martini I ever tasted?'

'No, who?'

'Pew Weston.' She sighed. 'That young man is exactly like my Ernst, why on Earth did David send him away?'

Jemima turned away, her face a deep red.

'Of course I remember LAC Weston, how could I ever forget him, you never stop going on about him,' she said.

'He is so like my Ernst,' April said, sighing.

'I'm sorry, darling, I should have told you sooner than this April. I feel frightful now. Weston was not sent away, he's been here all the time.'

'Do you mean he's been in Bravemouth all week and you didn't let me know?'

'I thought you were getting over him, darling, he's

only a common erk you know, he'll do you no good, April.'

April didn't want to fall out with her best friend, so she kept quiet and just stared out of the window, her heart racing at the thought of seeing Weston again.

Jemima made the Martinis, handed one glass to April, and they carried them to the terrace in silence.

'April, when's Edwina coming up from London, is she coming by train again?' Jemima said, changing the subject. 'The charity dinner and ball's on Saturday evening you know.'

'Don't try to change the conversation, Jemmy. I do love you and I don't want to fall out with you, but I really think you've been horrid. You could have told me Weston was staying on here. However, this only reinforces my belief that God sent him in answer to my prayers. If he hadn't, David would have sent him away. Don't worry about the charity ball, everything's in hand.'

'Sorry, April, I do wish I'd told you, I feel dreadful now.'

'I should think you do, I tell you everything,' April said, lying.

'Forgive me, darling.'

'I shouldn't really, but what the hell, if Weston's here to stay, I'm over the moon happy. Edwina's driving to Bravemouth on Friday, that's tomorrow, she'll probably get here around eight in the evening. She phoned on Sunday to say we can all go together in her new car. She's bought a Standard Vanguard, it's large enough she says to hold five or six adults. However, she doesn't want to drive to the ball; she wants us to find someone to chauffeur us.'

'I don't know of anyone other than David, and I really don't think we should ask him, he's so bad tempered behind the wheel. I suppose we could ask

David to get the camp's fifteen-hundred weight driver to take us.'

'No, no, Jemmy. I don't want to be driven there by a lorry driver.'

'Why don't you go down to the base and ask David yourself, he'll do anything for you. You may even get a glimpse of your sexpot.'

Weston followed the rest of his crew up the vertical iron ladder to the yard. Wittingham, the base clerk, was standing at the top.

'Pew old boy, Toddy wants to see you in his office now, he means now, he said pronto.'

'What does he want to see me for?'

'How the hell would I know? But I can guess.' He sighed deeply. 'She's with him, that bloody gorgeous, sexy Mrs Ferrimins. I think everyone in the base, with the exception of Mr Greenwith, has got a bloody hard on. That woman does strange things to me. I shall have to go somewhere again to get my hormones straightened out again.'

Weston knocked on the C/O's office door, and walked in.

'You wanted to see me, sir? Oh, good afternoon, Mrs Ferrimins; didn't expect to see you here.' He thought, Witty's right. April was looking fantastic; she was dressed in a short red cotton skirt with a low fronted white cotton draw stringed blouse, showing quite a lot of her suntanned breasts.

'I see you don't salute now, Weston.'

'Sorry, sir, seeing Mrs Ferrimins, I didn't think.'

'Good afternoon, Weston, you look well,' April said. 'You told me you were going away, what changed your mind?'

'I asked the same question, Mrs Ferrimins, but I didn't get an answer.'

'Enough of that talk, Weston, remember where you

are.'

April's eyes flashed; she didn't like to hear David talking to her Eagle like that.

'I've been informed by the marine tender coxswain that you hold a full driving licence, is that true, Weston?'

'Yes, sir. I do have a licence but I don't think it's what you call a full one, sir.' Why the hell did Richard have tell him I had a licence? he thought.

'If it's not a full one what groups does it cover?'

'Not sure, sir, just cars and motorcycles, I think.'

'Could you drive a Standard Vanguard saloon with it?' April said.

'Yes, I like Standard Vanguards, my father owns one and I drive it quite often, why?'

'We want someone to chauffeur us to a Dinner and Ball at a naval station on Saturday evening; do you think you are up to it?' the C/O said.

'I'm not sure that I'm the right man, sir. I'm not a chauffeur, sir, wouldn't it be better if Gabley drove you, sir.'

'No, Mrs Ferrimins says she doesn't want to be driven by a lorry driver.'

Weston looked from one to the other.

'Well, Weston. Will you do it? Spit it out man.'

'I suppose so, sir.'

'Thank you very much, Weston. I really appreciate this,' April said, getting to her feet. 'I would like you to come to my home on Saturday evening, say at six o'clock, and we'll take it from there.'

'We are going to a naval base, Weston; make sure you are smartly turned out in your best blue uniform. We can't let the air force down in front of the navy. Right, Weston, that will be all.'

'David, do you think LAC Weston could drive me home, my car's nearby, you know how I hate driving.'

123

'Yes, of course, he's nothing better to do. You can drop me off at my place as well, Weston.'

April's car was a Jowett Javelin, a car Weston had always wanted to drive. He dropped the C/O off at his home and drove on and parked outside Rowanberry House.

The C/O's wife was standing outside Rowanberry House gate looking very glamorous, wearing a large white sun hat, white shirt style dress and high-heeled shoes.

Weston got out of the car and opened the door for April.

'Good evening, LAC Weston,' the C/O's wife said. 'April darling, I forgot to remind you earlier, we are going with the vicar to Plymouth this evening; we promised to support his orphanage charity.' April's eyes flashed.

'I can't possibly go with you now, Jemmy; you will have to go alone.'

The vicar, with Mrs Heimer sitting alongside him, drove up in his Morris Minor.

'I'm going in, before the vicar sees me,' April said. 'Give him my apologies. Come along, Weston.' They ran down the path together.

Weston made them a substantial ham salad, poured April a Martini and opened a bottle of beer for himself.

'We've the whole evening to ourselves,' April said, sitting down to eat.

'No I can't stay, I'm sorry, Mrs Ferrimins, I will have to go back to the camp. I've had a message from Corporal Geordie to say I had to see him tonight. I can return here later if you want me to.'

'Very well, but don't be long, I made plans for us tonight.' Her eyes sparkled. 'You can take the car.'

Corporal Geordie was sitting alone in the mess when Weston walked in.

'Pew, I've bought a couple of rump steaks in town this afternoon, think you could you manage one?'

'Steaks, my word, of course I could.' He didn't mention having a ham salad with April.

'Right, while I've got you here, Pew, Barbara's cousin Tamsin phoned me today; she wants to meet you, Pew.'

'So she wants a date with me, does she?'

'Not quite a date, Pew. She wants me to arrange an outing or something so she can meet you casually. She doesn't want to be with you alone. I've told her what a womanising bugger you are, but she still wants to see you.'

The steaks arrived each with two eggs and a few chips. It didn't take long before their plates were clean.

'Well, Pew, what do you think about seeing Tamsin again?'

'Yes, great by me. I'll leave it with you to arrange something.'

'I think she's a fool, a beautiful girl like her going out with a womanising bugger like you.'

'What womanising have I done?'

'Quite a lot. I know everything that goes on regarding you and those posh women in Bravemouth. My lads tell me everything they see; you've been seen with the lovely Mrs Carrington-Townley in her bloody big car. You've also been seen with the beautiful Doctor Wendover. Yes you've even been seen going into her big house in town. Then again where have you been tonight? My lads tell me they saw you driving Mrs Ferrimins to her home in her car. Still, forget about that, what do you think about the four of us, me and Barbara and you and Tamsin, having a day out together in Truro? We could have a meal, see a film and get the late bus back.'

'Sounds great to me. When are we going?'

'What about Saturday?'

'Sorry, Saturday's out. I've got to drive the C/O and his friends to some charity ball at some naval base.'

'Why you? You're not a qualified chauffeur.'

'Better ask the C/O. I don't want to drive them.'

'Oh I can see what the attraction is; you'll be out with those bloody married women again. I bet they told the C/O we wanted LAC Weston, the one with a big dick, to drive them.'

'I've not been invited to the ball, I've only been told to drive them there. I'll be stuck in the NAAFI on my own all evening. What about Sunday, can't we go then?'

'No, Sunday's out. Tamsin works away in Exeter, she's a trainee something or other. She lives with one of her aunts during the week and only comes home on Friday afternoon. She goes back to Exeter on Sunday night. Tell you what, I'll lay it on for next Saturday.' He stood and picked up the empty plates.

'Next Saturday it is then, Geordie. If only you'd told me this yesterday. I would have had a good reason to turn the C/O down.'

'Right you are, Pew,' he sighed loudly. 'Leave it with me, I'll sort something out, don't forget to keep a week on Saturday open.'

Meanwhile, Dennis, or Stanley Laurel as his mother thought of him, was reporting on the day's events at Rowanberry House to his mother. He stopped talking when he noticed Weston getting out of Mrs Ferrimins' car outside Rowanberry House, this time out of uniform.

'I'll phone you later, Mother. That airman I told you about, he's here again, this time out of uniform.'

'Find out who he is and what he's doing there,' she said. 'I don't want any complications at this late stage.' Dennis left the house, intending to meet Weston

126

casually.

Weston pushed open the gate and looked up as per usual to the top of the hedge.

'So you've come back have you?'

'Yes, you are very clever noticing that, but this time I've come back for you my sweetheart. I'm going to come round to your place and give you a big kiss.'

'Oh go away. I can't talk sense to you. What are you doing here again?'

Dennis stood by April's car, but could not make out what Weston was saying.

'The trouble is, my darling,' Weston said, 'all the ladies of Bravemouth are in love with me and I have to try to share it out equally.'

'Don't talk such utter stupidity. I'm an old woman and I'm certainly not in love with you.'

'Oh yes you are, and I've found out your name, it's Mrs Cousins, and I've been told that you are madly in love with me. Underneath that hard exterior of yours, I know there's a heart of gold and it's all mine.'

'Go on you fool, get in to your hussy. I bet she's in bed even now waiting for you.'

Weston opened the unlocked front door and walked in.

'Pew, will you be ever so good and put my car away? My garage is No. 22 in the block of garages across from the RAF camp,' April shouted. 'I won't need it again tonight.'

She's even treating me like a chauffeur now, Weston thought as he returned to the car.

A tall extremely thin boy in RAF uniform walked up.

'Hello, do you want a lift back to camp?' Weston shouted. Dennis saw in this a chance to find out who this man was. He climbed into the passenger seat and started up a conversation, but it was a complete waste of time; all he discovered was the fact that Weston had only been in Bravemouth for a few days. Dennis got out in the town centre. Weston drove on to the garage, put the car away and walked back to Rowanberry House with the keys.

'You again, can't keep away from her can you?' the old lady shouted as Weston opened the gate.

'Mrs Cousins, you are trying to get me into trouble with Mrs Ferrimins?' The old lady chuckled.

'The truth cuts deep, doesn't it? I see she's left the door open for you again, I bet she's waiting for you in bed, looking all beautiful.'

Weston walked in and crossed the drawing room to the open French windows he could see. April, wearing a white bikini, was stretched on a lounger looking as beautiful as any film star.

'I've put the car away and brought the car keys back, Mrs Ferrimins. I will see you on Saturday.'

'No, Pew, don't leave yet.' She ran across and took him into her arms. 'Hold me tight, Pew. Don't you realise now that I have found you I want to keep you forever.' She kissed him deep and long, until they fell back onto her sun lounger, where they made Weston's special type of love until they climaxed together.

It was a most happy contented April who saw Weston off her premises that night.

Weston looked at his watch to see it was half past midnight when he finally made his way back to the camp.

Chapter Twenty

Saturday morning's pleasant cooling breeze had blown itself away by lunch time, leaving in its wake a hot, close afternoon. Weston, his forehead glistening with sweat, checked himself in his best blue uniform in the billets mirror before he set out. He couldn't help thinking about how he could have been in Truro with Tamsin and the others at this very moment. He sighed, as he thought what a fool he'd been in agreeing to be their chauffeur.

It was exactly six o'clock when he eased himself through a narrow gap left by a badly parked black Standard Vanguard saloon car outside April's home.

He glanced to the top of the hedge and he wasn't disappointed.

'Hello, young man, you look very smart today, for a change. Did you know her sister's arrived here? Should be nice for you, having them both in bed.' Weston looked at her with a question mark on his face, but didn't say anything.

'It is her sister, at least I'm pretty sure it is. She must be. They are as alike as two peas in pod, except her sister's got this beautiful long red hair. That's her car outside. Do you know her sister?'

'No, I didn't know she had one.'

'Oh yes and she was here last week. She looks a proper minx to me. I don't trust people with red hair.'

Weston rang the bell.

April, looking ravishing wearing a white satin dressing gown, opened the door.

'Come in, Pew, good to see you.' She leaned over the stairs, and shouted, 'Edwina, Weston's here, come up and meet him, bring the car keys with you.' She gave Weston a peck of a kiss. 'She won't be long, darling. I must get on, Kathleen's helping me to prepare the nips and sips for this evening.'

Weston stood there, wishing he hadn't arrived so promptly on time.

'Have you seen Edwina yet, Pew?' April shouted.

'No, not yet, Mrs Ferrimins.'

'So it's not April today?' She said, walking into the hall. 'Perhaps you're right. Yes, call me Mrs Ferrimins and I'll call you Weston. Especially in front of your C/O and his wife.'

'April darling,' a deep tobacco rasping husky voice from down the stairs shouted. 'I can't come up at the moment. Can't you send the fellow down?'

'That was my sister, Edwina. Sorry, Pew, you don't mind going down to her room do you? She's in the guest room, the second door along on the bottom landing.' Weston found the room and was surprised to see the door was open; however, he still knocked.

'Is that you, Weston? Come in and close the door behind you,' a husky voice shouted.

Weston closed the door behind him and stopped dead in his tracks.

'Sorry, I'm so sorry, Mrs Weatherington, I thought you said come in. I didn't realise you weren't dressed.'

'I did say come in.' April's sister was indeed a sight to behold; she was sitting in a white Lloyd loom chair smoking a cigarette in a very long holder, her long silk covered legs resting on the dressing table and, other than the stockings, she was only wearing a suspender belt.

'Surely you've seen a woman in her underclothes before?'

'But you're not even wearing underclothes,' Weston said, his face bright red.

'So what's the deal, you're either a man or woman. I've breasts and you haven't, or have you?' She

130

laughed. 'Where's this birthmark of yours April's told me about?'

'I'm sorry, I shall have to go.'

'Go? You've only just arrived. Don't be silly, I only want to see this birthmark.' She stood and slipped her feet into a pair of high-heeled shoes.

'Edwina, what the hell do you think you are doing, what's going on?' April shouted. She'd seen it all while standing in the doorway.

'Nothing really, darling. I only wanted to see his Eagle birthmark.'

'Edwina, you should be ashamed of yourself. Put your dressing gown on; cover yourself up.'

'It's rather late for that, don't you think.'

'Give Weston the car keys and stop embarrassing the poor boy.'

Edwina, a smirking smile on her lips, picked up an envelope from the dressing table and, not caring about her body being in full view, walked over and gave it to Weston.

'Here are the car keys and three pound notes; I want you to fill the car with petrol.'

'Thank you, Mrs Weatherington. I I I think I'll be going,' Weston said, hurrying out onto the landing, April following.

'Don't mention her horrid behaviour to any of the others, Pew. I don't want her to spoil the evening before it starts. Tell you what, Pew, put the money she's given you into your pocket; it will do for your expenses. I'll give you the money for petrol. Will you be an angel and call at the Todmarsh-River's on your way back and bring them here? I'm having a few friends in for drinks before we go.' She pushed his hair back from his face.

'Don't take offence with Edwina, Pew. I despair with her at times. She always acts like that; she does it

131

to make sure you will remember her.'

'If that was her intention, Mrs Ferrimins, she succeeded beyond her wildest dreams. I will never forget her.'

'I'll get you the petrol money.' Weston waited until she returned with the money – four pound notes. 'Make sure you fill it to the top; we don't want to be pushing it home, do we?'

Weston climbed into the Standard Vanguard; to his surprise Kathleen, April's daily help, was sitting there.

'Mrs Ferrimins said that you would drop me off at my home on your way to fill the car,' she said. She was a tall pretty girl with red hair.

'You're Taffy's friend, aren't you?' Weston said, smiling.

'Yes and I know your name, it's Pew Weston.'

'That's right. Where do you live, Kathleen?'

'In one of those cottages near to the RAF base. Taffy's told me you possess strange powers over women, and every women you meet falls in love with you. Is that true?'

'I don't think so; you're a woman and you're not in love with me, are you?'

'I don't know, well no not yet, but I don't know, I might be.' Her face flushed red. 'I think you're lovely and I'd love to go out with you. Yes I think Taffy's right...'

'You can't love both me and Taffy can you?' She didn't answer; however, she unnerved Weston a little by looking into his face.

Weston drove through the town and dropped her at a pretty colour washed cottage she pointed out to him. She got out and took hold of Weston's hand.

'Thank you, Pew. Is it true you've not got a girlfriend?'

'Yes that's true at the moment, but I am going out

with a girl from East Bravy next Saturday, her name is Tamsin. I don't know her other name, do you know her?'

'No, I don't, but I wish I was her. She must be the luckiest girl in the whole world.'

Weston drove on to the garage feeling flattered and puzzled by what the girl had said. He filled the car tank and drove on to the C/O's house.

The C/O, looking very distinguished in his dress uniform, came to the door.

'You're rather early, Weston.'

'Yes, sir. Mrs Ferrimins asked me to pick you up early, she's prepared pre-dinner drinks at Rowanberry house, sir.'

'Very well, wait in the car. Must say, you are well turned out Weston, well done, good show, can't let the air force down in front of the navy. What?' He looked out of the door. 'Bloody typical, it's started to rain. You'd better wait here while I find a brolly or two.' Mrs Todmarsh-Rivers came into the hall; she, like April, was a fine looking woman. Her pale skin, dark eyes and hair were set off by her long low-cut pale lemon satin evening dress.

'Good evening, Mrs Todmarsh-Rivers,' Weston said, at the same time thinking, I wonder what April and Edwina will be wearing? This could be a good evening after all.

'Evening, LAC Weston,' she said, speaking in a deep cultivated voice. 'Where on Earth is my husband?'

'It began to rain so he said he would see if he could find an umbrella or two, Mrs Todmarsh-Rivers.'

The C/O returned to the hall with two umbrellas; he handed one to Weston.

'We've been invited for pre-dinner drinks at April's, darling, are you ready? Do you think you should wear your fur, or a waterproof?'

'It's far too hot for my fur, darling. I'll just take my lace wrap. Weston can hold the umbrella for me, the rain isn't heavy.' She smiled at Weston.

Weston eased the Vanguard into the kerb outside Rowanberry House; he found just enough room behind Dr Wendover's selfishly parked shooting brake.

'Judy's here I see, that's her monstrosity of a car,' the C/O's wife said.

Weston held the umbrella over Mrs Todmarsh-Rivers as she walked down the path to the house. The C/O followed, carrying the other unopened umbrella.

Once inside April's hall, Weston kept to the background while April gushed over her friends, giving them her usual hugs and kisses before ushering them into the drawing room.

April was looking fantastic, her fair hair and green eyes set off by her long almost backless black silk evening dress. Lucy popped her head round the drawing room door; seeing Weston, she came into the hall. She was also looking extraordinarily lovely, in a long pale blue low cut evening dress.

'I see you've managed to procure the services of Weston for the evening, April?' she said.

Dr Wendover followed Lucy into the hall; she was wearing a long dark blue velvet dress, which showed her breasts to their advantage.

'Hello, Pewsy, how's the cut in your head?' she said.

The C/O shot Weston a questioning look.

'What cut, when did you cut your head, Weston?'

Weston thought, oh hell, now it will come out about me being at Lucy's cottage. However, before he could answer, Dr Wendover came to the rescue.

'Surely you've not forgotten that nasty gash he received when he was assaulted outside the camp. You

134

must remember, David?'

'Of course I remember the assault; however I wasn't aware you cut your head, Weston?'

'It was a very nasty wound. I had to put several stitches in. You should look after your RAF Eagle a little better, April.'

'Weston, an RAF Eagle?' the C/O said, laughing. He'll never be that as long as he's got a...well, I'll say no more. He lost all opportunity of being an Eagle when he refused to train as aircrew. He might now, with a bit of luck, make a web-footed Seagull one day.' Everyone laughed.

Weston scowled; he didn't enjoy being the butt of a joke.

Edwina came up the stairs to make her grand entrance. She was certainly looking wonderful; she was wearing a long over one shoulder green satin evening dress with a slit up the right-hand side which almost reached her hip. She'd arranged her hair to cascade in deep waves around her face and over her shoulders.

She smiled at Weston.

'What was all that merriment about? Were they taking the proverbial out of you, Weston?'

'It was nothing, Eddy,' Judy said. 'I called Weston April's RAF Eagle, and David said if he was lucky he might make it as a Seagull one day.' They laughed again.

'I shouldn't worry about that, Weston; an Eagle may be handsome and magnificent, but the Seagull is both handsome and successful.' She glided through the hall, her right leg showing to the top of her thigh as she walked up the stairs into the drawing room. The others followed.

Weston, now alone, sat on one of the old oak un-upholstered hall chairs.

I might not know much about Eagles or Seagulls, he

135

thought, but I can see that fine feathers make fine birds. He waited, half-listening to the inane chatter from the drawing room and the rain hammering on the windows.

'Ladies and gentlemen,' a man's voice Weston didn't know said. 'I would like to take this opportunity to thank April for providing this kind reception. Will you all be upstanding and raise your glasses to our very dear friend, April.'

Weston thought, that must have been either Lucy's, or Dr Wendover's, husband.

'Gentlemen,' he heard his C/O say. 'I would like you to raise your glasses to our wives. I give you gentlemen, "The Five Leaf Clovers".'

Mrs Weatherington came to the door.

'Weston, will you come into the drawing room?'

Self-conscious of being just a bottom of the pile airman in that salubrious company, Weston followed her in. She handed him a Leica 35mm camera with a flash attachment.

'I want you to take some photographs for me, Weston.' Weston took lots of pictures, as directed by Edwina.

'April, what is this weird fascination you and your sister have for calling men after birds?' a tall slightly built bald-headed man said. He must be Lucy's George, Weston thought.

'I rather fancy they would like to pluck the bird. What? Ha?' said the other gentleman, a tall cadaverous looking man.

'I think birds are a nice metaphor,' April said, smiling broadly.

'Perhaps one of you would like to pluck me?' Edwina said. The men didn't answer.

Weston handed the camera back to her and returned to the hall.

After about half an hour the party began to break up.

Lucy and Dr Wendover, together with their husbands, were the first to leave. They were travelling in Judy's shooting brake.

The C/O, holding his umbrella over April and his wife, followed. Weston held the other umbrella over Edwina as they walked to the Vanguard.

'David, I want you to sit in the back with April and Jemima,' Edwina said. 'I shall sit in the front with the driver and navigate.' She climbed into the car, removed her lace wrap and dropped the centre armrest down.

She obviously knew the way well, giving Weston directions well in time for him to act. The Standard Vanguard saloon was a softly sprung car and it dipped into every tight corner. On one extra steep corner, Edwina, who must have lifted the arm rest, slipped down the bench seat until she hit Weston. In the pretext of pushing herself back, she felt his penis.

Weston, not expecting it with the car full of people, involuntary jerked back with the shock and the car swerved.

'Careful, Weston, keep your eyes on the road,' the C/O snapped.

'Sorry, sir.' However, he could see Edwina was smiling when she again dropped the armrest down.

He drove on through the gleaming wet Cornish roads, it was only eight o'clock, yet it was almost dark.

'This is it, we have arrived, just drive down here, Weston. Pull up behind the other cars and join the queue.'

Weston waited his turn.

The naval sentry, his wet waterproofs gleaming in the bright arc lights, beckoned him forward to the gatehouse. Weston opened the window and the sentry pushed his head in and looked around.

'Good evening, ladies and gentlemen. May I see your tickets?'

137

Edwina gave Weston the tickets and he handed them over, the rating checked them and gave them back.

'Tell me this, driver, how do you get into the bloody air force? I've not seen so much beautiful talent in one place before,' he whispered, albeit loud enough for all to hear. Then in his normal voice he said, 'Thank you, driver, go down this road until you see another rating. He will direct you to the venue.'

Weston joined the queue of cars waiting to drop their passengers at the long awning that led to the hall. It was raining heavier than ever when his turn came. He was just about to get out and open the doors when a group of naval officers, who obviously knew whose car it was, ran over and opened the doors. With laughter and kisses all around, and completely ignoring the C/O, they escorted the three ladies down the awning.

The C/O, now alone, got out.

'Don't stray too far, Weston,' he muttered. 'We might require you to take us home early. Can't say I like the way this evening is developing.' He walked away from the car, leaving the door open.

'Follow this road until it veers to the right,' another navel rating said, closing the door. 'You will find the car park on your right. A room has been made available at the venue here for the drivers. The NAAFI is also open if you want something to eat; you'll find that on the far side of the car park.'

Weston parked the car on the far side of the car park. The rain was now coming down heavier than ever.

He saw the C/O's umbrella on the floor and picked it up and was just about to get out when the door opened and a Wren looked in.

'I thought it was you, Brylcream. I saw you drive by. You do remember me don't you?' She climbed in. 'I'm Sonia, the petty officer on the train to Polcastle.'

138

Sonia? How could he ever forget her; wasn't she the one who said he owed her a new pair of silk stockings when she showed her stocking tops to everyone on the station? Before he could answer, she kissed him square on the lips.

'Didn't think I'd have the luck to see you again, Brylcream,' she said. 'What are you doing here?'

Weston explained how he'd agreed to chauffeur his C/O and his friends to the evening's charity ball.

'I'm glad you did, Bryly, come on, you're coming to my room. You've got to get out of this wet uniform.'

'You always want me undressed.'

'I know, perhaps I should have said I've got to get you out of that uniform. Only thinking about you and keeping you well. I wouldn't like you to be ill with a chill, my lovely Bryl. Listen to that, I'm now a poet.' Her eyes twinkled.

'Well you'll not make a Wordsworth, so don't make up anything about daffodils, but what I do know, Sonia, is that the last thought in your mind is about me catching a cold.'

'Well, we had you naked on the train, didn't we, and who had a lipstick covered dicky do-da afterwards?' They laughed.

'I never did buy you those black silk stockings, did I?'

'So you did remember me after all. I thought for a while you hadn't. Come along, I can hang your uniform in our boiler room, it will soon dry there.' Weston gave her the umbrella.

'Here you have this umbrella, I can't get any wetter.' They ran down the road holding hands.

'In here, Brylcream.' She took him into the end room of a long barrack block.

'Won't you get into trouble if they find me here?'

'They are not going to find you, my sweetheart.'

139

It was a comfortable room with one bed each side of a table.

'You're very lucky to have a room like this, who sleeps in the other bed?'

'Sarah, she was the tall girl with dark hair on the train with me?'

'No, I can't place her.' Weston shook his head.

'It doesn't matter. She's away in London this weekend so we've the whole place to ourselves. Take your uniform off and I'll hang it in the boiler room. You know you've nothing down there I've not seen before.' She laughed and picked up a face cloth. 'Here, you can cover your dicky with this.' She laughed again. 'I'm sure it will be big enough.'

Weston took off his crumpled uniform; it was in a mess, and he'd looked so smart when he'd set out.

'Take those underpants off as well. By the way I've still got a pair of your underpants in my drawer somewhere, they'll be dry. Get into the bed. I want you to give me a real good shagging, and I'm going to make sure I get it. I won't be long.' Weston thought every woman I meet wants me for sex, but I don't care. He slipped naked into the bed, feeling quite excited; he lay back and awaited the onslaught. A few minutes later, Sonia came back. She was wearing practically nothing. Within a minute she was in bed with Weston. Two hours of frantic sex later they sat up.

'Brylcream, I think I must have died, I'm in heaven, you're fantastic at making love.'

'I'd better be getting back to the ball venue, the C/O will be looking for me, if I'm not back...'

'The ball doesn't finish until one o'clock, it's only eleven o'clock.'

'Shall we have it again,' Sonia said, feeling his......... 'I just don't believe this, you're ready again.'

140

It was turned midnight before they finished this time. Weston leapt out of the bed. Sonia sat up with her well-shaped breasts on show.

'That was wonderful for me, Bryly. How was it for you?' Weston smiled.

'I shall have to go, Sonia.' The door opened and a Wren officer walked in.

'Good God man, you're stark naked,' she said, looking horrified. 'Cover yourself up and get dressed at once. You, yes you, petty officer, you can do the same. Having a man in your room as you know is against all the rules. Never mind taking him into your bed. I could put you on report for this. Who is this person?'

'I don't know his name, Mam.' Sonia giggled. 'I call him, Brylcream.'

'Well, Brylcream, do you come from this base; are you in the navy?'

'No, sir, I'm LAC Paul Edward Weston, RAF. Sir.'

'Don't call me sir. What are you doing here, sharing one of my Wren's beds, LAC Weston?'

'I drove my C/O and his party from Bravemouth to here for the ball, Mam. I'm their driver.'

'How did you get to know this Wren?'

'She was in charge of a group of Wrens who raped me on the train last week, Mam.'

'Is he telling the truth, petty officer?'

'Yes, Mam, it is true that we had good time but I wouldn't say we raped him, Mam.'

'Well, well, well, what am I going to do about this pretty pickle? Shall I do the right thing and call out the guard to have you two locked in the guardhouse?'

The officer looked into Weston's eyes and she melted. 'No, his party would have no one to drive them back. You've been very naughty you know.' She smiled at Weston. 'I will overlook this breach of discipline this time.' Without another word she walked

141

out.

'What happened, Sonia; how did she know I was here?'

'Someone must have let her know. I'll find out who it was. Don't you worry. Mind you, did you see her face, that bitch fancies you for herself.'

'I'd better go now, Sonia; it's been a most unexpected but enjoyable evening. I fully thought we were for the high jump with that officer. Even so it's been nice seeing you again.'

'Yes, we are just ships that pass in the night, Bryly.'

Weston kissed Sonia goodbye and ran all the way back to the venue. It was still raining. The C/O was waiting just inside the awning.

'Ha there you are, Weston, jolly good show. I'll collect the ladies, bring the car around.'

Weston drove the car to the awning and opened the door.

Edwina once again insisted, to the C/O's obvious annoyance, that they use the same seating arrangements for the return journey.

Weston checked his watch against the clock in the car; it was just one o'clock. The rain had almost stopped, leaving just a few fretful showers to make things awkward for the driver.

Weston drove fast on the quiet roads. The rear seat passengers were soon asleep, obviously under the influence of an excess of alcohol.

Edwina first checked to see the others were asleep; she then began teasing Weston by playing with his......... which to her obvious pleasure quickly became erect. She eased her dress down and, taking Weston's left hand from the wheel, she placed it onto her breast. Weston couldn't do a thing, for fear of waking the others. He drove on one handed, his body in sexual torment. They arrived in Bravemouth and

142

Edwina replaced her breast into her dress and sat back. Weston pulled up first at the C/O's home. He got out and helped the C/O get Mrs Todmarsh-Rivers into the house; she was so intoxicated. Afterwards, he drove on the couple of hundred yards to April's home.

'Park Mrs Weatherington's car outside my garage, Weston,' April said, showing some of her old arrogance. 'Then return here for a nightcap. You do know that you are stopping the night here, of course.'

'No I didn't, sorry but I can't, I've brought nothing with me...'

'You have no excuse, Weston. I've bought a pair of new pyjamas for you to wear and a new toothbrush and razor. I'll have no argument.'

Dennis, who had been on the lookout at Rowanberry House all the night, stood out of sight and watched Weston drop April off at her home. He left at once; he couldn't wait to tell his mother. He ran back to the house he'd rented to phone her. He didn't even wait long enough to see Edwina get out. He was also so busy removing his fingerprints from around the holiday home that he also missed seeing Weston walk back and go in.

April had left the door open, and Weston went in and shut the door behind him.

'Is that you, Pew?' April shouted.

She was standing on the first landing in her evening dress. His heart missed a beat as he looked down at her; she really was a beauty with hair falling loosely around her face.

'Come down to the first landing and I'll show you to your room, Pew.'

She opened a door; it was the same room they'd made love in earlier in the week.

'These are for you.' She handed him a cellophane

143

packet containing a pair of pure silk navy blue pyjamas. She also gave him a small leather case. 'The new toothbrush and razor I promised you.'

'Get out of that damp uniform, Pew, you'll find a dressing gown behind the door. I'll wait outside while you change. I know how shy you are. Be quick though. Mrs Weatherington is making nightcaps for us in the drawing room. Do you like cognac?'

Weston had just taken his uniform off when the door opened and April popped her head around.

'Nice to see little more of you, Pew, you can hang your uniform in the bathroom next door, it will dry there.'

He changed into the pyjamas and dressing gown. They walked together up to the drawing room. Mrs Weatherington was standing looking through the French windows at the harbour. She smiled and handed them a balloon glass of cognac each.

'Pew's uniform was so damp he had to get out of it, so I gave him the new pyjamas,' April said, smiling.

Mrs Weatherington held out her glass.

'Here's to young handsome men the world over,' she toasted. 'May their pencils be forever hard and sharp. Drink it down, come along.'

April emptied her glass in one go and to Weston's surprise she collapsed onto the sofa. Edwina walked over and calmly felt her pulse.

'She's alright, she can't hold her drink, Westy. She never could.'

'Don't you think we should take her to her room, Mrs Weatherington?'

'Do call me by my name, it's Edwina; I hate being called by that frightful term Mrs, it sounds so old.'

'What are we going to do about April?'

'Oh to hell with her, you can take her to her room if you want. But she won't be any good to you. I put two sleeping pills in her cognac. She'll be out for hours.'

Weston carried April down the two flights of stairs to her room, dropped her on the bed and threw the covers over her. He didn't return to the drawing room, instead he went straight to his newly appointed bedroom. After what had gone on in the car, he wasn't in the least surprised to see Edwina wearing just a short see-through nighty, lying on the top of his bed.

'Surprised to see me, Westy? Get those bloody pyjamas off, I'm looking forward to experiencing what it will be like to be fucked by April's Eagle.'

Chapter Twenty one

Weston looked at her; she was certainly a beautiful picture waiting to be painted with her long flame coloured hair cascading around her lovely face, over her well-shaped breasts and lovely slim body.

'Do you think we should be contemplating having sex in April's home?' he eventually said.

'Oh for crying out loud, Westy, don't try to upset me and for goodness sake don't start feeling guilty. I've been looking forward to this all night. Forget all about April, she's so deep in slumber land, she won't bother us for hours.' She sighed. 'Come along, Westy, don't give me any aggravation, I want you to give me the best fucking I've ever had in my life.'

'Why are all you women in Bravemouth so foul-mouthed?'

'Grow up, Westy, don't start acting the naive child with me. What you need is educating in the ways of women and sex. Guess what, Westy. I think I'm the woman to do it. For starters get those bloody pyjamas off. Let's get on with it.' She leapt from the bed and pushed him down onto the bed. She removed the offending pyjamas and with a smile of achievement she kissed him. She then proceeded to kiss him down and down until she reached his more than ready primed weapon, which she caressed with her lips. The body kissing had been pure rapture for Weston; he was disappointed when she rolled off, indicating to Weston to do the same to her. Placing his fingers on her clitoris, she said 'And I want you to kiss me here and keep on kissing.'

From that moment, they slipped into that strange timeless, mind-blowing sensual world of shear unadulterated sex. They used every sexual position in

146

Edwina's vast knowledge of sex and lots she must have invented. In fact they tried anything and everything. Edwina just had orgasm after orgasm after orgasm, but she wanted more. Eventually, although reluctant to do so, they reached that final moment of truth which neither Edwina nor Weston could delay any longer. Their night of passion finished with the inevitable Earth-shattering satellite-crashing fully shared orgasm. Afterwards, physically and mentally exhausted, they fell into a deep satisfied dreamless sleep.

Weston was woken by the sunshine streaming through the bedroom's east-facing window. Hell, it's late, he thought. He checked his watch; however it was only five o'clock. Mrs Weatherington, looking lovely, was fast asleep. She's not gone back to her room, he thought. Hell fire, what would happen if April was to come in now? Her arm was wrapped around him; he carefully slipped himself out. He needed to take a trip to the bathroom badly. He didn't want to wake her; he knew if he did she would have demanded more and more sex. For a fleeting second, he was tempted to wake her. I'm sure I could manage it again, he thought. What a night they'd had, what a fantastic woman she'd proved to be. Once she'd realised he could keep going, she became more and more insatiable. I wonder how many times she came, before we had the big one, went through his mind. She was far more experienced at sex than any of his other conquests – April, Judy, Lucy and Sonia; they were all beginners by comparison. Edwina instinctively knew how to please a man and how to organize a man into doing the things that pleased her.

He eased the bedroom door open as quietly as he could and ran naked the short distance to the next door bathroom. After relieving himself, he dressed in his still damp uniform and crept along the landing to the stairs; he wanted to be away from Rowanberry House, before

147

either April or Edwina awoke.

'Careful, you punk! Bloody careful, you stupid awkward bastard, slow down not so F...ing fast.' Weston froze in mid-stride; it was a man's voice trying to whisper from down the stairs.

He looked over the landing. To his amazement two men were coming up the stairs, carrying someone on a stretcher.

'Is that Mrs Ferrimins? Is she ill?' Weston shouted.

'Who the hell's that shit? You said she was alone in the house. Get the bastard Dennis, before he gets us caught,' someone shouted.

Weston went to run, but before he could move a piece of cloth soaked in chloroform was placed tightly over his nose and mouth; he quickly passed out.

April and Weston were loaded into the makeshift ambulance.

Edwina slowly awoke from her blissful sleep and opened her eyes. She stretched and sighed with a sweet contentment she'd not known in years. What a wonderful night she'd had. She put her arm out for Weston, but to her disappointment he'd gone. What a bloody shame, she thought. I've just not enjoyed sex like that before in my life. She glanced at her gold Rolex wristwatch and it said seven thirty. I'd better shower and dress. I'm not looking forward to driving to London or flying on to the states later. Westy, what a man, what a lover, he certainly whets a girl's appetite. She pouted at the thought of leaving him behind with April.

Rebecca reported back to the Head of Earth affairs and informed him about the kidnapping.

'Watch closely over your charge, but otherwise don't interfere; you are Weston's Guardian, not April Ferrimins',' he said unhelpfully.

Edwina, now dressed in the white silk riding blouse

148

and tight beige trousers and boots she always wore for driving, stood feeling apprehensive outside April's bedroom. She was unsure of what her reception would be. She opened the door and, to her surprise, the bed was empty, but the covers were lying on the floor.

What the hell, she thought. She's gone to her cottage and taken Weston with her. Weston's having a good time shagging me all night and April all day. Can't say I expected this, still I can't really complain; I had a good night with him. I'd better get back to London. Franklin Junior will be waiting.

The phone rang; thinking it was April, Edwina picked it up. It was April's husband.

'April darling is everything chucky boo there?' Captain Ferrimins said.

'Hello, Michael, this is Edwina, April's not here.'

'Not at home? Where the devil is she, Edwina?'

'I don't know. I've just been to her room to let her know that I would be leaving for London in a couple of minutes. Her bed was empty. I don't know where she is.'

'Surely she wouldn't go without letting you know. Where do you think she is?' Edwina thought, shall I tell him about Weston? Yes, I suppose I'd better, what the hell.

'I really don't know, Michael, and that's the truth, but April, against my wishes, did invite the young RAF boy who chauffeured us to the ball last night to stay over at Rowanberry House. His bed is also empty, but where they've got to I really don't know. I'm sorry I can't be more helpful, but I must go, Michael, we are flying to the States later today. I think everything will work out, don't worry, she won't be far away.'

'Mmm, this sounds a little strange to me; however I will soon see. I've just received permission to use the board's new helicopter. I shall be in Bravemouth in a couple of hours, have a pleasant journey and flight, Edwina.'

Chapter Twenty Two

April and Weston, while still unconscious and dead to the world, were taken in the phoney ambulance to a large house, which was situated on a creek somewhere close to Falmouth. Before they had left Bravemouth, the gang had posted a large envelope through the police station letterbox containing April's cloverleaf ring and her engraved Rolex watch together with a ransom note for £75,000.

The ambulance pulled up just as Weston was coming out of his chloroform-induced sleep. He was dragged headfirst out of the van and thrown, dumped would be a better word, into what could only be a cloakroom. April, who was still unconscious, the result of Edwina's sleeping pills, was carried up the stairs and thrown on to a mattress in a large empty bedroom.

'I think we should cut one of her fingers off and send it to them; that will hurry them along with the ransom,' Harry said.

'No, we're doing nothing like that,' Graham said. 'We are not mutilating her, no one must be hurt as a result of this job, mother said.'

'Where the hell is your mother?' Charles snapped. 'She's not done much in regard to this kidnapping.'

'I'm right here behind you, Charles, and don't you dare criticize me,' Mrs Ruby Kingsley said, holding her nose and pushing Harry aside. 'Take a shower, Harry, and put some clean clothes on, you stink. Remember this, Charles, I've done all the donkeywork for this job and it's gone bloody well.'

'I still think we should send her husband one of her fingers, blood always gets the money flowing,' muttered Harry. 'I don't mind cutting it off.'

April came round and heard this part of the

151

conversation. Terrified of what she thought they were going to do to her, she wanted to run; however, sense prevailed and she lay unmoving, trying to piece together who these people were and where she was. The last thing she could remember was having a nightcap with Edwina and Weston.

'She's coming round; whatever you do don't let her see your faces,' Mrs Ruby Kingsley said, ushering them out. 'Wear your masks the next time you go in. I'm going now to phone the police, to see what they intend to do about her.' They nodded and she left to call the police from a phone box. She was back within a couple of minutes.

Weston, now fully conscious, stood and felt around for a light switch; it was pitch black in the cloak room. He tried the door but it was locked. He sat on the toilet and pondered, realising he'd somehow got mixed up with a gang who must have kidnapped April.

'We're going to Bravemouth to collect the ransom money, we'll take both my car and the ambulance; we can dump the ambulance afterwards. Harry, I want you to stay here and keep your eye on Mrs Ferrimins.' She crinkled her nose. 'And for goodness sake take a shower.'

April waited until she heard the door close before opening her eyes. She sat up and looked around. They'd put her on an old ripped smelly mattress in what must have been a bedroom and her dress was torn. She attempted to swallow, but couldn't; her throat and mouth was bone dry.

The door opened and a man who stank of sweat came in wearing a grotesque children's mask.

'Who are you, where am I?' April croaked.

'Shut up, slut,' he said, striking her hard across her face. April felt blood running from her lips.

'One more f…ing word from you and I'll teach you

152

a real lesson.'

'I'm so thirsty,' she said, her voice barely audible. He stuck his finger in front of her face. 'I said shut up bitch, so do so.' Nevertheless he went out and returned with a large bottle of lemonade, which he threw at her.

'Drink that, it's all I've got, now stop bloody moaning. I'll cheer you up in a minute or so. You're going to get this.' He held his groin. 'I'm going to shag you until you're sore, but you will have to wait a while until the others have gone to Bravemouth.'

Meanwhile Rebecca, having found the ambulance parked outside a large house, went in and searched the place. She soon found Weston sitting in the dark on the lavatory in the cloakroom. She unlocked the door.

'We'll be back in about three hours, Harry,' Mrs Ruby Kingsley shouted. 'Don't you dare try anything on with that woman; I'll kill you if you do. Behave yourself.'

Weston heard the car engines start up and leave. He tried the door again; to his surprise it was unlocked. He came out into in a large hall with tall windows and what must have been the front door.

April drank the bottle of lemonade and, leaning back into the corner of the room, she let her body slide down the wall to the floor.

The door opened and the same smelly man, this time without the mask, came in. April could see he had several days of growth on his chin and large sweat patches under his arms. The acrid smell of his sweat filled every corner of the room, making April feel sick. He grabbed her by the hair.

'I've always wanted to shag a society dame,' he said, leering. 'You're a lucky girl. My dick's bubbling with desire, it's going to fill you with ecstasy my dear.'

'Leave me alone, you brute. You smelly, horrid man. Keep away from me you dirty filthy fellow,' April yelled.

He slapped her across her face again and, still holding her by her hair, he dragged her down the stairs and pushed her through a door into a large empty room. April staggered in backwards.

'Take those things off, slut,' he shouted, dragging a camp bed from the wall into the centre of the floor. April ran across the room to where she saw another door; she opened it and saw it led down to a cellar. Before she could get away he caught up with her.

'No one can hear you here and there's nowhere for you to run, my fine lady. What's wrong, you're going to enjoy this. Take them f...ing things off, before I rip 'em off.'

'No, no, I can't, no, no, no,' April screamed, dropping to the floor and pulling her legs up to her chin. 'Leave me alone.'

'You're having this whether you want it or not.' He held his groin.

'Please, God, please help me, help me now,' she whispered under her breath.

'Off with those bloody things, or you'll feel this.' He brought the piece of rope he'd been using as a belt down hard across her legs.

'Stop it, stop it.' She got to her feet. 'Help me, God, please, father, help me.' She stood, feeling helpless.

'Take them f...ing things off.' He swung the rope again.

'Lie down on the f...ing bed...move...now...' She cagily walked around the bed trying to keep out of the range of the piece of rope.

With a hint of a smile, he removed his sweaty shirt and dropped his trousers. April, willing to grasp at any straw, saw the slightest chance when he got his feet entangled in his trousers. She sprinted across to the door on the other side of the room and ran down the

154

stairs into the cellar; removing the key from the door, she locked it from the inside. He cleared his feet and followed her down. He pushed a light switch by the door and tried to look through the keyhole, but she'd left the key in.

April was startled when the single un-shaded light bulb came on. However, it proved to be a great help to her; she could now see another door with a key in its lock, the other side of the cellar. With the lemonade bottle in her hand, she ran over and turned the key. The door led out onto a flight of stone steps leading up to a creek-side garden. She ran out, locking the door behind her. She stood in the garden breathing in the warm fresh air.

Weston, completely unaware of what was happening to April, and wondering where he was, stood outside the cloakroom door. He was about to walk across to the front door when he heard a door open, and he saw a naked man run across to the front door. Weston followed him out into the garden, where he saw that the man was running towards a woman. He saw at once it was April; she was standing in her torn dress with her back to the creek holding a large glass bottle in her hand. Weston knew that he couldn't get to her before the man did, so he waited, watching April. The man ran up to her and was just about take hold of her when April hit him on the head with the bottle; he fell poleaxed to the ground.

'April, it's me,' Weston shouted, running across the garden.

'Pew, Pew I'm so frightened, how did you find me?'

'April, thank goodness.'

'That monster, did you see him, he was going to rape me. Hold me, Pew.'

'He certainly stinks,' Weston said. 'Hell I can smell him from here.'

155

'He's one of the gang, they left him behind, I hit him with that. She pointed to the bottle. 'The rest of the gang have gone to Bravemouth to collect my ransom. How did you find me?'

'Never mind about that, let's get away from here before they come back. Here put this on, your dress is ruined.' He took his uniform tunic off and gave it to her. The garden he could see ran down to a creek, where a slipway with several boats lying on it had been built. Weston could see the tide was ebbing; however the water was still half-way up the slipway. He realised that going down the creek in one of the boats was about their only way of escape. He had three boats to choose from; he chose the largest, a seventeen foot open boat with a gaff rig and a short bowsprit. He could see it had an inboard engine. He dipped the fuel tank; it was full.

'April, give me a hand, let's push this boat into the water.'

'What about him?'

'I think we can forget him, he's well and truly out, thanks to you.'

Between them, they managed to move the boat down the slipway until it reached the water. Weston held on to the painter while April clambered aboard.

'I'm going back to the house to see what food I can find, I'll tie the boat to that tree until I get back,' he shouted.

'See if you can find something to drink, my mouth's bone dry.'

A couple of minutes later Weston came running out carrying a shopping bag.

He threw the bag in the boat, undid the painter and, pushing the boat out to midstream, he jumped aboard.

'I've put two bottles of lemonade in the bag and I've emptied their food cupboard,' he said, breathlessly. The ebbing tide took them broadside on down the creek at quite a pace.

Weston used the oars in the boat to keep the boat in the centre of the waterway. After about fifteen minutes, they rounded a bend and Falmouth Harbour, with the sea in the distance, came into view. He turned the petrol on and, after cranking the engine a few times, it burst into life. Feeling quite elated at getting away so easily, he set a course across the harbour to the open sea and then on to Bravemouth.

There was little shelter from the spray flying back from the dipping bows.

'Do you think they'll come after us, Pew? I definitely heard one of those men say he'd cut my finger off if Michael didn't pay up. Do you think they would have gone through with it? Oh dear, it makes me feel sick to just think about it. He struck me across my face you know.' She sat down on the bottom boards. 'You won't let them catch us, will you, Pew?'

'No way, they'll need a fast boat to catch us now. I'll see how fast this one is.'

Weston opened the throttle and the boat leaped forward; it had lots of power, but it also made the spray worse than ever. They were heading into a fairly strong south-westerly wind; he eased the throttle back. However, the spray eased when they left the confines of Falmouth Harbour and entered the open sea with the wind abeam. Weston set a course for Bravemouth and hoisted the sails, but he left the engine running. The boat was now much steadier with the wind abeam. She sailed well, Weston thought, if this wind holds they might make Bravemouth by five o'clock that evening. They were wet, cold and hungry; neither April nor Weston had eaten since the previous evening. Weston made sure the sails were set right, lashed the tiller and opened the shopping bag. He spread the food he'd stolen, bread, butter and boiled ham, along the centre

157

thwart. April, though still strikingly good looking, did look a sorry sight with her lips swollen and a nasty red wheal across her right cheek.

Chapter Twenty Three

Ruby Kingsley and her motley crew arrived in Bravemouth just as the church clock was chiming twelve. They parked the ambulance outside the hospital but left the car parked on the road; she made a phone call to the police station from a nearby phone box.

'Yes, Mr Ferrimins is in Bravemouth, he arrived an hour ago,' the police sergeant said. 'Yes, he's managed to get the money, it's all in used notes; they opened the bank especially for him.'

'Who is going to deliver the money?'

'He wants his private detective to do it, where do you want him to deliver it to?'

'I hope it really is in used notes for his wife's sake. Tell him he must wear a bright red shirt or sweater and a sailor type peaked cap. He must take the money to the telephone box at the edge of town by the four turnings. Remember I don't want to see any policemen around, if we do, we will damage her. Once the detective gets to the phone box, tell him he must pick up the phone as soon as it rings. I will give him further instructions. He had better get himself moving and I repeat: if we see any sign of the police, we will do her harm.'

She dropped the phone and ran to the ambulance. Her so called "job" was coming into fruition.

'Right you two, Graham and Dennis, take the red sweater and shirt with the sailor cap, and go into that narrow alleyway that runs from the station road down to the harbour. I've leased a small holiday cottage there. Here's the keys; leave them in the cottage. Wait in there until Mr Ferrimins' courier arrives with the money. Overpower him, tie his hands and tape his mouth. Afterwards, see if he's wearing a red shirt or sweater. Graham, you put on the same with the cap and take the case of money. You must get to the top of town as quickly as you can. I will be waiting with the car. With a bit of luck we could all be aboard "Mother's Boys" sailing for Holland with £75,000 in our pockets by five o'clock this evening.' Hoping they wouldn't make a mess of things, she returned to the hospital and, using a pay phone, she rang the number of the designated phone box and waited.

Chapter Twenty Four

While not exactly enjoying their bracing coastal sail to Bravemouth, Weston and April were feeling a little more human after having eaten something. Weston was sitting on the stern deck steering with the tiller and April was sitting between his knees.

'How did they manage get hold of you, Pew? I don't remember anything; do you know why I was unconscious?'

'They took me at the same time as you. I caught them red-handed; they were carrying you up the stairs on a stretcher. The next thing I knew, I'd also been chloroformed. I didn't come round until they dragged me out of the ambulance and stuck me into that closet in the house.'

'They never mentioned you to me, why was that?'

'I think they'd forgotten about me.'

'Oh, Pew, I feel so ill, my legs are aching. I think I'm going to die, I must lie down.' She stretched out on the bottom boards and slept for over two hours. It was turned five o'clock when Bravemouth Harbour came into view. He altered course and shook her awake.

'We've arrived, April; you can see your house from here, won't be long now.'

'No, no, don't go into Bravemouth, Pew. I've just dreamt they were waiting on the town quay and they cut my fingers off. Don't go in please.'

'It was only a dream, they won't be there.'

'Don't go into Bravemouth, please, please,' she begged.

'If we don't go in there, where can we go?'

'We can sail along the coast to Judy's place; it's only a couple of miles. You can see her house with its white gable from out at sea; it's the only house for miles around. Oh my head's beginning to spin I feel so dizzy.' She held onto the mast while Weston altered course.

They sailed on, until like she said a white gabled house came into view. It was exactly as April had described it. When they were abeam of the house, Weston pushed the tiller hard down and the boat turned into the shore, and as the wind filled the other side of the sail its boom swung over catching April on the side of her head. Weston's hands were so full in guiding the boat through the rocks to the small beach that he completely forgot about April for a moment or two. He dropped the jib and the main sail, and at the last minute he revved the engine high to drive the boat up the beach. Oblivious to what had happened to April, he went to help her out of the boat; to his surprise she was unconscious on the bottom boards. She came around briefly when he picked her up.

'Where am I?' she said. 'Oh my head, I feel terrible, who are you?' She passed out again Oh hell, she could die on me and I'll get the blame, Weston thought, what the heck's happened to her? I shall have to get her to Dr Wendover as quickly as I can. From the beach he could see a flight of uneven steps had been cut into the rock which led to the cliff top. He thought about leaving April in the boat and going for help. However, he decided he couldn't leave her, not in her present condition. No matter how he did it, he had to carry her to the top. He struggled to lift her across his shoulders. He then began the slow tortuous climb. He was almost at the top when his right foot slipped and his right leg went down the side of the rough cut steps. This mishap gashed the entire inside of his leg from ankle to groin. He recovered his composure enough to make one final effort to get to the top. From the top he could see Dr Wendover's house. Dr Wendover and two young ladies were standing outside. They saw him at once and Dr Wendover shouted something before they ran towards him.

'Pew Weston, is that April you've got with you?' she shouted.

'Yes, doctor but she's passed out, would you have a look at her?'

'So the kidnappers kept to their word and they let her go when they received the ransom, did they?'

'No, we didn't know the ransom had been paid, we escaped and we've sailed up from Falmouth in a small boat, it's down there on the beach.'

'Why on Earth, did you bring her here?'

'Because April insisted, she wouldn't let me sail into Bravemouth. She begged me to bring her here.'

'She looks bloody awful, what have they done to her, what happened? Susan and Penny darlings, run back and bring a stretcher to take Mrs Ferrimins to my surgery. How are you, Pewsy?'

'I'm alright I suppose, but I think I've cut my leg. I slipped near the top of the cliff. Why are you all naked? I don't know where to look.'

'I'm afraid April's suffering from a severe shock to her system; you don't look so good either, Pewsy, did you say you fell?'

'No I didn't fall I slipped and I think I've cut my leg, but it doesn't hurt.'

Dr Wendover attempted to look at his wound but his trouser leg was so thick with blood, it wasn't possible. She would have to cut them off.

The young ladies returned with a stretcher and they gently placed April on it.

'Put Mrs Ferrimins into treatment room No 1, Penny, then bring another stretcher and some strong scissors. I shall have to cut these trousers off to get to his leg.' She undid Weston's belt, but his trousers were so soaked in blood she couldn't get them off. She bent down for a closer look.

'Is it very bad, Dr Wendover?' Weston asked.

'It looks terrible, but I won't know until I've removed your pants. How on Earth did you carry April up that cliff with a wound like that?'

'It's funny, doctor, but it's only just beginning to hurt.'

Penny and Susan returned with the stretcher. Weston was placed on the stretcher while they carefully cut the trousers away from his leg.

'Is your name really Pewsy? It's a funny name for a man,' Susan said.

'No, not really. I have to tell everyone this, it's my initials, my name's Paul Edward Weston, it's not a funny name. Dr Wendover's always called me Pewsy. I don't mind. But tell me this, why are you all naked?'

'This is Dr Wendover's naturist farm; clothes are not allowed to be worn here.'

'What about her husband, does he go round with nothing on, or only you girls?'

'No, don't be silly, everyone must be naked. Dr Wendover's husband never wears clothes; however, at the moment, he's away in Kenya on business.'

'Your leg's in a bloody mess, Pewsy. I don't like it at all. In fact I'm worried that you could easily lose it,' Dr Wendover said. 'I just hope I can save it for you. Take him into the bathroom, girls. Lay the stretcher over the top of the bath and, using the small spray, clean all that sand and debris from the wound; be gentle, I don't want him passing out on us. I'm going to be busy for the next few minutes. I must phone April's husband and then the police to put them in the picture and then I suppose I must ring Pewsy's commanding officer.' Penny and Susan were still cleaning the wound when Dr Wendover came in.

164

'You have done a good job there, girls, you've really cleaned it well. Pewsy, are you still with us, good show? We are now going to try to suture your leg. It's such a mess; I'm hoping we are up to it. Susan, go and collect all the penicillin powder and ointment we've got on stock and fetch it here. Thank goodness I've plenty of local anaesthetic, the poor lad's going to need it.' Susan returned with the penicillin; she was a tall girl of about eighteen with a well-shaped firm figure, pretty face, brown eyes and short dark hair. Penny was of similar age but smaller with green eyes and long fair hair.

'How long have you known Dr Wendover?' Penny said, trying to start a conversation.

'I met her for the first time this week and she's already treated me twice in fact since I've arrived in Cornwall. I always seem to be being treated by her, oh, oh hell that really hurt.'

'Sorry,' the girls said in unison. 'But we've got to get these small grains of sand out of the wound.'

'Do you like being in this nudist camp, do you ride the horses naked?'

'No, of course not. Dr Wendover wouldn't allow that,' they giggled. 'You see, we ride along the same bridle paths that the general public use.'

The door opened and Dr Wendover, looking very officious and down to business wearing her white overall, came in.

'Pewsy, darling, get this into your tiny brain, we don't run a nudist camp here; this is a naturist farm, there's a huge difference.'

'A small brain, usually means a big.........'Susan said, giggling.

'Well we can see that isn't true,' Penny said.

'We don't want that sort of talk here you two,' Dr Wendover said, smiling. 'By the way, Pewsy, April's suffering from amnesia; she's lost her memory she can't even remember her name. I've spoken to her husband on the phone and he's told me he will not be leaving her here in my charge. He's sending her to a private clinic somewhere abroad; he wouldn't tell me where. There's an ambulance on its way for her now. The police have also phoned; they are sending a detective to interview you. I'm sure they think you're somehow involved in the kidnapping. I told them about your leg and how I would not allow you to be moved, so they are also sending a police doctor over to examine you.'

Chapter Twenty Five

Captain Ferrimins, obviously in deep thought, put the papers he'd been reading down with a frown on his face. It was his private detective's report on Weston, and it made him think the real danger to his marriage was LAC Weston. Determined to destroy Weston's credibility with his wife, and to try somehow to involve and incriminate him with the kidnappers, he phoned for his private detective to come to see him. When the detective arrived, he gave him a small parcel to take to the post office. The parcel contained £2000 in old banknotes and a scribbled note on perfumed paper saying "Thanks for your help old boy and this £2000 is for you, couldn't have done it without you".

'I want you to take the next train to London and post this parcel at a post office there.'

He watched the detective leave before climbing into the private ambulance he'd hired to take April from Judy's farm, a clinic in Europe. He was no fool; he knew his wife was so beautiful she could have any man she wanted, which was the reason he put the private detective on his payroll, to follow her and report on all her movements. The final report he'd received from the private detective was about an RAF boy he'd observed going several times to her home, and leaving late. The captain quickly put two and two together and realised her new lover was no other than this Paul Edward Weston. He was now only interested in Weston's downfall. He really hoped his plan to implicate Weston in his wife's kidnapping would work. In fact he was elated when he was told that Weston had not brought April back until after the ransom had been paid. April's amnesia was turning out to be a godsend to him; it meant she couldn't be questioned at the moment.

167

Chapter Twenty Six

Dr Wendover and the two girls managed to transfer Weston from the stretcher onto the long surgery table. This was where they were going to begin the marathon stitching of the wound in his leg.

Dr Wendover spread all the penicillin she had into the wound and injected his leg with painkiller.

They prepared themselves for the long job of stitching the whole length of his leg.

'I think there will be about ten or eleven inches for each of us to sew, girls; when we've done that, I want you to help me encase the leg in plaster. If we don't it might reopen. He won't be able to go to the toilet for a while, so Susan will you bring a new catheter from my surgery, but don't put it in until we are finished here.'

Later, after what seemed forever, Dr Wendover and the girls eased their backs and looked at their handy work.

'You can sign his plaster now girls. You were very good, Pewsy.'

'He's turned a terrible colour, I think he's passed out, doctor,' Penny said.

'Yes, oh dear, he's cold and clammy to touch,' said Susan. 'Feel him.'

'Let me have a look.' Dr Wendover took her stethoscope and she frowned when she listened to his heart. 'His heartbeat's very faint. I can't understand it. Help me rig a saline drip for him. Perhaps he's lost too much blood. Take my car, Penny, and go to the hospital and bring back all the blood they can let you have; luckily they'll have his blood group there.'

'The ambulance for Mrs Ferrimins has arrived, Dr Wendover,' Susan shouted. 'Captain Ferrimins has come with it. He wants a quick word with you, Dr Wendover.'

'Tell him to come into the surgery.'

'I sincerely hope I've not upset you, Judy, by sending April to a specialised amnesia clinic on the continent,' Captain Ferrimins said as he walked into Weston's room. 'She will get the best treatment in a place like that, Judy. Sure there are no hard feelings.'

'It's entirely up to you, Michael; she's your wife. After all she's only one of my best friends.' She said this, thinking, the shit; he obviously doesn't think I'm good enough to look after her.

Dr Wendover and Susan stood and waved from the door as the ambulance taking April to the mystery clinic left.

The police arrived in two cars, followed by Lucy with Weston's C/O and wife in her Ford Pilot.

A tall, painfully thin cadaverous man and a large well built man carrying a doctor's bag walked into Weston's room, unannounced.

'You must be Dr Wendover?' the tall thin man said. 'Is this LAC Weston, the man in question?'

'I am Dr Wendover and this is my clinic. Don't you think it customary to knock on a door, can't you see I'm busy with a patient? Yes this is LAC Weston.'

'I'm Chief Inspector Polpain and this is Dr Botomly,' he said, ignoring Dr Wendover's outburst.

'May I,' the doctor said, taking hold of Weston's wrist.

'He has a very little pulse; what drugs have you given him?' he asked, shaking his head and looking at the inspector.

'Other than penicillin, none whatsoever. However, I have given him several injections of a local anaesthetic. His leg's in a terrible state, it's a real mess, deeply gashed from his groin to his ankle. He could very easily lose it.' Doctor Botomly got his stethoscope out from his bag and listened to Weston's heart.

169

'It's not his leg that I'm concerned about, doctor; I think his life's at stake here. I've seen this reaction before.' He looked gravely at Dr Wendover. 'He's either one of those rare people who can't take local anaesthetic, or else he's extremely allergic to penicillin. There's not a thing you can do about it, Dr Wendover. You will have to leave him to his own resources to pull him through. Were you not aware of any allergies he may have had? He should have carried a card.'

'I told him exactly what I was going to do and he didn't say anything.'

'Well what are we going to do about him?' the inspector said. 'He's my one and only lead in this case. I shall have to question him, I will arrange for an ambulance.'

'You will do nothing of the kind,' Dr Wendover said. 'He's not leaving my care until I say so, and if you insist on moving him I will hold you personally responsible, inspector.'

'Very well, if that's the way you want it, I shall have to leave a constable here; your patient from this moment on is under arrest.'

'I can't stop you from doing that, inspector, but I shall insist on your constable conforming to my rules.'

'What rules?'

'This is a naturist farm and the rules state that anyone who isn't a casual visitor like yourself must be completely naked at all times.'

'Very well if that's the way you want to play it,' the inspector said, smiling. He walked out, but was back within five minutes.

'Very well, Dr Wendover, you win; I can't get any of my men to agree to strip and show all. However, I am going to post a constable in a car at the end of your drive for as long as it takes. Come along, Dr Botomly, I've a report to type.'

'That means we will have to leave here as well, Jemmy,' the C/O said. 'We shall have to go back with the inspector. Lucy's staying on here.'

'If Lucy's staying, then so am I,' Jemima said. 'I will phone you tonight, dear.'

Penny returned from the hospital with the blood.

'Thank you girls for helping me with Weston,' Dr Wendover said. 'You've been a wonderful help to me today, would you mind putting that catheter in for me before you go home? Mrs Todmarsh-Rivers and Mrs Carrington-Townley will help me now.'

Chapter Twenty Seven

That evening Lucy, Jemima and Judy were sitting around the desk in Judy's surgery enjoying a glass of Martini. Lucy had taken a shower and was wearing an unfastened long Chinese silk dressing gown, exposing most of her body. Judy had taken her white coat off and was sitting naked.

'I think I'm the only normal person here; you two are always exposing your bodies,' Jemima said, sighing noisily. She shook her head and picked up her Martini. The others ignored her outburst and carried on sipping their Martinis. The conversation lagged and the faint sound of the sea breaking on the foreshore, the seagulls screaming and owls hooting came through the open window.

'I enjoy being in the nude,' Judy said, pouring what was their fourth Martini. 'Clothes always pull tight on me, actually they annoy me.'

'April didn't like being naked, did she?' Lucy said. 'You and April are so alike, Jemmy, you don't like being naked do you? I'm like Judy, I love being naked and I certainly love to see nude men. These Martinis are good, Judy. April would have enjoyed one of these; she loved a Martini heavy with gin.' The others nodded in agreement.

'Do either of you think LAC Weston had anything to do with the kidnapping?' Jemima said. 'I want to believe that he didn't, but I can't be sure.'

'I don't think he did,' Judy said. 'He said to me he'd helped April to escape and I believe him. The police have got it wrong. I hope he pulls through; he's growing weaker by the minute. If he dies, it will be my fault; it will be my stupidity that killed him.'

'You weren't to know he was allergic and couldn't

take certain treatments,' Lucy said.

'Do you think if he does pull through he will go to prison?' Jemima said.

'Oh you two, you're pessimists. Change the subject,' Judy said. 'Tell me this: do you think April had him in her bed?'

They didn't answer, but Judy frowned and placed her glass on the table.

'I must check on my patient.'

'We'll come with you,' Lucy said.

It was warm in the treatment room and Weston was lying on the bed covered by a single sheet. Judy changed his drip.

'Look at him, the poor thing,' Lucy stated. 'It's hard to think that this is the man who took me to my seventh heaven. I've never known feelings like the ones he gave me when we made love. It was like floating on a wonderful magic carpet, right up to that most fantastic explosion I felt inside me, when we climaxed together.' She sighed. 'He's the most fantastic lover ever. Don't you look at me like that, Jemmy, this man's bloody good.'

'I'm just shocked to hear you talk this way, Lucy,' Jemima said. 'He's only a twenty year old national service erk, and you're a married woman. You are a cradle snatcher. I don't suppose you've missed out in having sex with him either, Judy. When did you take him into your bed? Good grief, look at your guilty face; so you have also had him in bed, Judy. You're both old enough to be his mother.'

'Well so what? I've never denied that I like sex,' Judy said. 'This boy's a master at sex, there's no doubt about it. He really is wonderful. For the first time in my life I have had multiple climaxes and when we did eventually finish we came together, in one huge explosion. He is certainly a fantastic lover.'

173

'I'm pretty sure April's been to bed with him too, it's obvious from the fuss she makes of him,' Lucy said.

Rebecca, sick with worry, reported to the Head of Earth affairs.

'I'm worried about my charge, sir. He's growing weaker by the minute. Is there anything I can do to help him?'

'No, leave him; he'll pull through in time. The main thing is to keep his brain fully occupied; don't let his mind shut down, not even for the shortest period of time.'

'How can I do that, sir?'

'Send him a dream, a powerful dream about something that will intrigue his mind. Send him a dream about what might have happened or could have happened yesterday, had the kidnapping not taken place. You can do that without visiting him.'

'Come along girls, let's have another Martini. It's at times like this that I feel inadequate,' Judy said, putting the cocktail shaker back on the shelf. 'I honestly don't know what I can do to help him.'

'Well I'm beginning to see double; how many Martinis have we had?' Lucy said.

'Who's counting?' Judy said.

'We have had quite a lot, but who cares?' Jemima said, slurring her speech.

'I'll get another bottle of Gordon's,' Judy said. 'I feel like getting drunk tonight. I'm so depressed, I wish I could help him.' She left and came back with a new bottle of Gordon's, refilled the shaker and topped up their glasses.

'Here's to, no let's drink to Weshon pulling thue,' Lucy said, holding her glass out.

'Yeth we'll do that,' muttered Jemima. They clinked their glasses.

174

'Weston is something special,' Lucy said. 'And I know now what April sees in him. Look girls, look,' Judy shouted. 'The colour's returned to Weston's face and his expression's altered. I believe he's now dreaming.'

Weston did look a lot different. Not only did his face have colour, his lips and eyelids were moving. Judy brought her stethoscope.

'His heartbeat's improved immensely. Yes he's dreaming now. Well girls it's turned midnight. I think we should take it in turns to watch over him. I'll go first,' Judy said. 'We'll do two hours each?'

'No, I think we should watch over him together. I vote we all have a large scotch or brandy now to warm us.'

'Very well. I'll get a bottle of cognac, but one of us must stay awake at all times,' Judy said.

Chapter Twenty Eight

The dream sent to Weston by Rebecca began where he awoke in April's home with the bright sunlight shining through the east-facing window to find Edwina was still in his bed.

He eased himself out from under her arm and ran naked to the bathroom, where he dressed in his damp uniform. He had a strange feeling he'd done this before. The rest of his dream was not continuous; it was composed of small snatches here and there. In one of the snatches he found himself on April's terrace talking to Edwina.

'Why didn't you wake me this morning?' Edwina said. 'I could have had sex with you again.'

'Yes, I know we could have done it again and again and again, and again, and again. We could have been at it right up until now.'

'Wasn't it heaven though, darling? I can't wait to take you to bed again, and again, and again.'

They were still laughing when April came out; she didn't speak at first, she just glared at them.

'What's so bloody funny?' she eventually muttered. 'I hope you two are not laughing at me?' She sat down, not smiling, on a sun lounger. 'Pew, I want you to answer me one question.'

Edwina began to titter.

'That's enough of that, Eddy, this is not funny. Pew Weston, did you rape Mrs Weatherington last night? She said you went uninvited into her bedroom last night and forced yourself upon her against her will.' Weston was taken aback by this; he was flabbergasted.

'No, no I did not,' he said, albeit unconvincingly. *'No, I couldn't do anything like that; I couldn't do it, no I couldn't force myself on anyone.'*

'You two sound so funny, you should hear yourselves; anyone would think I'd stolen the Crown Jewels, instead of your little boy's virginity. It's no good April, I've won, I've had your little boy in bed and there's not a thing you can do about it.'

'You red-headed bitch, Edwina, you, you rotten egg, you did put something in my drink last night didn't you? You did it to give yourself a clear run at Pew. You even had the audacity to seduce him in my home. You went to his room, didn't you? I knew it wouldn't be the other way around.'

'Sorry, darling, can't wait around and talk, must leave now, flying out later today you know, remember April, all's fair in love and Weston.' The doorbell rang.

'I'll answer it myself, you wait here.'

'I never thanked you for last night, Westy,' Edwina said. 'What a night, it's a night I will always remember.'

The very next moment, Jemima and Weston's C/O Todmarsh-Rivers came out onto the terrace.

'What are you doing here, Weston?' He snapped.

'He's here because I invited him,' April snapped. 'Edwina wanted to thank him personally for driving us last night. What can I do for you, David?'

'I've brought your car around, you said you wanted me to drive you and Jemmy to Morton this afternoon.' April looked surprised.

'Sorry, David, completely slipped my mind, forgot all about it. You will have to wait while I change.'

'I must leave now,' Edwina said. 'I've a long drive ahead of me and that bloody endless flight to the States later. Goodbye, everyone. Thank you for a wonderful weekend darling and you too, our chauffeur, thank you for everything.' She smiled at Weston.

Weston became restless; he began tossing from side to side.

177

'He's stopped dreaming,' Judy said. 'He'll now either come round or take a turn for the worse.'

'No he's not; he's dreaming again,' Lucy said.

In the next snatch of the dream, Weston was driving April's "Jowett Javelin." He had April and the C/O's wife sitting in the back.

Her car handles well, he thought, much stiffer on the corners and easier to steer than the "Standard Vanguard." April gave him the directions in between chatting about the various naval officers they'd met the previous evening. Edwina's name was not mentioned.

He drove on, thinking about how dreadful he and Edwina had been, using April's home to have sex in.

'We'll drop Mrs Todmarsh-Rivers off first at her sister's home, Weston,' April stated haughtily. Her sister's home was an elegant manor house approached down along a tree-lined drive. They dropped Mrs Todmarsh-Rivers outside the house and April gave Weston the directions to her country cottage, which was a mile or so farther on.

"Mountain-Ash cottage" was a dream of a place, standing in its own grounds. Weston opened the two hardwood varnished gates. A sign written in Oldie English said, "Mountain Ash Cottage." He drove down the longish drive and parked the car outside the large two car garage.

'Bring the picnic basket, Pew, and the key to the cottage is also on the car key ring; open the door. Sorry I forgot, you poor thing didn't have a lot of sleep last night, did you? Oh, Pew, how could you let Edwina do that to me?'

Weston was unable to answer her cutting remark. He put the key in the lock, but before he could open the door, she pushed by him without speaking.

'Make a pot of tea, Pew Weston, the kitchen's that way.' She pointed. 'I'm so incredibly thirsty. I don't

know what bloody drugs you and Edwina used on me last night.'

'Now this has gone far enough for me, Mrs Ferrimins. You were with me last night, right up to you drinking that nightcap. How could I have had anything to do with it? Edwina told me she'd crushed a couple of her husband's sleeping pills into your brandy.' She frowned upon hearing this but didn't answer.

He made the tea and took it on a tray into the living room. This room, like the one in Lucy's cottage, had a cool Cornish slate floor, covered with loosely scattered oriental rugs. It had a comfortable looking chintz-covered sofa and two easy chairs were placed in front of a stone inglenook fireplace. Under the large window, which looked out onto the front garden, was a mahogany dining room suite. On either side of the fireplace were two well filled bookcases.

Like her home in Bravemouth, this one also had a painting over the fireplace. However, this one was a large oil painting of a white painted liner in a gold frame; the brass plate was inscribed, "R M S, Magnificent."

He placed the tray on the table and poured her a cup of tea.

'Where's your cup of tea, Pew?'

'I thought I'd wait, until we had lunch.'

'Fiddlesticks, have a drink of tea. I don't want to have the picnic for a while. You are always hungry; don't they feed you at that camp?'

'I was waiting to have my lunch when you phoned.'

'We will have the picnic after you have made love to me, not before.'

'But I'm hungry, really hungry.' The three ladies in Dr Wendover's kitchen distinctly heard Weston shout. They ran back to his room. However, Weston had settled down and was apparently dreaming again when

179

they arrived.

'He's becoming very unsettled,' Judy said. 'Come along, let's leave him in peace for a few minutes.'

Rebecca listened, pleased with Weston's progress.

Weston was again dreaming that he was with April in her cottage.

He could see she was wearing the same white wraparound skirt and white silk shirt over her bikini top that she'd worn the first day they'd met.

'I know what you're thinking, Pew Weston.'

'What?'

'That I was wearing these clothes the first day we met. Well, my unfaithful Eagle, what did Edwina call you? She told me you were her Seagull.'

'I'm not going to talk to you about your sister, Mrs Ferrimins. I'm sorry, I didn't make last night happen and now I sincerely wish it hadn't.'

'Tell me and be brutally honest, is Edwina's figure as good as mine?' She stood in front of him. 'Well is it?'

'I can't see any difference, you're both beautiful women; if anything you're the more striking, because you are taller, and why either you or Lucy or Judy want to know me, just a common Erk, is a mystery.'

'Did she flaunt herself in front of you?'

'No, it was not like that at all. I found her lying on my bed when I came back to my room after carrying you down and putting you to bed.'

'So you carried me to my room, Pew? The bitch didn't tell me that.'

'Yes, after you collapsed after drinking that nightcap.'

'Were you disappointed?'

'Well yes I was. She told me you couldn't hold your drink.'

She jumped to her feet without speaking, undid his

shirt and dropped his shorts. She then pulled him to her and kissed him; they just dropped to the floor.

'I want you to fuck me, Pew Weston, and I want you to do it now.'

'No not now, I'm so hungry. Let's eat first,' Weston shouted again.

'He's still hungry, poor fellow,' Lucy said. Weston became restless and tossed and turned. He finally settled down.

'You are so mercenary, Pew, killing this magical moment by talking of food.'

'Sorry but I am still very hungry,' Weston again shouted.

'He's getting agitated, he will be waking shortly,' Dr Wendover said. 'Look, he's settled down to dreaming again.'

'Very well, bring the basket,' April said. 'We'll have the picnic in the paddock.'

The garden had been laid mostly to lawn, with beds of flowers down the sides and either side of the wide flagstone path, which ran down the centre.

'You are so like my Ernst, Pew,' she said, kissing him. 'I could love you to death.'

The paddock was a fenced off area at the end of the garden, approached through another five barred gate. It was about two hundred and fifty yards long by a hundred and fifty yards wide; it had a large natural pond, almost a small lake, at the top.

She put on her sunglasses.

'We shall have our picnic there by the pond.' She nodded to a garden table with a bench either side. She took out a yellow and white check tablecloth and laid it across the table. 'Open the wine, Pew, I put two bottles in the basket.' She laughed.

'It's good to hear you laugh, April.'

Later on, after demolishing the picnic and feeling

181

slightly inebriated, they lay together in the sweet smelling grass, listening to the bees and grasshoppers. She kissed him passionately.

'Anything Edwina can do, I can also do and you must call me, April; don't you dare call me Mrs Ferrimins again.'

She rolled onto her back and outstretched her arms and legs.

'Pew, my sweet darling, shall we be naughty and do it out here?'

'No, I don't want to do it outdoors. Let's go back to the cottage.'

She rolled on the top, kissed him and, leaping to her feet, she pulled his shorts down. With a shriek of laughter, she leaped to her feet and ran around the edge of the pond, waving his shorts over her head.

Weston, feeling both awkward and foolish, watched her convulsing with merriment.

'Enjoying yourself, LAC Weston?' He froze, it was the voice of the C/O's wife; he attempted to cover himself with his hands.

'It's too late now to hide your………, LAC Weston. I've been watching you two for the past two minutes...'

'Lucy, Judy, here quickly,' Weston distinctly heard the C/O's wife shout. 'LAC Weston's coming out of his coma.' Weston opened his eyes to see Mrs Todmarsh-Rivers, Lucy and Dr Wendover standing around his bed.

'Jolly good, it's nice to have you with us again, Pewsy,' Dr Wendover said. 'It's four o'clock Monday afternoon and you've been out since this time yesterday, almost twenty-four hours. How do you feel?'

'Welcome back to the land of the living,' Lucy said, picking up his bed sheet which had slipped off.

'I'm thirsty, my mouth and throat are so dry.'

Weston gulped down two cups of almost cold tea

182

and lay back.

'What's happened to me, have I broken my leg?'

'No, it's not broken and very little has happened, darling,' Dr Wendover said, sticking a thermometer in his mouth. 'I'll give you a good check over.' She gave him a detailed examination. 'You seem fine now. How do you feel? You had me very worried.'

'I'm still hungry.'

'You shouldn't feel hungry on that drip.' She pointed. 'It's full of nourishment.'

'Don't tell me,' Weston said. 'Tell my stomach. Why is my leg in plaster, can you take it off?'

'No, not yet. I'll see about getting you something a little more substantial to eat, it's good to see you feeling your old self again, Pewsy.'

But Weston wasn't listening, he'd gone back to sleep and was dreaming again. He was back with April in the paddock.

'Here, Pew, use this to cover yourself.' She threw him her wraparound skirt. Smiling broadly, she ran to her friend and they did their usual greetings before walking to the cottage together. Weston, holding her skirt in front of himself, followed at a discreet distance. He waited outside the cottage, listening to their conversation.

'April darling, you weren't really going to have sex with that erk, were you?' the C/O's wife said. 'Remember this, April: he's nothing but a common airman.'

'Yes I was, I bloody well was, that was until you spoilt everything. Pew's my friend, he's not an erk, he's the answer to my prayer's, Jemmy, he's my Eagle returned to me by God.'

'Don't fool yourself, April; that man has neither money nor position in life. Your wealthy aristocratic German Eagle has gone; he died a long time ago.'

183

'No, Jemmy, you're wrong. Pew Weston is not an Erk, he's a gentleman and he's so like my Ernst it's frightening. I don't want to hear you call him by that name again.'

Weston began to toss back and forth again and suddenly sat up.

'Back with us again, Pewsy?' Dr Wendover said. The room door opened and Penny came in.

'Hello, Penny, are you here for the day?' Dr Wendover said.

'Yes, doctor. How's Pewsy today?'

'He's out from his coma. Will you make him something light to eat? I don't want to overload his stomach for a while.' Penny prepared a plate of ham salad and took it in.

'Dinner time, Pewsy,' she said, kissing his neck and shaking his shoulder.

Weston looked at her.

'Did you say dinner? This is yet another green salad. I'm sick of green salads.' They laughed.

Chapter Twenty nine

'Penny, will you and Susan give Pewsy a bath and a nice close shave? Make him as respectable as you can. The police have just been on the phone; they are on their way over to interview him.'

The girls looked at Weston and giggled.

'Don't get excited, you two; you are not giving me a bath.'

'Why not? We did it after you fell, we are both junior doctors,' Penny said. Susan left and returned with a bowl of warm water and a large sponge.

Half an hour later, Weston, whether he wanted it or not, was looking like a new pin, washed, clean-shaven and even wearing pyjamas. He waited for the police to arrive

'You may have one hour, Inspector Polpain, provided, and I mean this, you don't upset him. Remember he's only just come out from the coma,' Dr Wendover stated seriously, showing the inspector and Dr Botomly into Weston's room.

'May I check him over before we start, Dr Wendover?' Dr Botomly said.

'Very well, if you think it's really necessary, but I'd like a word in private with you first.' She led Dr Botomly into her surgery. 'Look here, doctor, don't pronounce Weston fit to leave, at least until after I've removed that plaster cast.'

The inspector was frowning with impatience when Dr Botomly eventually joined him.

'What did she want, doctor?' he asked offhandedly.

'Just a little professional medical advice, nothing to do with this case and nothing for you to bother yourself about, Harry.' He set about checking Weston's pulse and heart. He stood back. 'You can question him now.'

'LAC Weston,' the inspector began. 'I am of the opinion that you aided the gang of criminals who abducted Mrs April Ferrimins. I must warn you now that anything you say can be taken down and used in evidence against you.'

'How many times have I got to tell you? I did not help those people, I caught them red-handed carrying Mrs Ferrimins up the stairs in her home. That's when they overpowered and chloroformed me. I was taken or kidnapped at the same time as Mrs Ferrimins.' Weston shouted this.

'Right, LAC Weston. I think you've wasted enough of our time this evening. Come along lad grow up and cooperate, tell me the names of the gang and where they are hiding. If you do, I can promise that you will not get more than five years in prison. If you don't and you do get sent down for kidnapping, you could get ten years minimum.'

'This is the last time; I'm not going to tell you again. I was kidnapped at the same time as Mrs Ferrimins,' Weston shouted again. 'How many times do I have to tell you? I had nothing to do with the kidnapping, why don't you believe me?' Weston fell back in frustration. Dr Wendover came running in.

'What's all this shouting about, have you upset him, inspector? That's enough, gentlemen, sorry you must leave. I can't have you upsetting my patient.'

'Patient indeed, he's nothing but an unconvincing profound liar, but I shall carry on questioning him again in the morning.' The inspector got to his feet. 'Come along, Doctor Botomly; good evening to you, Dr Wendover.'

The following morning, Penny and Susan were working in the hospital. Consequently, to Weston's dismay, Lucy, helped by the C/O's wife, bathed and shaved Weston before his meeting with the police…

186

Doctor Botomly and the inspector arrived at ten o'clock, and after a curious, seemingly spurious, examination by Dr Botomly, the questioning started again. Weston appeared to be holding his ground. In fact he had a feeling he was getting through to the inspector.

Dr Wendover showed Squadron Leader David Todmarsh-Rivers, who was carrying a small parcel, into the room.

'LAC Weston, this registered parcel was delivered to the base this morning; it's addressed to you,' his C/O said, throwing the package to Weston. 'I thought it might be important, so I brought it over.'

'Where did it come from, sir?' Weston said.

'Open it and you'll most probably find out,' the C/O said, sighing in fake desperation.

Weston ripped open the package without a thought, and dozens of used £5 and £10 notes cascaded out onto the bed.

'What the hell's this, laddie?' the inspector said, picking the notes up and counting them. 'There's two thousand pounds here and, mmmm, what's this?' He picked up a handwritten note and put it to his nose.

'This is scented,' he muttered. 'Must have come from a lady. Listen, I'll read it to you. *This is your share old boy, thanks for your help, couldn't have done it without you.* It is signed from a friend. I think this just about wraps up this case good and proper. I'll take care of this money; have you a bag, Dr Wendover?'

'No, I don't think you should take that money, inspector,' Weston said. 'That money was addressed to me, so until it's proved otherwise, it's mine.'

'Not if it's the proceedings from a kidnapping. My word you are in big trouble now, boy.'

'But I've not been proved guilty, inspector. So the money's mine. I don't know where it came from, but it

187

was addressed to me.'

'Where did that package come from, David?' Dr Wendover said. 'Can you read the postmark?' The C/O picked up the wrapping from the bed.

'It's stamped Tilbury, London.'

Dr Wendover gave Weston a cold piercing look.

'Tell me the truth, Pewsy. What do you know about this? Where did it come from?'

'I honestly don't know, doctor. I can assure you I had nothing to do with the kidnapping. How could I? It's ridiculous to think I had. I've only been in Bravemouth for a few days. I think someone's trying to get me sent to prison. Why does no one believe me?'

'Right calm down, Pewsy. I for one believe you,' Dr Wendover said. 'I'm going to phone my solicitor; you're going to need a good lawyer.'

'He certainly is going to need a good lawyer. By the way, the magistrate's court is set for ten o'clock next Monday morning,' the Inspector said. 'I think he should accompany me now to the station; this money has changed the equation.'

'You're not taking Weston out of my care, not until I say he's fit enough to be moved, and don't argue with me, the boy's still wearing a catheter. If the magistrate's court is set for ten o'clock Monday morning, he will remain in my care until then. I shall personally deliver him to the court on time next Monday morning.'

'Sorry, Doctor Wendover, it's more than my job's worth to let him stay here now without security.'

'Then I shall give you security, inspector. Will a cheque, with next Monday's date for a thousand pounds be enough? I shall expect it to be returned when he shows up at court.'

'Very well, but I think you're being stupid sticking your neck out for him, he's guilty as hell.'

188

'That's my business, inspector. Will we be seeing you here again?'

'I don't think so, not now you are appointing a defence solicitor for him. I'll see you Monday next?' He looked appealingly at Weston. 'Why don't you make a clean breast of it laddie? It could save us all a lot of money and time.'

Weston didn't answer and the inspector and Dr Botomly left.

Dr Wendover and Squadron Leader Todmarsh-Rivers, not looking very happy, went into the kitchen, where Lucy was waiting.

'What's the matter, Judy, you look glum?' Lucy said. 'Have you upset her, David?' The C/O shook his head.

'David's not upset me,' Judy said. 'It's Pewsy; the poor boy's been told he's to appear at the magistrate's court next Monday morning.' Jemima popped her head around the door. 'I've decided to go back with David, Lucy, he's borrowed Mr Greenwith's car, are you coming back with us?'

'No, Jemmy. I'll stay on for another couple of days to help out. Give me a ring tonight.'

The C/O and his wife left.

'Do you think you will be able to manage on your own Lucy? I've got to go to Bravemouth, it's one of my clinic days today,' Judy said.

'Of course I can, just think of it; I'll be alone at last with my heartthrob.'

'He'll be no good to you, not while he's wearing that catheter. I'll see you at around seven o'clock tonight. Good bye.'

'What do you think, Weston?' Lucy said. 'Do you think you'll be any good to me?' She pulled the bed sheet back and stood looking at him.

Penny came in.

'Penny, darling,' Lucy said, surprising Weston by lying through her teeth. 'Dr Wendover's just told me to tell you, you must pull this catheter out.'

'No, she did not; don't believe her, Penny. Dr Wendover didn't say that,' Weston said. 'I don't think you should touch this catheter.'

'I agree with you, Pewsy; she didn't say anything to me,' Penny said.

'She told me, and that should be good enough for both of you, now take it out.'

'Well, but it will be on your head, Mrs Carrington-Townley. I don't think it should come out,' Penny stated as she removed the catheter 'You will have to get out of bed to go to the lavatory now, Pewsy.'

'May I?' Lucy said. With a twinkle in her brown eyes, she began fondling his now unrestrained penis. 'You sexy beast, you're already responding,' she said.

'Lucy, what the hell do you think you are doing?' Dr Wendover shouted. 'It's a good job I came back, who took the catheter out?'

'I did,' Penny said. 'But Mrs Carrington-Townley said you told her to tell me to do it.'

'Right then, Lucy, perhaps you could put it back in. No forget that, I'll do it myself. Sorry about this, Pewsy. I'll try not to hurt you,' Dr Wendover said. 'You've been through enough lately.'

The following morning, Weston's defence solicitor arrived.

'This is Miss Rosemund Devenish, your defence lawyer, Weston,' Dr Wendover said, showing her into Weston's room. Dr Wendover, realising the seriousness of the situation, was for once wearing a red and white batik sarong. 'You don't need to retain her services if you don't want to. However, she is one of the best solicitors in her field, which is defence.'

Miss Devenish was a small thin lipped petite woman

with shoulder length fair hair and bright blue eyes. Weston guessed she must have been around thirty to thirty-five years of age.

She shook hands with Weston.

'Do you think you will be fit enough to go to the magistrate's court by next Monday?' she said. Weston shot a questioning glance at Dr Wendover.

'I'm asking you, not Dr Wendover, and I expect you to answer.'

'How could I know that? I'm not the doctor.'

'Will he be fit, Dr Wendover?'

'Yes, I'm sure he will.' Lucy came in; she was topless, wearing only her shorts.

Miss Devenish gave her a disdainful look.

'You're almost naked, Mrs Carrington-Townley, this is disgusting.'

'I'm well aware of it, Miss Devenish; however, we are on a naturist farm. How did you know my name?'

'I recognised you from the inspector's description.'

Lucy pulled out her tongue and brushed past her to the door.

'LAC Weston, from what I can see about this case you've not got a great deal going for your defence. Why don't you take this chance to plead guilty and receive a lighter sentence?' Weston was astonished by this outburst from his defence lawyer.

'You are supposed to be my defence lawyer, Miss Devenish, yet you've not asked me one question about my side of this affair, yet you want me to plead guilty. I don't think I want you to defend me. I want someone who at least thinks I'm innocent.'

She looked deeply into Weston's eyes and, perhaps unfortunately for her, her entire attitude changed.

'Don't be hasty, LAC Weston. It's my job to investigate every avenue. Tell me all you know from the beginning and I'll see what I've got to work on.'

191

Weston couldn't tell her anything different from what she already knew, and when she left she wasn't looking very happy.

'She's gone, thank goodness,' said Lucy, tripping in and lying on Weston's bed.

Dr Wendover followed her in and scowled.

'Get off his bed, Lucy. I'm going to take the plaster off now.'

Within five minutes Weston's leg was revealed in all its glory; the wound had healed well, but the cast had left his leg emancipated, shiny and bright red, but to Doctor Wendover's relief there was no infection.

'You have wonderful healing flesh, Pewsy. I'll take the stitches out on Friday. But we must find some way of hardening your skin off. It's a lovely day; how would you like to go for a swim in the sea? The salt water will do it a lot of good. Coming with us, Lucy?'

'No, I'll wait here with a Martini, I'm not keen on swimming.'

With help from the doctor, Weston slowly made his way down the rock steps to the cove, where he'd left the boat.

'What happened to the boat?'

'Your C/O, David Toddy, and his boys took it back to Falmouth; it had been hired by the kidnappers along with the old house. You never know, you'll probably be up in court again shortly for stealing it.' They laughed.

'I'll race you out to that rock.' She pointed to a small rock a hundred yards out from the cove. 'Come along, Pewsy.' She was a powerful swimmer; she completely outclassed him. She was treading water, holding onto the rock for what seemed an age, before he swam up to her.

'I can't keep up with you, Judy, but I do think this is doing my leg good.'

'See the flat topped rock with grass growing on the

192

top?' She pointed. 'I'll give you a hundred count start and I'll race you to it. I've got in mind some different exercises for you to do when we get there.' It was almost dark when they got back.

'I don't suppose you two have been swimming all this time, I bet you've been shagging on the beach,' Lucy said. 'See how I think of you. I made a hot meal for you both and I've been keeping it warm.'

'I'll get a couple of bottles of wine from the cellar,' said Judy, smiling.

'Is she better at sex than me, Weston?' Lucy said, looking him in the eye.

'Lucy, you know very well I don't talk about my friends, but I will tell you this: I don't know what I would do without you lot of gorgeous women looking after me.'

'How do we compare to April and I mean in bed?' Lucy said, smiling

'I'm not comparing anyone; don't put me on the spot,' Weston said.

Later the three of them sat naked on the patio, enjoying the warm evening air caressing their bodies, sipping a glass of one of Judy's good cognacs.

'Well, Pewsy, Lucy tells me you won't discuss April with us, perhaps you'll tell us about your dream,' Judy said

'What do you want to know?'

'Everything.'

'Well, it began exactly as it really happened on the day of the kidnapping. In real life I awoke, I looked across the bed to see Edwina hadn't returned to her room. She was still asleep in my bed. I went to the bathroom, dressed and was about to leave for the camp when, like I told you, I was kidnapped along with April.'

'Whereas in the dream...'

193

'So you really did have Edwina in your bed, in April's home?' Lucy said, looking at Judy. 'I've always admired Edwina for her sheer cheek.'

'I wish I hadn't told you that now. Oh what the hell. I'd better start at the very beginning. It started after we got back from the charity ball. April told me to park Edwina's car outside her garage and then to return to her house to have a nightcap with her and Edwina. She also said she would have no arguments and that I was to stop the night there. The door to Rowanberry House was open when I got back from parking the car, and I was met by April in the hall. She told me Edwina had prepared nightcaps for us in the drawing room. We went up and Edwina gave us both a balloon glass of cognac. She said we had to drink them right down. April did so and a couple of minutes later she was out to the world, lying fast asleep across the sofa.

Edwina didn't want me to, but I carried April down to her bedroom and pulled the covers over her. Afterwards, I didn't go back to the drawing room, I didn't even drink my nightcap. I went straight to my room, where I found Edwina, wearing nothing but the briefest nightdress, lying on my bed. She told me to forget April because she had drugged her by crushing two sleeping pills into her cognac. I suppose you've guessed the rest. Edwina and I spent the night together. I awoke to find Edwina still in my room and I went along the landing to the bathroom to dress; that was when I was chloroformed and kidnapped along with April.'

'Why didn't you tell the police how Edwina had drugged April?' Dr Wendover said. 'You should also have made it clear about April inviting you to stay the night. I can see it clearly now; you are innocent. I wonder where all that money came from though.'

'I've got my own thoughts about that money, but I

can't involve Edwina in my case; it could destroy her marriage. Then again, I can't let Captain Ferrimins know that April not only invited me, but demanded that I stop the night. That would probably ruin April's marriage. I'm afraid that is my dilemma and I don't want either of you telling anyone about what I've told you tonight.'

Chapter Thirty

With Penny and Susan's help, Dr Wendover made a most exaggerated show of getting Weston from her shooting brake into the wheelchair. It was her intention to make the court think Weston's leg was much worse than it was. All three of them pushed Weston into the court at precisely ten o'clock. Inspector Polpain was waiting and he immediately gave Dr Wendover her un-cashed cheque. Rosemund Devenish was also waiting and she didn't appear to be happy.

'I'm very sorry, LAC Weston,' She said. 'I have not been able to offer anything new in your defence, so it's now a forgone conclusion that you will have to stand trial.'

Weston, even though he'd half expected it, was devastated by this news and found he couldn't think straight. He'd never been in any sort of trouble in his life, yet here he was, innocent of any crime, waiting for a kidnapping charge to be brought against him. Rebecca was also upset because there was nothing she could do to help him.

LAC Paul Edward Weston,' the clerk shouted. 'You have been charged with aiding people unknown in the kidnapping and ransoming of Mrs April Ferrimins. How do you plead? You may remain in the wheelchair.'

Weston stared blankly around the court.

Rosemund whispered, 'Say, not guilty.'

'Oh nnot ggguilty,' he managed to get out.

'Is your name Paul Edward Weston?'

'Yes, sir.'

'Is your address the RAF Marine Craft Unit, Bravemouth?'

'Yes, sir.'

'Paul Edward Weston, you are committed to appear at the assize courts in four weeks' time. Would LAC Weston's commanding officer, his defence and prosecuting lawyers approach the bench?'

Weston was wheeled away to the court cells and Miss Devenish followed him down several minutes later...

'LAC Weston?' Miss Devenish said. 'Dr Wendover offered to put up bail for you. However, your commanding officer objected to it on the grounds that if it was granted he would still have to send you into detention. So a compromise has been made. Lucky for you, Dr Wendover is still treating your leg, so it's been decided to remand you in the cells of Bravemouth police station until the trial. You can appeal against this, but my advice is to accept it.'

'Thank you, Miss Devenish,' Weston mumbled, still wondering, why me? I've not done anything wrong.

Weston, feeling like a convict, was placed in the rear of a black police van and taken directly from the court to Bravemouth police station. He hoped no one from the RAF base would be around when he arrived. The police sergeant, who appeared to Weston to be a rather pleasant man, wheeled him through the station to the cell that was to be his home for the next four weeks. Weston looked around and he wasn't very impressed with it. The cell had dark magnolia painted walls and there was a complete lack of privacy due to the open steel barred door. In its favour it did have a small unbarred window overlooking the harbour. The only furniture in the cell was a low bed alongside the riverside wall.

'You'll be alright here, boy,' the sergeant said. 'The food's good, my misses cooks it.'

'Alfred, what on Earth are you doing with that young man?' a shrill voice screamed out. The sergeant scowled and looked around.

'It be true, boy, a policeman's job is not a happy one. That be my misses,' he mumbled in his Cornish accent.

'Alfred,' his wife again shouted. 'Don't you put that boy in the cell with an iron barred door. Put him into the cell with a proper door; he's got to have some privacy while he be holidaying here.'

'Holidaying??? Very well my sweetness and light, anything for a quiet life,' the sergeant said, shaking his head and letting his breath out with a sigh.

The sergeant backed Weston in his wheelchair out from the cell and, muttering to himself, he pushed him down a short passage into another cell.

'I be leaving you here, boy. Get yourself settled in.'

He's gone to have harsh words with his wife, Weston thought.

This new cell was much larger than the other one and it had a solid wooden door. It also had a proper bed and a large unbarred window overlooking the harbour. The sergeant had left the cell's solid wood door open; this gave Weston a view right through the station and out through the main door into the high street. He was miles away in thought, watching the day-trippers walking by, when Lucy, wearing a bright yellow sundress, came clip clipping in, in her extra high-heeled sandals. Weston felt a little better at seeing a friend, but he also noticed the police sergeant was enjoying the view of Lucy's suntanned cleavage.

'Hello, Mrs Carrington-Townley,' the sergeant said. 'Always a pleasure to see he.' He turned and winked at Weston. 'Come to visit your new neighbour?'

'Yes, sergeant, your lodger and my new neighbour is a very dear friend of mine. Hi there, Weston. Isn't this wonderful, I only live next door. If you want anything, and I mean anything, just let me know. By the way, sergeant, Dr Wendover asked me to give you this. It's a note giving you the authority to allow Weston to leave the station for his treatment.' The sergeant took it and frowned.

'Yes, well, yes I suppose,' he said slowly. 'But you see I don't have a constable free at the moment. It says he's to have this treatment for as long as Dr Wendover deems necessary. I be sorry about this maid, but I can't let him leave the station until I've a constable to go with he, it be more than me job's worth, what if he were to escape.'

'We don't need a constable; you won't escape, will you, Weston?'

'Afternoon, sir, afternoon Doreen,' the sergeant said, stiffening his back. Lucy and Weston glanced round to see a police superintendent and his wife walking into the station.

'I've only called in to see how you were coping with having a detainee in your cells. Do you think you'll be able to manage?'

'Hello, Muriel,' the woman who had to be the superintendent's wife said. 'Isn't this exciting? We've never had vicious kidnapper in our custody before, have we? Where is he? Oh, hello. I didn't see you there, Lucy.'

'This is our vicious criminal,' Lucy said, laughing and pointing to Weston in the wheelchair. 'By the way, sergeant, I've been up to the camp and brought Weston's civilian clothes down here for him. He can't wear that thick woollen uniform all the time. Would it be alright if he changes before we go to the hospital?'

The sergeant shot a glance at his superintendent.

'Yes, of course he can,' the superintendent said. 'I've not come to Bravemouth to see you especially. I have really come to see the harbour master, but I thought I'd look in on you. Coming to the harbour

199

office with me, Doreen?'

'No, you go on, dear. I'll see you later. I want a chat with Muriel; I've not seen her in weeks.'

Lucy pushed Weston into his cell, closed the door and helped him out of his uniform. However, never a person to miss an opportunity, she took hold of Weston's.........

'Stop it. Stop doing that please, Lucy,' Weston whispered, not wanting the others in the station to hear him. Lucy chuckled.

It felt good to be wearing a sports shirt and shorts again, even if his leg was still bandaged.

He's just one big cuddly toy, she thought; I can't wait to get my hands on him again, Lucy thought.

'May I take Weston to the hospital, sergeant?' Lucy said, looking at the sergeant with her large limpid brown eyes.

'Sorry, but no. I can't spare a constable at the moment.'

'Do I really need an escort, Hillary?' Lucy said, looking askance at the superintendant, who she knew very well as a friend. 'How can he possibly escape in a wheelchair?'

'No, you won't need an escort, but if you do try to do a runner, my boy, you'll miss out on all of this. You'll be sent to a real prison.'

Lucy and the sergeant helped Weston into her large car and they put the wheelchair in the boot.

'Remember when I first did this to you, Weston? You were so shocked.' She slid her hand up his shorts leg.

'Please, Lucy, no, stop that.' He looked out from the window. 'This is not the way to the hospital, and for goodness sake stop doing that, get this car turned around please,' Weston said.

'No.' She laughed. 'This is the way to my double

200

bed in Kings Landing.'

'Now then Lucy, let's be sensible. What if Dr Wendover was to phone the station, and they didn't know where I was. I'd be sent to a real prison. I'm sure you don't want that, do you?'

'No I suppose not, but it would have been nice.' Lucy kissed him, then, pulling a long face, she reluctantly turned the car and without another word she took Weston to the hospital.

'Where the hell have you been, Lucy? I told you two o'clock,' Dr Wendover said. 'It's now quarter past, I was just about to phone the police station.'

'Weston wanted a drive to get some countryside air. But remember, all's fair in love and Weston, Judy.'

'Where's the wheelchair?' Dr Wendover said.

'It's in the back of the car, why?'

'It's my own fault. I should have gone for him myself. Why didn't you wheel him here? I'm going to take you to my private treatment clinic, Pewsy. I can't treat you in this place; I'll have no peace here. Pass all my phone calls on to the clinic, nurse.'

'Last time you took me there, you abandoned me naked without a stitch to wear. Sure your husband won't arrive again?'

'He's not due back from Africa until the end of the month.' She laughed. 'You never did tell me how you got out of that mishap, did you?'

'Didn't I? Well, I'll tell you this, doctor, it won't happen again, I can assure you of that.'

'Right you can go home now, Lucy. I'll wheel Weston down to my clinic; it's going to take a lot of my special physiotherapy to put his leg right.'

Two hours later, after some of her very special physiotherapy, which helped to unwind her as much as Weston, Dr Wendover wheeled Weston to the police station. He was surprised to see what a transformation had taken place in his cell. Its single bed now had a bright gingham bedspread, and alongside it was a bedside table with a reading lamp and a pile of magazines. Pretty gingham curtains had been placed on the window and a soft brown woollen rug alongside the bed.

'How do you like your room now, boy?' the sergeant's wife said. 'The super's wife, Doreen, and I did it this afternoon. Your dinner's not quite ready, so if you want you can sit outside and watch the ships in the harbour. There's a fishing rod somewhere. I'll find it for you tomorrow. I'm going to make your "holiday" here as comfortable as I can.'

'He be here on remand, Muriel, he not on holiday,' the Sergeant shouted.

'Oh shut up, misery guts. Take no heed, boy,' his wife said. 'Here, take this cup of tea and these biscuits out with you. I'll shout he when dinner's ready. If you're a lucky boy you might catch a glimpse of Mrs Carrington-Townley sunbathing; the lads tell me she does it in the nude.'

Weston wasn't bothered about seeing Lucy sunbathing. He lay back and relaxed in the deck chair and watched the boats sailing in the harbour.

'Is that you, Weston?' He looked up to see Lucy looking over the dividing wall.

'That our yacht over there.' She pointed. 'It's called "Never Never land".' He looked to where she pointed.

'What that big one, the one with two masts?'

'Yes, that's the one, would you like to go out to it? There are some fabulous bunks aboard her. Wonderful, for you know what.'

'Lucy, it may have escaped your notice, but I'm here on remand; I can't go gallivanting off at the drop of a hat.'

'No, it's a crying shame, especially with George

202

away in London for a week or so, leaving me with nothing to occupy my mind.'

'Lucy, you know I'm not free and I don't think you want your mind occupied.'

'Leave it with me, Weston. I've no idea what I'm going to do, but I'm going to make hay with you while George is away.'

He looked longingly at her small well-shaped breasts barely covered in her sundress. If only, he thought.

'I'd go to bed with you this very minute if I could, Lucy, but you know my circumstances.'

'Weston, you don't realise just how excited I get when I know I'm going to see you. I'm not on my own either, all the Five Leaf Clovers, well except for Jemima, are head over heels in love with you.'

'Five Leaf Clovers; yes I remember someone making a toast to the Five Leaf Clovers at April's home the night of the ball. Who and what are they?'

'It's us five, Edwina, April, Judy, Jemima and me; we called ourselves that at boarding school. All our parents, well except Jemima's, lived and worked abroad in the old British Empire. Therefore, we spent all our young life in England, at boarding school. However, we did spend all our wonderful school holidays every year with Jemima's parents in Falmouth. Still you don't want to hear about this sort of thing.'

'Yes I do, please carry on.'

'Well, we were all enrolled into the same boarding school as five-year-olds on the same day, except for Edwina, who had already been there for a year; she's a year older than the rest of us. And we five have been the best of friends ever since. At first, we called ourselves the Five Woodbines. You could buy a packet of five woodbines for two pence those days. Jemima's mother was furious when she found out and she suggested we change it to the Five Leaf Clovers. To make sure we did what she said, she bought each of us a ring with a cloverleaf motif. We still wear them; look.' She showed him hers, and sighed. 'I've been thinking about your court case, Weston; if only April could get her memory back, she would clear your name.'

'I don't think so, Lucy; April knows less about the kidnapping than you do. Remember, she was under the influence of Edwina's drugs at the time.'

'What if we could persuade Edwina to go to court; she'd clear your name I'm sure.'

'I don't know about that. I somehow can't see Edwina standing up in court, telling the world how she'd drugged her sister to enable her to spend the night with a lowly RAF erk. Then again I don't think anyone has seen or even heard from her since the kidnapping.'

'She left England for the states the day April was kidnapped,' Lucy said. 'I'm going to have a word with Judy. The court must be told all the facts. If you won't help yourself, perhaps we'll be able to persuade Edwina to stand up for you.'

'Dinner's ready, boy,' the Sergeant's wife shouted. Weston stood.

'I shall have to go, Lucy.'

'Bye, see you tomorrow. I love you, Weston. I'm taking you to the hospital for your "treatments" again tomorrow, bye bye…'

Lucy's plans appeared to be dashed when Dr Botomly made an unscheduled visit to the police station.

He was busy examining Weston's leg when Lucy came in. When she saw what he was doing, she at once phoned Judy.

A few minutes later Dr Wendover appeared.

'I wasn't informed of your visit, Dr Botomly. I could protest to the superintendent about this. Weston's my patient and I've not asked for a second opinion.'

'Get off your high horse, Dr Wendover. I was passing through town, so I thought I'd call in and see how he was getting on. Must say you've done a wonderful job on his leg, congratulations. He could have lost that leg, if not his life, if you hadn't treated it so well. Is there any special treatment you would like to try? The leg's still quite emancipated,' he said, with a twinkle in his eye.

'Regular bathing in salt water is probably the best treatment for both his skin and muscles.'

'Very well, yes, I can see that doing him good, but don't wear him out.'

'The beach below my Treroscoe farm surgery would be perfect for him.'

'Very well, Dr Wendover. I'll write you a note giving you permission to take him there every afternoon, provided he's back in his cell by six o'clock.'

'May I take him this afternoon? The weather's perfect.'

'Why not; will that be alright with you sergeant?'

'So long as he's back for Muriel's dinner by six, I don't mind.' Dr Wendover couldn't wait to tell Lucy the good news.

'So you'll be "swimming," if that's your new name for it I suppose, with Weston every day?' Lucy said, looking crestfallen.

'You can take him on Monday, Thursdays and Saturdays. I'll do the other days.'

'Can I come with you today? I've nothing better to do.'

'Of course, make sure that you are ready for one o'clock.'

'Do you know, Judy, I've done nothing but fantasise about Weston ever since I set eyes on him, have you?'

'I've no time for fantasies, Lucy, but I've lots of energy for the real thing. See you at one o'clock.'

A young lady came running up the street.

'Is Pew Weston locked up in there?' she asked Dr Wendover

'Yes he is, my dear, and who are you?'

'I'm Barbara, Pew's girlfriend's cousin. Do you think I could see him?'

'I suppose so,' Dr Wendover said. 'Go in and ask the sergeant.'

'Young lady here to see you, Pew,' the sergeant's wife said, showing Barbara into the cell.

'Hello, Barbara. Tamsin not with you?' Weston said. 'Still, I'm not surprised, she's not even written to me.'

'That's what I've come to see you about,' she blurted out. 'She's got a new boyfriend and without even asking me or Geordie she invited him to go to Truro with us...isn't it awful, Pew, you being locked up? I'm always thinking about you being locked in here; it looks very nice but you're still in prison. I've brought you a homemade pasty. Geordie gave me the meat, but I made it. I've also got a card for you; it's signed by everyone at the camp, but Tamsin's not signed it. Do you think you'll have to go to a real prison? Tamsin's dad says you will; he says it's all you're fit for. But then he doesn't like you, does he?'

'Doesn't he? I didn't know.'

'No, he hates you; it was her dad who made her dump you. He said you were a no good philander.'

'That's not very nice, why does he hate me?' Weston said. 'I've never met him.'

'I don't know, Pew, but I do know you won't go to prison. You'll get off with a caution. You didn't mean

206

to help those people, did you? You just got yourself mixed up with a bad crowd, that's all.'

What chance have I got when my own friends believe I was involved with the gang? Weston thought.

'I don't like Tamsin's new boyfriend. He's tight with money; he won't pay for anything. I don't think Tamsin's all that keen on him either.' They laughed.

'Is this young lady your girlfriend?' the sergeant's wife said.

'No, but she's still a very good friend.'

'You're only allowed ten minutes visiting, dear; I'll show you out.'

Dr Wendover and Lucy called at the station just after one o'clock. Weston was waiting for them.

'Lucy, what are you going to do while I give Weston his therapy? Perhaps you could prepare a meal for me?'

'I see, so while you're giving Weston his, or is it your, physiotherapy, I'll be flogging myself to death over a hot stove.'

Dr Wendover stopped the car outside her farmhouse; they could quite clearly hear the seagulls screaming and the surf breaking on the rocks.

'All's fair in love and Weston, Lucy,' Dr Wendover said, smiling. 'Come along, Pewsy, you know my rules regarding clothes and that goes for you too, Lucy.' Dr Wendover, who as per usual was wearing only her white overall, was naked in a flash. Lucy undid her shoulder ties and let her dress drop, revealing she was also naked underneath.

These women don't wear much in the way of underclothes, Weston thought.

'I'll race you to the beach, Pewsy, and call me Judy when we are alone,' she shouted, setting out.

'I can't race you; I'm a wheelchair patient,' Weston shouted.

207

'Bollocks, you're fine now, Weston; I should know, I'm your doctor.' Weston threw his clothes into her car and Lucy gave him a kiss.

'Stay just a moment or two with me, Weston, please,' she said.

'Sorry, Lucy, I've got to go.' He tore himself away and ran after Judy. Judy, looking like a Greek statue with her breasts held high, was waiting below on the beach. She saw Weston on the cliff top and set out swimming past the rocks guarding the cove. Weston was no match for Judy at swimming. However, later, while he was having his special treatment on the grass-covered rock, he was more than her equal.

Chapter Thirty one

Weston was becoming more and more morose as the date for his trial came closer.

Captain Ferrimins had made extensive inquires and questioned everyone he thought knew his wife, in an effort to discover more facts about his wife and Weston's affair. He was now more determined than ever to get Weston convicted and sent to prison. With this in mind, he instructed his private detective to take to Mr Haley's hardware shop, where the duplicate keys had been cut, various pictures of Weston, which the detective had taken without Weston's knowledge, to help the shop owner point out Weston at the trial.

The morning of the trial, Weston was taken to the court in a police van; even though he knew he was innocent, he knew there were lots of people around who thought of him as a criminal. He'd actually become quite famous locally; consequently, a small but silent crowd had assembled outside the police station to see him leave for court.

Rebecca's superiors had told her quite bluntly that she was not to use her powers to help Weston. She, however, knew the only hope Weston had of proving his innocence was to find Edwina, April's sister. Rebecca spent a week searching for Edwina and she eventually found her in a hotel in Tahiti where she and her husband was holidaying.

Rebecca couldn't wait to tell Edwina about April and Weston. Nevertheless, she held back, not wanting to rush in and spoil things for Weston.

She watched and waited until Edwina was sunbathing alone on an empty beach. With the conditions right, Rebecca entered her mind and sent her a dream.

In the dream, Edwina found herself walking down a long corridor which had doors on either side and at the very end was yet another door. I must be in some kind of a hospital, Edwina thought. She opened the door at the end of the corridor. To her surprise she saw her sister April sitting up in bed. She was talking to a man who must have been a doctor.

'Mrs Ferrimins,' she heard the man say. 'This is going to take a very long time unless you are prepared to help me; this is a two way battle. I can't do anything without your help.' Edwina ran across the room to her sister's bed.

'April, why are you in bed, are you ill?'

'Eddy, I recognized you,' April said. 'Doctor I know this is my sister'.

'Why shouldn't you? I am your bloody sister, now April for goodness sake, buck yourself up.'

At that point Edwina awoke; the dream had been so realistic, it left her bewildered and shocked to find she was lying on a Tahitian beach.

'I've got to get in touch with April at once, Franklin; I think she's ill,' Edwina said to her husband. 'How can I do it from here?'

'This is rather sudden, darling, how on Earth did you discover she was ill?'

'I don't know, but I've just had what I think was a dream. I have got to get in touch with April as quickly as possible. In my dream she was in some kind of hospital. I think she may have had a nervous breakdown or something similar. I've just got to see her.'

'We can always phone darling, however it may take a couple of days, but we'll get through eventually. Or you could send a cablegram; that would be quicker.'

'I'll do both. That's what I'll do; I'll send four cablegrams, one to April and one each to Judy, Lucy, and Jemima. I can let them know where I am and tell them I'm on my way back to Britain. I will also try to phone April, that's if I can. But in the meantime I've got to get back to Bravemouth, please make the arrangements. I'm sorry about this, darling, but we can always have another holiday.'

'It was only a dream, darling; look there can't be anything amiss with April, darling. This letter arrived this morning from head office in New York. Michael's sent us tickets for the second inaugural voyage of the cruise liner, "RMS Monarch." The liner is being returned to passenger service after being used as a troop ship. Michael says that he asked the board of directors if he could be her "Captain" for this one voyage. They agreed and they gave him eight complimentary first class stateroom tickets for his friends; he's sent two to us. Not one word about April being ill.'

'There is definitely something wrong with April, I know that dream was true. I've got to get back to England.'

'Of course, darling, we have got to go anyway; the cruise ship is sailing from Southampton in just over a week's time. I'll make the arrangements.'

Chapter Thirty two

Weston, his mind a maelstrom of wild unrelated thoughts, stood in the courtroom hardly listening to what was going on.

The jury had been sworn in and the prosecuting Barrister, a Mr Woolton, was standing in front of the court.

'I would like to call my first witness, your honour; Chief Inspector Polpain.' The inspector took the stand.

'You are Chief Inspector Polpain, the officer in charge of the kidnap investigation?'

'Yes, sir.'

'Would you please tell the court what happened when you questioned LAC Weston at Dr Wendover's Treroscoe farm, clinic?'

'I found it a waste of time, your honour. LAC Weston is a profound liar and I feel sure that he's in cahoots with the kidnap gang, albeit by an opportunist meeting. I also went to the naval base where Weston had driven Mrs Ferrimins and her friends to the charity ball. I found out that LAC Weston had five hours to kill there. Consequently, I thought he might have used that time to meet up with the gang to finalise the kidnapping. However, it was also a waste of time; all I found out was that Weston was a philander. He spent the entire evening with some Wren in her room. However, LAC Weston, who is a very deviously clever fellow, could have done this deliberately, just to throw Captain Ferrimins' detective off the scent. LAC Weston is a liar, albeit a clever one; he even tried to use the fact that Mrs Ferrimins had been set free after the ransom had been paid to further his own ends. He thought he could make himself a hero by telling everyone how he'd organised and participated in Mrs

212

Ferrimins' escape.'

'Thank you, inspector. Would you also tell the court about the package someone unknown posted to LAC Weston from Tilbury, London?'

'Yes, sir. I was in LAC Weston's room in Dr Wendover's private hospital when his commanding officer brought the parcel in. It had been posted to the RAF camp. I don't think he could have been thinking coherently at the time because he opened it in front of me and two thousand pounds in used notes cascaded out onto his bed with a note saying, "Thank you for your help."'

'Where do you think that money came from, inspector?' the judge asked.

'That money could only be payment for his help in the kidnapping, your honour.' His next witness was Mr Hailey, the owner of the hardware shop in Bravemouth. He was a small grey haired man of about sixty, with a pronounced stoop.

'You are Mr Hailey and you own the hardware shop in Bravemouth?' Mr Woolton, the barrister, said.

'Yes, sir.'

'Mr Hailey, I would like you to look around the court and see if you can see the man who brought Mrs Ferrimins' keys into your shop to have duplicated? If you can see him, will you point him out?' Rebecca thought; he's not going to blame Weston for something he has not done. I don't care what they say in the Earth Department. She carefully slipped into Mr Hailey's mind and guided him to look around the court room a couple of times before suddenly pointing to Squadron Leader Todmarsh-Rivers.

'Yes, sir, that be the man there,' he said, in his Cornish accent.

'Thank you, Mr Hailey. Your witness, Miss Devenish.' He sat down to loud laughter before he looked at the person his witness was pointing to. He then leapt to his feet. 'Sorry, your honour, there must be some mistake.'

'Sit down, Mr Woolton, he is now Miss Devenish's witness.'

'Are you one hundred percent sure that is the man who brought the keys into your shop, Mr Hailey?' Miss Devenish said.

'Yes, I'm one hundred percent sure.' Rebecca eased herself out from his mind and the court again erupted into laughter.

'Thank you, Mr Hailey. No more questions for this witness, your honour.'

'You may step down, Mr Hailey,' the judge said.

Mr Woolton, looking very bewildered, called his next witness, Squadron Leader David Todmarsh-Rivers, to the stand.

'You are Squadron Leader David Todmarsh-Rivers?'

'Yes, sir, and before we go on, may I say that I am not guilty of having Mrs Ferrimins' keys duplicated in Mr Hailey's shop.'

'Quite? hm, hm.' He cleared his throat. 'You are LAC Weston's, commanding officer?'

'Yes, sir.'

'Would you tell the court your opinion of LAC Weston?'

'Objection, your honour; this man's personal opinion of my client has nothing to do with this case.'

'Choose your questions with a little more thought, Mr Woolton.'

'Sorry, your honour. I'll rephrase the question. Squadron leader, would you please tell the court why, when you were informed that LAC Weston was being sent to your unit, you tried to get him posted away? I have also learned that you even considered sending him

214

on a twelve week diving course with the navy.'

'There wasn't anything personal in my decision, your honour. I thought a person such as LAC Weston might disrupt my unit. From what I could find out from his papers, he was far too intelligent a man to serve as motor boat crew on a launch. A man of his intelligence should have been at least in aircrew and an officer, not an LAC deckhand.'

'Is that the only reason you had doubts about this man?' said the judge.

'I think you're grasping at straws, putting this man up as a witness, Mr Woolton. Have you finished with him?'

'No, not yet, your honour.'

'Get on with it then, man.'

'Sorry, your honour. Squadron leader, would you please tell the court how LAC Weston came to be acquainted with Mrs Ferrimins?'

'April, I'm sorry your honour, I mean Mrs Ferrimins, is my wife's best friend. She asked me if I could send someone to her home to do some jobs for her. Actually, the work involved lifting a carpet and putting that and some other items away in her attic.'

'Why did she need an airman to do work like that?' the judge said.

'She'd tried for weeks apparently to get someone from the town to do the work, but had failed. So she came to me to see if I could help her out. Weston had just been posted in and was on a loose end, so I sent him.'

'That was six days before the kidnapping. So is it possible that the gang approached LAC Weston on that day?'

'Objection, your honour. How could the squadron leader know whether LAC Weston was approached or not?' Miss Devenish said, smiling.

215

'Yes, I agree with you,' the judge sighed. 'Choose your questions with more care, Mr Woolton.'

'Sorry, your honour.'

Miss Devenish put her thumb up to Weston.

'I have no more questions for this witness, your honour. Your witness, Miss Devenish?'

'No questions, your honour.'

'You may step down, Squadron Leader Todmarsh-Rivers. Your next witness, Mr Woolton?'

'Captain Michael Ferrimins?'

'Captain Ferrimins, I believe you had a brief conversation with your wife outside Dr Wendover's private hospital, before she finally lost her memory?' That remark ripped deep into Weston's mind; he shot a glance across the court to Dr Wendover. Neither Weston nor the doctor had known of this.

'Yes, that is true,' the captain said.

'Would you tell the court what she said?'

'My wife was hysterical at the time. However, she kept on repeating and repeating over and over again "my fingers my fingers. They are going to cut my fingers off." I asked her who was going to cut them off and she said, "My Eagle, Pew Weston. Oh Pew, Pew. Oh, Pew, look after me." I asked her who her Eagle was and who was this Pew Weston. She said, "It was awful; he had garden secateurs in his hand, he was going to cut my fingers off." She passed out at that point and when she recovered consciousness her memory had gone again.'

'Thank you, Captain Ferrimins. No more questions, your honour. Your witness, Miss Devenish.'

'Thank you, Mr Woolton. Captain Ferrimins, is it not feasible that Mrs Ferrimins' remarks could be construed into her thinking LAC Weston would protect her from the people who were threatening her?'

'No, I can't see that at all; she was obviously in

terror of the man.'

'But you told us your wife said, let me quote from what I've written down, "My Eagle, Pew Weston, oh Pew, Pew look after me."'

'What are these names, "My Eagle" and "Pew"?' the judge inquired.

'They are Mrs Ferrimins' affectionate terms for LAC Weston, your honour,' Miss Devenish said.

'I see, thank you, Miss Devenish, now things are becoming a little clearer. You may carry on with your questioning.'

'Captain Ferrimins, I think you want everyone to believe it was my client your wife was accusing. However, I put it to you, sir, that LAC Weston had nothing whatsoever to do with the kidnapping. In fact I believe he was the only person your wife could look to for help. No more questions, your honour.'

'Captain Ferrimins, what do you think your wife meant by those affectionate terms?' the judge asked.

'I've not the slightest idea, sir. I don't think she did either; she was rambling at the time, your honour.'

'Very well, you may step down. We will adjourn for lunch and reassemble at two thirty.'

'All stand,' a court official shouted and the judge left.

'Come on, old lad, it's the cells for you,' the constable said, taking Weston by his shoulder. Dr Wendover, looking very important in her tight fitting white overalls, followed them into the cell.

'I've got to talk to you, Pewsy. I've told the court I need to check your leg, listen carefully.'

'What is it?' Weston asked.

'I've just received this cablegram from Edwina; I'm so excited I could scream.' She showed Weston the paper and whispered, 'She's been on holiday with her husband in Tahiti, but she's now on her way back to

217

Bravemouth. It also says she tried to phone April at Rowanberry House but couldn't get an answer. She wouldn't; Michael's not at home, he's staying at the Bravemouth Hotel. I somehow don't think she's heard about the kidnapping. Nevertheless, she's given me a phone number to ring in New York. I don't care what you say; I'm going to phone her now, even though I don't know what the time is over there. I don't care if I have to get her out of bed; I'm going to tell her about this court case. I'm sure she'll take the stand on your behalf. Come along, get those trousers off, I shall have to go through the motions.' The officer opened the door again and Lucy came in. She was carrying a picnic basket. She was looking more like Peter Pan than ever, wearing a stylish white fitted shirt and a short straight black skirt.

'The sergeant said we could eat in here with you, Weston, after Judy's finished her examination. For goodness sake, put your trousers on, Weston. I'm going randy just looking at your bare legs.'

The door was opened yet again and Rosemund Devenish came in.

'Weston, the prosecution have just informed me that they have a new witness, a Flight Sergeant Fenship. Do you know him?'

'Flight Sergeant Fenship, I know that rotter,' Lucy said. 'He's a lecherous person. He approached me once on the town quay; he was reeking of beer and cigarettes. When I told him I was a married woman, he said it was my loss and that he was one of the only men in Bravemouth who could guarantee to satisfy me.'

'I wasn't asking you about this man Mrs Carrington-Townly, I was asking LAC Weston; do you know this man?' Miss Rosemund said. 'If you do, I want you to tell me all you know about him; I think he could do you a lot of harm.'

'Yes I do know him, he's a horrible man.' Weston told her everything he knew, including the fact that every man at the RAF base knew that Flight Sergeant Fenship was head over heels in love with Mrs Ferrimins. Miss Rosemund took everything down in shorthand.

Weston was brought into the court again at two thirty. For the first time, he was thinking clearly and he had a good look at the jury. To his disappointment, he saw it was comprised mostly of men; he could only see two women and they looked like a couple of battleaxes.

'You have another witness to call I believe, Mr Woolton?'

'Yes, your honour. Call Flight Sergeant Fenship to the stand.'

The Flight Sergeant, wearing his best blue uniform and his commander kite moustache freshly waxed, came in; he looked at Weston and smirked.

'You are Flight Sergeant Fenship?'

'Yes, sir.'

'Would you tell the court exactly what LAC Weston told you about Mrs Ferrimins on his second day at Bravemouth?'

'Well, your honour, we were on our way to Plymouth in the high speed launch. The lads in the engine room had told me how LAC Weston had been going around the base saying Mrs Ferrimins liked him. I knew it couldn't be true, so I went to see him. At the time he was on the helm of the launch. He laughed into my face and said it was true and that she'd begged him for sex. I told him to keep away from her; he wasn't good enough for her.'

'So you told LAC Weston in no uncertain terms to keep away from her. What did he say to that?'

'He laughed and said he'd do what he liked.'

'What happened after that, flight sergeant?'

219

'I just repeated what I'd told him before and said that if he saw Mrs Ferrimins again I'd give him a good hiding. Two men had given him a good going over the previous night for taking their wives to bed.'

'Thank you, flight sergeant. Your witness, Miss Devenish.'

'Just one moment, Mr Woolton,' the judge said. 'Your witness Flight Sergeant Fenship has just made a statement that LAC Weston had been given a good going over, well they were his words, by some husbands for taking their wives to bed. Does this mean that your witness is inferring to this court that LAC Weston goes around making a habit of philandering? If so, please tell me what bearing it has on this case?'

'None, your honour; it shouldn't have been said. I'm very sorry, your honour.'

'Jury, strike out those remarks and disregard them. Carry on, Miss Devenish.'

'Flight Sergeant Fenship,' she said, slowly reading from the notes she'd made with Weston. 'Is it true that you have a great dislike for my client and that you have disliked him ever since you first met?'

'Objection, your honour.'

'Overruled, Mr Woolton. I do think this is very important to the case. Carry on, Miss Devenish.'

'Would you answer my question, flight sergeant?'

'Yes it is true. I don't like him; he's too smarmy for me.'

'I put it to you, flight sergeant, that the only reason you don't like LAC Weston is not because you think he's smarmy, but because Mrs Ferrimins likes him. I think you will do and say anything to get him into trouble. Your testimony in this case is worthless. No more questions, your honour.'

'You may step down, flight sergeant. Have you any more witnesses, Miss Devenish?'

'Yes, your honour. I would like my client LAC Weston to take the stand.' Weston hadn't expected this. Rosemond smiled at him.

'LAC Weston, we've patiently sat through and heard all these stories the other witnesses have told us. Would you please tell the court your side of this case?'

'Where do I start?' Weston asked.

'I think you should take it from where you left Rowanberry House to park Mrs Ferrimins' sister's car outside her garage.'

'Well, your honour, when I returned from parking the car I found the front door had been left open and Mrs Ferrimins and her sister had gone to bed. I went in and I also went to bed,' Weston lied under oath, but only to protect April and Edwina's reputations. 'The following morning, I was about to return to the camp for breakfast when I heard voices from down the stairs. I looked over the gallery and saw two men carrying someone on a stretcher. I shouted, "Is that Mrs Ferrimins, is she ill?" and someone shouted, "Get the bastard." The next moment I had a cloth soaked in chloroform pressed onto my face and I passed out. When I came to I was in this place with no light; it was pitch black. I felt around and found I was in a closet-cum-cloakroom in a strange house...' Weston told the court how he'd found Mrs Ferrimins in the house garden and how between them they'd launched the small boat and sailed it up the channel to Dr Wendover's farm.

'Thank you, LAC Weston. Your witness, Mr Woolton.'

'No questions, your honour.'

Next on the stand was Dr Wendover; she told the court how Weston, after sailing the small boat up the coast, had against all odds carried Mrs April Ferrimins up a sixty foot cliff, despite his leg being ripped open from groin to ankle.

Penny, followed by Susan, were also called and they repeated more or less what Dr Wendover had said.

The judge summed up the evidence to the jury. He finished by saying, 'No matter what else you think about his case, the only real cast iron evidence we have to prove that LAC Weston took part in the kidnapping is the note that came with the two thousand pounds. You must consider the facts; LAC Weston has not given a satisfactory explanation for this money. Was it a gift or was it his pay off?'

The jury was about to retire when Miss Rosemund Devenish approached the bench.

'I would like to ask for an adjournment, your honour. This telegram has just arrived.' She handed it to the judge.

It read: "Vital evidence, regard to LAC Weston in the Ferrimins kidnap case stop. Can't get to the court until two thirty pm Friday stop. Edwina Weatherington. (Sister of April Ferrimins.)

The judge frowned and called the clerk of the court over. They had a few whispered words. He then stood.

'This case will be adjourned until two thirty pm, Friday.'

Dr Wendover rushed over and had a word with Rosemund Devenish.

'Excuse me, your honour,' Miss Rosemund said. 'Dr Wendover wants to know if it would be possible for LAC Weston to return to the cells in Bravemouth. His leg is still in a poor condition and she would like to try a new treatment. The judge half-turned and stopped in his tracks.

'If the prosecution agrees, I've no objection. Make sure he's here by two thirty, Friday afternoon.'

'I've no objections, your honour,' Mr Woolton mumbled.

Weston was standing outside the police van when Judy, Jemima and Lucy came out.

'Hello, can I take this opportunity to thank you ladies for standing by me, when even my own family deserted me. I don't know what I would have done without you.'

'Pewsy, we are all on your side,' Dr Wendover stated. 'I've spoken to Edwina and she's going to go on the stand for you. However, the only damning thing about this case is that money, where do you think it came from?'

'I could hazard a guess. I suppose.'

'Well, let us know?' Lucy said.

'I'm probably wrong, and I know none of you will agree with me, but I think it came from the captain.'

'Ho no, what made you think that?' Jemima said.

'From that moment when he told the court that April was terrified of me, which you all know is an absolute lie.'

'Yes I was puzzled about that,' Dr Wendover said. 'But two thousand pounds is a hell of a lot of money to throw away.'

'He can well afford it; he probably had that amount left over from what he drew out for the ransom,' Weston said.

'I don't suppose we'll ever know for sure,' Lucy said. 'I sincerely hope that Edwina blows their case sky-high.'

Chapter Thirty Three

Friday afternoon proved to be another hot and sunny day. Weston walked into the court at two thirty precisely and the first thing he noticed was that most of the jury had taken their jackets off. He wondered if it would be alright for him to remove his tunic. However, he changed his mind when he saw the C/O was wearing his.

He looked around, but could see no sign of Edwina.

'All stand,' the official shouted and the judge came in.

'This new witness, Miss Devenish, has she arrived, is she in the court?' the judge inquired.

'Yes, your honour; however she's had a long drive from London. I would like you to give her a minute or two to compose herself. Also, I have had no time to bring her up to date with the case, your honour.'

'Can't be helped; perhaps we'll get the truth from her, if you don't enlighten her to the facts,' the judge said, looking at his watch. 'I'll give her two more minutes.'

Weston heard the door open and close and a low murmur ran around the court; he looked round to see Edwina making her entrance. She was looking fabulous, wearing the clothes she always wore for driving, a white long sleeved frilly fronted blouse and skin tight beige trousers tucked into highly polished dark brown boots. Her long red hair was tied back in a pony tail. Gosh, she looks even more beautiful than I can remember, Weston thought.

She looked towards Weston, smiled and blew him a kiss. Fully knowing she had the whole court room captivated, she pulled the ribbon tying her ponytail and shook her head. This allowed her hair to cascade down and around her shoulders. Looking like a top model, she walked across the court, holding her breasts high, to the witness box. There she turned towards Weston and blew him another kiss.

'I would like to apologise to the court for my state of dress,' she said. 'But I've had no time to change out of my driving clothes.' A ripple of laughter went around the court.

'Did I hear you say riding clothes?' the judge said. 'I take it you rode from London, Mrs Weatherington. Did you tether your horse outside the court?' More laughter.

'No, sorry to disappoint you, your honour,' Edwina said, doing an exaggerated curtsy towards the judge. 'I drove from London in my new Standard Vanguard saloon. Do I have to hold a bible or something?'

A court official handed her a bible and put her on oath.

'You are Mrs Edwina, Phoebe, Eunice Weatherington?' Miss Rosemund Devonish said.

'Of course I am. Who else could have such stupid names?'

'Would you please tell the court what your relationship is to Mrs April Ferrimins?'

'Her older sister. I don't like to admit this but I am one year older.'

'Mrs Weatherington, is it true that you attended the summer charity ball held at the naval base on the Nineteenth of May with April your sister and other friends?'

'Yes, I did. Everyone enjoyed it; we had a wonderful evening and April and I travelled with David Todmarsh-Rivers and Jemima, his wife, in my new car.'

'Would you tell the court who chauffeured you to the venue that evening?'

'Yes, we were driven by my,' she sighed, 'lovely Seagull, my I could eat that fellow…I'm sorry, your honour, I do mean LAC Paul Edward Weston.' She turned towards Weston and smiled.

'I suppose,' the judge said, sighing, 'that "my lovely Seagull" is your personal pet name for LAC Weston, Mrs Weatherington?'

'Yes, but only one of my many names for him, your honour; he is lovely in many ways.'

'Yes, quite; is it true that all the women who know LAC Weston have their own personal pet names for him?' the judge said.

'Yes, I think they do, your honour,' Miss Devenish said.

'Mrs Weatherington, would you tell the court what happened at Rowanberry House, Bravemouth, when you returned from the summer ball?'

'It was raining; actually it had rained heavily all the evening. Westy dropped Jemima and David…sorry, your honour, his commanding officer and wife, off at their home first and then drove on to Rowanberry House. I got out with April and April told him to park my car outside her garage, which was over half a mile away, and then to return to Rowanberry House for a nightcap. April had planned for Weston to stop the night by preparing a room for him. She had even bought him a new toothbrush and a pair of silk pyjamas so he would have no excuse not to stay.'

The noise in the courtroom was getting louder by the second. The judge banged his gavel for silence.

'So it is true that LAC Weston was invited to stay the night, by your sister?' Rosemund Devenish said.

'Yes, of course he was; were there doubts?'

'Oh yes, quite a lot. However, carry on Mrs Weatherington.'

'There's not much more for me to say except that I

had made up my mind that April wasn't having Weston in her bed that night. I was going to have him in mine. My beautiful sister April, who got all the new men first, wasn't going to have Westy that night. To make sure of that, I crushed two of my husband's sleeping pills into the glass of cognac I gave her; she knocked it back in one go. You should have seen Westy's face when she collapsed across the sofa. I wanted to leave her there; however, Weston didn't agree, and he carried her down the stairs to her room. While he was employed in putting April to bed, I slipped into his bedroom. There's not much more to tell, unless you want to know about our momentous night. I awoke in the morning, but didn't let Westy know I was awake. I saw him getting out of the bed. I looked at my watch; it was six o'clock in the morning. He thought I was still asleep, but I watched him leave and a few moments later I heard voices. However, I put that down to someone in the harbour. I went back to sleep and didn't wake until nine thirty. Westy hadn't returned, so I got out of the bed and I checked April's room. Her bed was empty; consequently, I jumped to the wrong conclusion that April had taken Westy out to her cottage on the moors. The phone rang and I answered it and it was Michael, April's husband. He said he wanted to talk to April. I told him she wasn't there and that I didn't know where she was. I showered and dressed and drove back to London. We flew out later that afternoon to the States.'

'Thank you, Mrs Weatherington. No more questions, your honour.'

'Mr Woolton, would you care to cross examine?'

'Yes, your honour. Mrs Weatherington, may I inquire what you know about a parcel containing two thousand pounds, which was posted in London addressed to LAC Weston?'

'Nothing, no nothing at all.' She shook her head. 'I

227

don't know anything about money. But I do know this: LAC Weston was far too busy in bed with me that night to have had anything to do with the kidnapping. I personally saw to that.'

'No more questions, your honour.'

The judge gave the jury a further summing up. This time he was obviously in favour of an acquittal, but he did point out yet again that there was still no satisfactory explanation for the two thousand pounds. 'If you think someone sent it to LAC Weston in payment for his help in the kidnapping, you must find him guilty. On the other hand, if you think some malicious person sent it solely to implicate Weston in the kidnapping, you must bring in a not guilty verdict.' The foreman of the jury talked to each member in turn.

'We don't need to deliberate on this case, your honour; we are unanimous in bringing in a not guilty verdict.'

'You have been found not guilty, LAC Weston. Is there anything you would like to say?'

'Yes, sir; if no one's claimed that money, which some kind or unkind benefactor sent me, may I have it?'

'It's yours, I believe, LAC Weston.'

Weston looked across the court to Captain Ferrimins, who wasn't looking very pleased.

Judy, Lucy, Edwina, Jemima and the C/O were waiting outside the court.

'Come along, Pewsy, we are going to celebrate your acquittal with a meal in the Bravemouth Yacht Club,' Dr Wendover said. 'It's my treat.'

'May I remind you ladies that LAC Weston cannot go to where and how he pleases; he is now once again under RAF orders,' the C/O said.

'Don't you dare spoil this celebration, David. If you do you'll have me to answer to,' his wife said. 'Weston is to be our guest to the Bravemouth Yacht Club; are you coming with us or not, David?'

'I'd better come with you, I suppose,' he muttered. 'Weston won't be able to buy you drinks and I'm not having you ladies going to the bar.'

Later, after enjoying a sumptuous meal in the yacht club, the ladies demanded a speech from Weston. He looked askance at his C/O, but his C/O made no comment. Weston got to his feet.

'I'm afraid I'm not a very good after dinner speaker, ladies. However, this opportunity does enable me to say a huge thank you to all you wonderful people who have stood by me during these past few weeks. If it hadn't been for you ladies and your unselfish help, I would be in prison now. Thank you all very much indeed.' He sat down. His C/O, looking very officious and important in his dress uniform, stood back from the table.

'Take your glasses, ladies, and may I stretch my imagination and call you a gentleman, Weston, let us drink a toast.' He held his glass out and everyone stood. 'To the ladies of the Five Leaf Clovers.' They drank the toast and Jemima, with a sparkle in her eyes, stood and held her glass out.

'I think we should toast our fifth member. Here's to my wonderful absent friend, April.'

'I'll second that, Jemima,' Edwina said.

The door swung back and Captain Ferrimins strode like a storm trooper into the yacht club. Seeing the gathered throng celebrating, he walked over.

'What on earth is this person doing in the yacht club?' he said, pointing to Weston. His remark was met with silence. 'Still spreading lies and deceit, are you, LAC Weston? I'm surprised at you, David; it's your responsibility to keep a man like this in his place, and that place is certainly not the yacht club.'

'I suppose you'd prefer him to be in prison,

Michael?' Lucy said. 'I'm coming around to your way of thinking, Pewsy.'

'I think we all are,' said Dr Wendover.

'By the by, I was talking to April's doctor this morning and he said she's finally responding to her treatment,' the captain said. 'Perhaps now we'll learn the whole truth about this, this Paul Edward Weston. Must say I was shocked by your revelations, Eddy; going to bed with this common bag of rubbish. What on earth will Franklin Junior have to say about that?'

'You're easily shocked, Michael, and why should I worry? I tell Franklin Junior everything. I have no secrets from him,' Edwina answered calmly, lying through her teeth. 'How would you like to sleep with me again tonight, Westy? I believe the beds in Rowanberry House are not being used.'

'No, Edwina, how dare you; that apology for a man will not be sleeping in my house ever again,' the captain uttered angrily.

'I'm afraid he's not your Westy or Pewsy anymore, ladies he's now just plain LAC Weston, and as such he'll be sleeping at the RAF camp tonight,' the C/O snapped. 'He might not think so, but he is still in the air force. LAC Weston, you had better return to the camp and prepare yourself for a week away from Bravemouth, you're going to RAF Aston Combe with your newly repaired launch tomorrow. I want that launch slipping, scraping and painting. I'm sending you and AC1 Cherry to do the painting and two engine fitters to overall the engines. Better say your goodbyes, girls. You will all be on the high seas cruising the world by the time he gets back.'

'Sorry, Michael. However, I'm afraid I can't accept your kind invitation for the cruise. The air force will not let me leave my post for three months. However, I see no reason why Jemima shouldn't go.'

The church clock was chiming seven o'clock when Weston finally set out from the yacht club. He first called at the police station to give his thanks to the sergeant and his wife for making his enforced stay there as pleasant and comfortable as it was.

He was finally on his way to the camp when he noticed three young ladies walking down the high street towards him. Seeing Weston, they began giggling.

It's Tamsin, he thought. She was looking very attractive, her short silvery blonde hair falling forward in curls around each temple. She was wearing a blue cotton skirt and a white sleeveless shirt style top. He waited for them.

'Hello, Tamsin, you look well. I'm so sorry about breaking our date in Truro.'

She blushed, and looked to the ground.

'Hello, Pew; have they let you out of prison?' she said, without looking at him. 'My dad said I've not got to have anything to do with you, you're a jailbird.'
Weston ignored her remarks.

'These girls, are they your friends?' he said.

They began to giggle.

Tamsin flushed a bright red.

'Where are you going?'

'Back to the ferry, there's not much happening in town this evening.'

'Look, it's only just gone seven o'clock, Tamsin; how would you like to have a meal with me? I've not had a bite to eat since breakfast,' he lied. 'I can walk you to the ferry later. I'm going away on the launch tomorrow for a few days.'

She looked at her two friends.

'I'll see you girls tomorrow, bye.'

'I thought you said your dad didn't approve of me,' he said, laughing.

'He doesn't, but what he doesn't know won't harm

231

him. I don't care.'

He took her hand, and looked down into her large blue eyes.

'Which café do you recommend?'

'I think the Anchorage café is the best in town.'

'You didn't visit me in the police station did you? But Barbara did.'

'Dad said I had to keep away from you, you're a bad lot and one day you'll finish up in prison. I did walk by the police station several times but I didn't see you. I don't think we should talk about it anymore, do you? If we do we'll finish up having a row.'

'Well never mind, let's go to the Anchorage café and get something to eat.'

He found Tamsin's company, after spending so much time with his married lady friends, quite refreshing. It was a pleasure to be talking to a girl nearer his own age, even though their conversation became a little strained at times, with neither of them mentioning the court case.

She talked about herself and how she worked in a large department store in Devon as a trainee buyer. She also told him she came home on a Friday afternoon and stayed until Sunday evening and that she lived with an aunt near Exeter during the week.

'Come along, Sweetie Pie. I must say I've enjoyed this evening.' He held her chair while she stood.

'Sweetie pie?' she said.

'Sorry, Miss Tamsin, it slipped out, don't you like being called Sweetie Pie?'

'Yes I do, Pew. I think it's nice. You are a gentleman; do you know I've never had my chair held for me, before?' Weston took her hand.

'Do you know something, Sweetie Pie? I don't even know your surname.'

'It's Tredinnick. Tamsin Tredinnick.'

232

'I like that. This way, Miss Tamsin Tredinnick, or should it be Sweetie Pie, I'll walk you down to the ferry.'

'If you go away tomorrow, you'll miss the first part of the regatta. I've taken one of my week's holidays just so I can be at home for the regatta.'

'We'll be back in Bravemouth by Wednesday or Thursday. I'll see you then. I'll pick you up at the ferry.'

The lads were lounging around the billet when he walked in.

'Look whose come home, lads; it's that bloody part-time airman, part-time criminal, full-time shagging machine, Pew Weston.'

Richard jumped from his bed ran over and shook his hand. 'Welcome back, Pew; good to see you again. I believe you and Peter are going away to RAF Aston Combe for a week or so to paint 7412? Mind you, I wish I was going with you. While you're away, we poor buggers have got to plant a new box hedge around the lawn.'

'I always thought you reprobates would make better gardeners than seamen,' Weston stated.

'Get the bastard and cut his balls off,' Tom shouted. 'We'll spoil his and his lady friend's fun.'

Chapter Thirty four

Corporal Barry the coxswain of HSL 7412 gently nosed the launch into position between the four stout steel poles on the launch cradle. Within minutes, the sixty eight foot launch had been hauled out and was sitting high and dry in the centre of the huge slipway.

Weston and Peter Cherry set to work without delay, using high pressure hoses and scrapers on the hull's infestation of marine growth before it dried out; they knew if it did, it would be almost impossible to remove.

LAC Gabley, Bravemouth lorry driver, came down the slip and parked his fifteen hundred weight truck alongside the launch and Corporal Barry and the skipper got in. The skipper shouted through the open window.

'LAC Weston, if you think you will have finished the work by Wednesday afternoon, ring the base before Wednesday lunch time and let Warrant Officer Greenwith know. We'll be here early Thursday morning to take you back. At least then you'll be there for the last half of the regatta.' They drove away, leaving Weston and the working crew behind.

'I don't know how I'm going to manage without having my regular sex, Pew,' Peter said. 'I'm already feeling horny. I'm going to miss Marion. Do you think you'll be missing your regular sex?'

'Me, miss sex? I've not had any for months; you forget I've been in prison for weeks, and before that in hospital with my leg. By the way, not one of you lot came to see me.'

'That's where you're wrong, Pew; Tom, me and Richard called in every evening after work, but you were always away having your leg seen to. Or undergoing some sort of sea water therapy. Well that's what the sergeant told us. It's like Tom said, you only know one therapy and that's women. Didn't anyone tell you we'd visited you?'

'No, because I don't believe you did. Come on, let's get this bloody job finished. I'm determined to get back to Bravemouth by Thursday.'

The cleaning of the underwater growth was finished well ahead of time by their reckoning, and the launch was ready for its first coat of antifouling paint. Pleased with their efforts, they removed their overalls and walked up to the NAAFI canteen for lunch.

The two engine fitters Walter English and Arthur Smith were busy fastening a carboy of water on the starboard side deck when they got back.

'What are you doing, Walter?' Weston shouted.

'It's those flaming boat builders, Pew. (Walter never used swear words as such.) They used up all the water; they've emptied the whole tank. There's not a drop of water aboard, so we borrowed this carboy from the battery store and filled it with distilled water; at least we can have a cup of tea now.'

They worked nonstop through the afternoon to finish the first coat of antifouling. After showering and changing into their uniforms, they walked up to the NAAFI canteen.

'I can't afford to eat here every day,' Peter said. 'I think we should go to the camp cook house, not here.' They walked through the NAAFI door and Weston froze in his tracks.

'I don't believe it,' he said.

'What is it?' Peter asked. 'What's the matter?'

Standing by the counter, looking very attractive in her Wren uniform, was Sonia. She heard his voice and turned.

'Brylcream,' she screamed. 'It's my Brylcream.' She ran over and threw her arms around Weston. 'My sweetheart, my Brylcream.' She kissed him.

Peter looked on, visibly embarrassed.

'I didn't think I'd ever see you again, Brylcream. This is fantastic, are you going to take me to bed? I'm aching all over for you.' She kissed him again.

'What are you doing here, Sonia?' Weston managed to get out, catching his breath. 'By the way, this is my friend, Peter Cherry.'

'Hello Peter, nice to meet you. Brylcream, let me treat you and Peter to something to eat. I had a good win on the nags yesterday.'

Both Weston and Peter ordered steak and kidney pie and chips.

Sonia brought their food over and they ate almost in silence.

Weston put his knife and fork down and sat back.

'What on Earth are you doing here, Sonia?'

'Drove my captain over to some meeting,' she giggled. 'Well that's what he tells me, but what meetings take place on a Saturday? I know what it is; he wants to look at a boat he intends to buy, he's out at sea in it now. He won't be back for hours.'

Peter finished his meal and sat back.

'Well, Brylcream, you haven't got me for long,' Sonia said. 'Are you going to shag me or not? I'd love you to do it, like you did the last time.' She looked into Peter's face. 'He's so good in bed, Peter; when he fucks a girl it goes on forever. Do you mind if I have a quick feel, Bryly?' She laughed as she felt his.........through his trouser fabric. 'Jolly good, I see you are keeping your pencil sharpened.' Peter, red-faced with embarrassment, got up from the table.

'I promised to phone Marion,' he said. 'I'll go now, Pew. I'll make my way to transit hut afterwards.' He looked at Sonia questionably. 'Thank you for the meal, Sonia. I, I think.'

'Poor thing, perhaps I shouldn't have talked about sex in front of him? But I had to get rid of him; I wanted to be alone with you, Brylcream. Do you know seeing you today has given me a huge thrill.'

'I don't know where we can go for sex, Sonia. Have you got a room here?'

She shook her head.

'Sorry, Brylcream. Oh bloody hell, my captain's come back; the bugger's early for once. Sorry I'll have to go.'

They left the canteen, holding hands.

'At least now I've seen you again, I feel refreshed.'

'I don't feel very refreshed.'

'Poor darling, there'll be other moons. You and me, Bryly, are like ships that pass in the night and we have to be happy with our little snatches of pleasure.' Her eyes twinkled. 'Well, goodbye.' She held him close for a moment, kissed him and then ran across to the captain's car. Weston, not normally an emotional man, felt as if something had gone from his life; he didn't know if he'd ever see her again. He made his way to the transit hut with a heavy feeling of sadness. Was the vivacious Sonia, like she said, just another ship that passes in the night? He hoped not; he liked Sonia and he enjoyed her lively company.

The weather remained perfect, which was fine for painting the launch's topsides. Weston and Peter, wearing only their old denim overalls, without a stitch on underneath, set to work with a vengeance, working nonstop until lunch time. They then downed tools, showered and went on to the canteen for a meal.

'Wonder if that sexy girlfriend of yours will be here again? Do you know she's the horniest woman I've ever had the good fortune of meeting? I've never heard a woman ask for it before, especially using swear words. How did you get to know her?' Weston thought,

237

the less he knows about Sonia the better; wonder how he'd get on with someone like Lucy or Edwina?

'I shouldn't think she'll be here today,' Weston said. 'She drives her boss all over the country; he's a top ranking naval officer, a captain I think.'

The weather remained good and by Wednesday morning Weston and Peter could see their hard work had paid off; the launch would be ready for the riggers to re-step the mast after lunch.

By half past eleven most of the work was practically finished. Feeling pleased, Weston walked up to the NAAFI to phone the base. It was answered almost at once.

'Bravemouth Bh12, Marine Craft Unit, Wittingham,' the base clerk said.

'Hello, Witty, this is Pew at Aston Combe.'

'Hello jailbird, have you finished the painting yet?'

'I thought I'd phone to let you know we're almost finished and we'll be ready to return in the morning.'

'Look, Pew, I'm glad you phoned. I've got a message for you from one of your lady friends; you know the one, the ravishing redhead, she told me she was Mrs Ferrimins' sister. I met her in town this morning. Hellfire, Pew, she's every bit as beautiful as her sister; she's left me all of a shake, even my legs are trembling.'

'Never mind about your bloody legs, what's the message?'

'She's given me a phone number, can you write it down? She wants you to phone her as soon as possible.' Weston found a pencil and wrote the number on the wall of the cubical. 'By the way, Pew, I met Tamsin at the fair last night; she was with Peter's girlfriend, Marion. They were having a hell of a good time with two sailors from the regatta guard ship. I told them I was going to tell you and Peter. Marion said, "Why should I stay at home? After all it's regatta week, and when the cat's away, I do play."'

'What did Tamsin say?'

'She just said, "Please yourself, tell him if you want, I don't care."'

'I shall have words with Miss Tamsin when I get back.'

'Mr Greenwith has just come in, Pew. LAC Weston's on the phone, sir.'

Weston heard the phone changing hands.

'Weston here, sir, we will be ready to…'

'Don't you mean LAC Weston?'

'Sorry, sir. Yes, sir, LAC Weston, we'll be finished and ready to come back in the morning, sir.'

'Well done, Weston, you and Cherry must have worked hard. I will let the C/O know as soon as he comes in.'

'Thank you, sir.'

Weston put the phone down and quickly dialled the number Witty had given him. He knew it was Edwina as soon as he heard her husky voice.

'Westy darling, so good to hear from you. I didn't know if I could trust that pimply faced youth to give you the message. Now listen carefully, I'm leaving for Southampton this evening. However, I was wondering if you and I could get together this afternoon. Captain Ferrimins has had to leave Bravemouth early, so he's trusting me to close both Rowanberry House and April's cottage on the moors. Did you know that he's going to be the captain of the cruise liner for this one voyage? I'd love to see you again before I leave. What do you think? I could send a taxi to Aston Combe to pick you up and take you to April's cottage this afternoon? Lucy told me you have Wednesday afternoons free, it's sports day or something.'

'It is sports day today, alright. The trouble is,

Edwina, when we are away on duty we don't have a sports day. However, I see no reason why I shouldn't take the afternoon off. We've finished most of the work here and no one's going to miss me.'

'Good, I'm already tingling with excitement at the prospect of having you in bed again.'

'What time do you think the taxi will arrive?'

'I'll phone for it right now. I'll tell the taxi driver to pick you up outside RAF Aston Combe, at say twelve thirty. Bye bye, my darling.'

Weston checked his watch; it was all ready a quarter to twelve. I'll change into my best blue uniform, he thought; good job I brought it with me. The service police might not stop someone wearing his best blue uniform from going through the gates. Weston, hoping his plan would work, walked as nonchalantly as he could through the gates at twenty five past twelve. No one gave him a second glance. Peter had been a mite curious when he saw he'd changed into his best blue. However, he didn't question anything when Weston told him he was going into town. The taxi arrived on time and the driver opened his door.

'I'm looking for someone called Pew Weston?' he shouted.

'Yes, that's me,' Weston shouted, running across. Fifty minutes later, the taxi pulled up outside Mountain Ash Cottage. Edwina, her hair tied back in a ponytail, came out; she was looking fantastic in her riding clothes. The taxi driver took one look at her.

'Bloody hell, is she your girlfriend?'

Weston didn't answer; he got out and waited while Edwina paid the driver. She kissed him and he slipped his arm around her waist.

'At least you're not dressed the same as you were the first time we met at April's,' he whispered into her ear. 'Mind you, I wish you were; I can remember exactly what little you had on that day.'

'What?' she laughed.

'Just silk stockings and a suspender belt, that's all.'

'I can remember what you said at the time. You said it in such an indignant manner. "Sorry, Mrs Weatherington, I didn't know you weren't dressed, I thought I heard you shout come in."'

'Well, what do you expect? I really was shocked.'

'Westy darling, that night I spent with you after the ball was the most heavenly experience of my life. Do you know I still wake up riding that magic carpet you created for me? The bedroom's up there.' She pointed to the stairs. 'You go up. I'll be up shortly; of course you already know, you must have been here before with April?'

'No, she never brought me out here.' Edwina, with a puzzled expression, kissed him.

'Carry me away and treat me to your special ecstasy, darling.' Two hours later, both happy but physically exhausted, they came down.

'I'm still glowing inside, Westy, let's go back.'

'No I'm hungry; I've got to have something to eat.'

'It's a jolly good job then that I packed a picnic basket for lunch. You are always hungry. April told me that. Shall we have the picnic in the paddock and afterwards who knows what we might get up to? By the way you didn't tell me when you were last here?'

'I've not been here before, this is the first time. Well I mean in body, but I did spend a half day here with April in an extremely strange dream that I had when I was in that coma. Now that I've seen the place in its flesh I realise how frighteningly real that dream was.'

'Shall we run through the garden to the paddock in the nude, Westy?'

'That's also curious, because in my dream April wanted us to run up the garden to the paddock in the

241

nude. But I wouldn't do it; I put my shorts on. After the picnic we made love in the long grass and April, feeling skittish, ran off laughing around the edge of the pond with my shorts and she threw them in. That was about the time Mrs Todmarsh-Rivers turned up and caught me stark naked. Both she and April couldn't stop laughing at me; in the end April took off and gave me her wraparound skirt to wear. So today I'm taking my trousers with me; knowing my luck, she's bound to turn up again.'

'It was only a dream, Westy. Jemima can't catch you out today; she's on her way to Southampton. Mind you I also had a strange dream about April being ill. So I won't disbelieve anything about dreams.'

The weather was hot and humid; there was a threat of thunder in the air and not as much as a breath of wind in the paddock. The swallows were swooping low over the pond, splashing down every second or so and the whole paddock was filled with the rich aroma of freshly cut grass and the buzzing of insects.

'Captain Michael cut the paddock yesterday before he left for London.' She laughed. 'Wasn't he good? Otherwise we'd have been lying in shoulder-high grass.'

'Perhaps it would be more reassuring if the grass was higher; I feel so exposed. I don't like being naked out of doors.' He dropped the picnic basket on the rustic table. There was no doubt about Edwina being beautiful. Even after all he'd gone through with the other ladies, he was still trembling with excitement at the thought of making love to her yet again.

She laughed. 'You're not the same shy man I met at April's are you?' She said, laughingly. She took from the basket a bright red table cloth and laid it on the table. 'Would you like to spank me? I'd like you to. Gosh, Westy. I love you so much. I want you to make

242

love to me forever.'

'I do agree with everything you say, but don't you think we should eat first? We're going to need our strength.'

Edwina had a good appetite and between them they quickly consumed everything in the basket. Weston drank the entire bottle of red wine to himself. Edwina wouldn't have any wine; she wanted a cool head for driving, she said. They lay back in the cool sweet smelling grass with the warm summer sun caressing their bodies.

Edwina nibbled his ear and whispered, 'Do you realise, Westy, that from tomorrow you will be on your own; not one member of the Five Leaf Clovers will be left for you in Bravemouth. We are all going on Michael's cruise. I do wish you were coming with us, but that wouldn't do, would it; we would be fighting over you.'

'I've still got Tamsin.' She glared at him and her eyes flashed.

'What? Don't tell me you still hanker after that uneducated fool of a girl. Lucy told me that she never came to see you when you were on remand in the police station. That girl thinks nothing of you.'

'Don't you think we are wasting time, Edwina? Shouldn't we be making the most of today, especially if you are going to be away for several months. Today's been, as far as I'm concerned, an absolute Godsend.'

She pushed him down onto the grass with a smile and, allowing her breasts to touch him first, she dropped on top of him. After half an hour or so, to Weston's surprise, she reached a massive climax. Afterwards, she lay alongside, breathing heavily.

'Westy, I can't settle; that dream of yours is upsetting me. Didn't you tell me that in your dream April threw your shorts into the pond?'

243

'Yes, but why now?'

'Because, I can't put it into words, but I think, yes I really do think, that even though you thought you were having a dream, you were really here in body. Can you remember the spot where April threw your shorts into the pond?'

'No, well not exactly; perhaps about fifteen yards in from this side of the pond. But it was only a dream, they won't be there.'

'There's something strange about these dreams, both yours and mine. There's too much factual evidence involved. I've never been to the hospital where April's a patient and I've no idea where it's situated. So how could I possibly have been there? Yet I have been there and I saw April; she was real. Then again, you know everything about this cottage, yet you say this is your first time here.'

'But what about April and Mrs Todmarsh-Rivers? They were both in my dream.'

'I don't know, Westy; there are so many answers I can't find, but to put my mind at ease, wade out and see if you can find those shorts; you've no clothes on and it can't be very deep.'

'No, it'll be cold and the bottom of the pond will be muddy and it will certainly pong.'

'Westy, get in there; you won't melt.'

'I'd much rather make love to you, Edwina.' He looked longingly at her naked form.

'There'll be plenty of time for that, you beast. I've got to know about those shorts; if they are there where you saw her throw them, at least I'll have one of the answers to my questions. I'm going out of my mind with the intrigue.' Weston began to wade out, apprehensively placing his feet in the soft mud of the pond bottom. He was up to his waist in the water when he felt something with his foot. He put his hand down and he gave an involuntary shiver when he lifted something from the bottom.

'What have you found?' Edwina shouted. 'Give it to me.' Weston threw whatever it was to her. 'Well it doesn't look like a pair of shorts. It's a table cloth; look, you can still make out the gingham pattern. It must have blown off the picnic table. Go on get back in, have another look.'

'No way am I going back into the filthy pond. There's nothing there. It was just a dream.'

'Yes I think you are right, Westy. Still, I had to know.'

'I bet you'll ask April to have the pond drained as soon as you get back from the cruise.'

'Yes, that's an idea. Come along, my heartthrob; let's have a final dip into that magical world of Westy's sex.'

'Well in my dream I was caught out stark naked by Mrs Todmarsh-Rivers. I have a feeling I'm being watched today.'

'Well that can't happen this afternoon; Jemima left for Southampton early today, with Lucy and Judy and their husbands. They've gone by train.'

'I still have a feeling that I'm being watched. I hate being undressed in the open air.'

'Do know what I think, Westy. I think, somehow, you were here at the cottage in both your mind and body. You lived that dream as if it was real and as far as you are concerned it was real. You saw someone or something you thought was April throwing your shorts into the pond. It couldn't have been April could it? Then again it could have been; she has no memory of these events. The more I think about what goes on in heaven and Earth, Westy, the more flummoxed I become.'

Rebecca looked on smiling.

Edwina leaned over and kissed him. 'Let's make love again, its five o'clock. We've not much time left. I've a long, long drive ahead of me.'

'I'm ready, if you are,' Weston said, rolling onto his back.

They froze; someone was running up the garden. The next minute Jemima, the C/O's wife, arrived, breathless and agitated.

'Quick, Edwina, cover yourself, and you, LAC Weston; get yourself out of sight. David will be here any moment.' Weston got to his feet, trying to cover himself. 'This is no time to feel embarrassed, Weston. David will send you into detention if he finds you here.'

Rebecca hadn't given much thought to Weston not being where he should be. Hoping to put matters right, she entered the C/O's mind and told him to have a few minutes rest and to go to sleep.

Edwina took the tablecloth from the table and wrapped it around herself, and even in this crisis of events she still looked quite fetching to Weston's eyes.

'I thought you'd gone with the others on the train, Jemmy?'

'No, I couldn't go without saying goodbye to my sister. But you know my nosey David; he misses nothing. He saw your car parked outside here so he stopped.'

'Right, Jemmy. Let's take the bull by the horns; we'll walk back and meet David coming up the garden.'

'You were right, Westy. You said Jemima would arrive and catch us naked. Better hide yourself behind that bush, Westy, just in case David does decide to walk up.'

Weston sat on the ground behind a tall laurel bush. He waited for half an hour, but no one came. He

246

thought he heard a couple of car engines start. But he wasn't sure. He was getting quite used to being abandoned stark naked by one of the Five Leaf Clovers. He decided to make his way back, if only to find out what was going on. He cautiously made his way to the cottage. He saw something had been pinned on the cottage door; it was a note from Edwina. He ripped it off. It said *"Sorry, darling, David was asleep in April's car when we got back. He's now returned to Bravemouth alone. Jemima has decided to come with me in my car to Southampton. I couldn't let you know because David insisted on waving us off. I have left the cottage door open, the keys are on the kitchen worktop. When you leave, will you lock the cottage door and push the keys through the letterbox? I've phoned for the taxi, it will pick you up at six o'clock. I've left some money on the worktop, use some to pay the taxi and the rest is for you, my darling. Sorry, my Seagull; I always seem to be ruffling your feathers, don't I? See you after the cruise. I can't wait. I shall have to go, lots of kisses, darling Westy. I love you. Eddy xxx."*

Weston looked at his watch; it was ten minutes to six. He was pleased now that he'd followed them down the garden, otherwise he could have missed the taxi. He found his uniform where Edwina had hidden it behind the sofa and quickly dressed. The taxi arrived dead on time.

Chapter Thirty five

It wasn't until he was in the taxi on the way back to Aston Combe that it dawned upon Weston the full gravity of what would have happened if his commanding officer had discovered him at April's cottage. I've got a lot to thank the C/O's wife for today, he thought. It also struck him how dull his life was going to be with April, Lucy and Judy gone. Although he hadn't always appreciated it at the time, it was probably the most wonderful era of his life, but it was now coming to an end. He paid the taxi driver outside RAF Aston Combe's gates and marched as smartly as possible into the camp. There were no guards posted and the camp appeared quiet; he didn't see a soul until he arrived back at the launch on the slipway. He checked around and he could see Peter had finished the last few jobs. Walter was standing on the deck; when he saw Weston he came down the ladder to the slipway.

'Where's Peter, has he gone for dinner?' Weston asked.

'I don't know, Pew; I've not seen him since five o'clock.'

'I'll walk down to the NAAFI,' Weston said, hoping no one had discovered his afternoon away from the camp with Edwina. 'Have you and Arthur eaten?'

'We had a bite at about half past five in the NAAFI, but Peter wouldn't come with us, he went to the cook house; he's broke, he told me.'

Peter's face was like thunder when he returned from the cook house.

'So you're back are you?' he said. 'I bet I know where you've been; you've not been shopping in town this afternoon, you've been to bed with some woman.' Weston shrugged his shoulders.

'You can think what you want, Peter, but can you prove it? Look, I'm going to the NAAFI for a meal, are you coming?'

'No I've no money left, I'll stop here.'

'Please yourself. I might go back into town again later. Sure you want to stay behind.'

Weston strolled up to the NAAFI and ordered himself steak pie and chips. This would be the first he'd eaten since his picnic with Edwina.

Having eaten, and wondering what to do with himself, everything around him seemed such an anticlimax after his stolen afternoon with Edwina. He turned the corner and there it was; he couldn't believe his eyes. Sonia's captain's car was parked across the road from the NAAFI. Where was she? He had to find her; she would be a wonderful answer to a lonely evening. He returned to the NAAFI and he'd only just sat down when Peter came running in.

'Pew, Sonia's here; she was looking for you.'

'Where is she?'

'I'm here, Brylcream.' She'd followed Peter. Weston looked at her and his heart raced; she was looking very smart and attractive in her uniform.

'Pleased to see me, Brylcream?' she said, giving him a peck of a kiss. 'Have you eaten?'

'Yes, but I could manage another meal. What would you like?'

'I'll leave you two with each other. I'm going back,' said Peter walking away.

'Brylcream, I'm all yours to do what you please with. My captain's gone away for a few days; he's sailing to Jersey with some friends on their yacht. He's booked me into a hotel for three days. How would you like to spend tonight with me in a hotel bed? Come along, if we leave now we can eat at the hotel.'

'I shall have to be back here by seven in the

249

morning, though. We are sailing the launch back to Bravemouth tomorrow.'

Sonia paid for a taxi to take them to the hotel. It was called the Drakes Arms.

They went in and Sonia collected the room keys.

'Do you want to go into the dining room, Bryly? I'm not hungry now.'

'Well I did eat in the NAAFI, so I'm not bothered. Shall we go up? I've got to have a bath or a shower.' The bathroom was next door to Sonia's room, so after twenty or so minutes in the bath together they peered out to see no one was around and, carrying their clothes, they ran to her room and leapt into bed. It was only eight o'clock.

Considering that Weston had enjoyed sex several times in the afternoon with Edwina, he still didn't disappoint Sonia.

They finally came up for air at ten o'clock.

'What a lover you are, that was fantastic, Brylly, but sex always makes me hungry,' Sonia said, kissing his neck. 'However, I think the dining room will be closed by now. Shall I find out?' She phoned down and a few minutes later a waiter arrived with a bottle of champagne, glasses and a large plate of ham sandwiches.

'Good old captain. He's paying for this,' Sonia said, touching her glass to Weston's.

Weston awoke at six o'clock. He didn't wake Sonia, who was sleeping soundly. He wrote her a note, thanking her for being his "Ship that passes in the night".

He had plenty of money from what Edwina had left at the cottage for him, so he walked through Plymouth looking for a taxi. He saw one and waved it down.

He was back in RAF Aston Combe by seven o'clock.

250

He quickly turned the lads out of the transit hut and they all made their way to the cookhouse for breakfast. After breakfast they set about making "7412" ship shape and Bristol fashion ready to go to sea.

Weston told Peter to take the paint they had left and the brushes back to the store, and he detailed the fitters to take the carboy of water back to the battery store.

Now alone with his thoughts, Weston walked around to the launches stern and sat down on the end of the cradle, staring across the river. The cold early morning chill had now gone; he removed his tunic, and laid it on the cradle. Its Eagle shoulder flashes stood out in the bright sun light. April had called him her Eagle, when she'd first seen them. April, yes April, it seemed years since he'd seen her. He thought about the last twenty-four hours and the wonderful stolen afternoon he'd spent with Edwina. He also remembered his night of passion with Sonia, his ship which passes in the night. A lone Seagull circled gracefully overhead, and landed close by. He watched it sidle up to some titbit it had spotted. It went through his mind what the C/O had said the evening he'd driven April, Edwina and her party to the charity dinner and ball. "RAF Eagle? Who Weston? Not a chance in hell, with a bit of luck he might make a web-footed Seagull someday." Edwina had spoken out in his defence that night. Didn't Edwina look fabulous in that green dress. What was it she said, "Don't worry Weston the seagull is still the handsomest and the most successful of all the birds."

He watched the seagull take off and was still following its flight when he heard the sound of a lorry.

'What's this, Weston, nothing to do? Where are the others?' the skipper said, walking down.

'They are taking various items we've borrowed back to the stores, sir; we will be ready to go to sea as soon as they return, sir,' he said.

251

'Must say you've done a good job on the old girl, Weston; she looks well.'

'Thank you, sir.'

'Right, Corporal Barry, let's get her into the water.' Gabley the lorry driver sidled up to Weston.

'Wittingham asked me to give you these letters, Pew.' He slipped them into Weston's hand. Weston knew who had written them and he disappeared up the ladder and into the fo'c's'le to read them.

The first one was from Edwina. *Darling Westy, by the time you read this I will be on the ship in Southampton, waiting to set sail. I'm going to miss you, my Seagull. I shall always think of you and treasure our stolen afternoon at the cottage. I love you. Must close now. See you when we get back, my Seagull. I do love you, Edwina x x x x x x x x x.*

The other letters were from Lucy, and Judy; they were written in a similar vein.

Now full of nostalgia, Weston placed the letters in his pocket.

Rebecca looked on, wondering what lasting damage she had done to Weston's mind by filling it with all those powers. She returned to the Earth office.

'Sir, may I be relieved of my duties now? The Bravemouth ladies have all left town.'

'You will not be relieved of your duties until I say so, Rebecca. No arguments. I want you to watch your charge closer than ever. I think we may have damaged the balance of his mind when we gave him those new powers. Stay close to him and don't let him out of your sight.'

Two hours later, RAF HSL No 7412 set sail for Bravemouth, fully refuelled and with her tanks refilled with water. The approaches to Bravemouth Harbour were crowded with yachts of various colours. A naval ship, a boom defence vessel was moored in the centre

252

of the harbour; she was acting as the Regatta guard ship.

'Where the hell's our f...ing flags, Weston? Why aren't we flying any?' the skipper shouted.

'There are none aboard, sir. They were removed when the boat builders were repairing the superstructure, sir.'

'Bloody hell, that's an oversight. Steer as close to that bloody navy ship as you can, corporal. You never know, they might not notice us.' Nevertheless, the navy ship had seen them and all her crew on deck came to attention and stood facing them. The skipper called his two-man crew to attention and he saluted from the bridge. Embarrassed by their lack of bunting, they slipped by and picked up their mooring. Its crew, at least, happy to be home in Bravemouth.

Chapter Thirty six

Six o'clock Thursday evening. Peter and Weston now wearing their civilian clothes, set out to the ferry landing to wait for Tamsin and Marion to come over. Weston, not wanting the letters he'd received from his lady friends to get into the wrong hands, placed them into the inside pocket of his sports jacket.

They waited for over an hour at the ferry landing, but neither Tamsin nor Marion came over. Finally giving up, they retraced their steps into town to have a drink.

They were standing with their drinks in their hands outside the Ship inn when a brass band playing the Cornish floral dance came around the street corner; there were groups of people dancing behind it.

'Look, Pew, there they are,' Peter shouted. Marion and Tamsin were dancing with two sailors. The girls had almost danced by when Tamsin saw them. She shouted something to Marion and pointed; they laughed and carried on dancing.

'I'm fed up, Pew,' Peter said. 'After the way we worked to get back here for today. I can't believe this is happening. I was looking forward to having sex tonight with Marion. If she was to come back now, I'd forgive her, provided she lets me have a bit of nooky. There's not much fear of that though now; did you see how handsome those Matelots were? Come on, let's have another drink. I'm having a pint this time.' It was well over an hour later when the girls, looking rather sheepish, came to see them.

'It took us ages to dump those Matelots, Pew,' Tamsin blurted out. 'Mind you, they were very dishy,' Marion said, laughing.

Peter grabbed hold of Marion, gave her a huge kiss

and whispered something into her ear; the next moment, without a word to Weston or Tamsin, they'd gone. Peter wanted his nooky, as he called it, and after all he'd told Weston, he would forgive her anything.

Weston and Tamsin eventually made up their quarrel and they walked into the Anchorage café for a meal. It was a warm evening, and Weston took his sports jacket off and lay it on an adjacent seat. The relationship between them improved immensely during the meal. So much so, they arranged dates with each other for the rest of the regatta week.

'I think it's about time you went home, Tamsin. I don't want to upset your dad by making you late. I'll go to the toilets then I'll walk you down to the ferry.'

Weston returned from the toilet to find Tamsin had left. His heart fell when he saw his jacket lying on the table with the three letters open on top of it.

He thought, why did I take my jacket off? He paid the bill and set out running to the ferry after her. He'd almost caught up with her when she climbed onto the ferryboat. He grabbed her arm and tried to pull her off.

'Go away, Pew. I don't want to know you; go and read your girlfriends' letters again.' Their differences unresolved, Tamsin sailed away.

Weston watched the ferryboat disappear into the darkness, thinking about how hard he and Peter had worked to get back to Bravemouth early to be treated like this.

Tamsin wasn't the same girl he knew; her attitude towards him had changed. He began to feel more and more despondent by the minute. He stared blankly across towards East Bravy and tried to work out what had happened between them. It can only be the fact that I almost went to prison, he thought. Captain Ferrimins has certainly done a good job on me. That man's taken away or destroyed everything I hold dear in life, even my credibility. I've got nothing left to live for. I can't go back to the camp feeling like this; I'm in no humour to see Geordie, or to listen to Tom and Richard's ramblings. Feeling rock bottom in self esteem, he walked along the esplanade towards the harbour entrance, his mind repeatedly going over and over all that had happened in the few weeks since he'd arrived in Cornwall. He crossed over the small town beach and climbed to the top of the cliff. There he stood above the castle, looking first out to sea, then down the harbour.

He shivered involuntarily in the cool evening breeze and the letters fell on to the ground when he put his jacket on. He retrieved them, wishing he'd left them behind in the billet. He looked down the harbour towards April's home, but couldn't make it out because of the brightness of the guard ship's lights. He now realised that everything that had made his life tolerable in Bravemouth had gone. Taken away by a man he hardly knew, April's husband Captain Ferrimins. His entire world was now lying wrecked and shattered around his feet. He decided that the best thing to do was to return to the camp. The alcohol he and Peter had consumed before the girls had returned was clearing from his head, making him feel even more miserable.

Rebecca was upset to see Weston in this state and she returned to the Earth Department office to see what she could do to help him.

'Please allow me to help him in his hour of need, sir. I've never known my charge to be so low in spirit and it must be our fault.'

'I agree with everything you say, Rebecca. However, rules are rules. Your request is rejected. Keep your eyes on him but do nothing more.'

Rebecca returned to her duties; however, as far as she was concerned, rules were made to be broken. Weston was her responsibility and she was going to help him regardless of anything those in high places said.

Weston, feeling extremely downright miserable, sat down on one of the bench seats that had been placed on the cliff above the harbour. He had never in his life felt as low as this. He wanted to finish his life, and with this in mind he stood on the edge of the cliff. One quick jump down there into that surf would end it all, he thought.

Rebecca, without a thought about the consequences, materialised alongside him and, taking his hand, she led him back from the edge of the cliff to the seat.

'Who are you and where did you come from?' he managed to say.

'Hello, Paul Edward Weston; I'm a very dear friend of yours,' Rebecca said.

'How do you know my name?'

'Like I said, I'm a very good friend of yours. I've been watching over you twenty-four hours a day. I know you were planning to do something very silly a few moments ago.'

'Who are you?'

'Let's say it's my job to see that no harm comes to you. I was a long, long time earning my wings and now after this debacle, letting you see me again, I will in all probability lose them again.'

'Where are your wings? The only ones I can see are on those earrings you're wearing.' He pointed to her gold earrings which were tiny little winged angels.

'No my wings are real. Do you like my earrings? If so, I will make you a present of them.'

'No, I couldn't accept them. Tell me, why you are here?'

'Because I must talk some sense into you, Paul Edward Weston. I want you to start thinking positively again. I want no more thoughts of doing yourself harm.

Will you promise me that, please?'

'Very well I promise, but you've not told me your name?'

She didn't answer, but she touched her lips to his and disappeared.

He shivered in the darkness; he was cold. Had he really seen his Guardian Angel or was it all in his mind? He wasn't sure, but he certainly felt a lot better.

Rebecca returned to the Earth Affair's office, where she was asked to explain her actions.

'I can only say I'm guilty of everything you say, sir.'

'Do you realise that by pleading guilty, Rebecca, I have the right to take your wings away? I will give you one chance to reconsider your plea. Please try to find a way of convincing me why you shouldn't lose your wings.'

'Sorry, sir, but I must tell you this: I would do it all over again. The only thing I can say in my defence, my Lord, is I've enjoyed every moment of being Paul Edwards Weston's Guardian Angel. I can't change and I will do anything within my power to help him, no matter what the consequences are for me. I was made his Guardian and my one and only duty is to look after him.'

'Rebecca I'm going to ignore your plea of guilty. I realise that your actions today were done solely in the interest of your charge. However, we would like you to keep to the rules in the future and for the present you may keep your wings.'

Earlier that day in Southampton.

April and her four friends, the Five Leaf Clovers, were sitting in the cruise ship lounge.

'Girls I have something to tell you,' April said, standing. 'I've decided that I shall not be going on the cruise with you. I'm going to leave the ship now before she sails. Michael will have to learn to get on without me. I'm taking the next train back to Bravemouth.'

'That's silly April,' Lucy said. 'What will you do in Bravemouth? You'll be bored out of your mind and you'll be on your own.'

'No, Lucy, you are wrong there. I'll not be on my own, I shall have my Eagle, or is he Edwina's Seagull, to keep me happy.'

'Yes, of course, Pew will always be my Eagle. However, Jemima, you were right when you told me my brave Ernst had died a long time ago. Paul Edward Weston may look like him in every way, but he's still a far different person. I loved my Eagle who died, but I also love Pew Weston. However, I don't think Paul Edward Weston has been very true to me. I'm sure every one of my so-called friends has been to bed with him in these last few weeks. I can always tell when you girls are sexually satisfied and the only man capable of doing that is Pew Weston. However, to hell with you all; it's now going to be my turn. First, Jemima, I want you to get your husband David on the phone and tell him that April needs to cash in the IOU he owes her. Tell him it will be in full and final payment. I want in return for it a full month's compassionate leave from duty for Paul Edward Weston, starting tonight. Will you do that for me, Jemmy, please?'

'No, I will not.' Jemima's face was livid. 'Why should I, what does he owe you for? What promise has he made to you, April?' Jemima said.

'Don't worry about that, my darling. I've not been to bed with him. There's nothing in that IOU for you to worry about. However, seeing as you are my dearest friend, will you please make that phone call before I leave?'

'I want to know about this IOU, April Berkshire,' a red-faced Jemima stated. 'I shall make the call.' She

259

was back within less than five minutes.

'Yes, April, to my surprise he agreed to your terms at once and he said he wouldn't cash in the IOU, because LAC Weston did need a long leave to get over his traumatic experience with the kidnappers. He also said, for what it's worth, you can keep your IOU and cash it in sometime in the future for something nice. What was that IOU for, April? Please tell me.'

'Thank you, Jemmy. I will now make a solemn promise to you, darling, that one day I will tell you. But today's just not the right time. Right, ladies of the Five Leaf Clovers, who is going to drive me to the station?'

'No one,' Edwina said, smiling. 'Here, take the keys to my car; it is parked outside the hotel. Drive yourself. You can do it, you can do anything you want to.' She threw the keys to April.

'I couldn't drive all that way, Eddy.'

'Yes of course you can, don't be silly, you've made a start; you are now going to stand on your own feet.'

'I don't know, Eddy. You sound exactly like you did that day in the hospital when I had that illusion of you telling me to help myself.'

A shiver ran through Edwina; she did actually see April in the flesh that day she was sunning herself on the Tahitian beach.

Weston, feeling a little better, but still feeling low and depressed, made his way slowly along the esplanade towards the camp. He could see the lights of the navy ship reflected in the sky as he walked along the dim gaslight illuminated narrow esplanade road. He walked by Rowanberry House; it looked forlorn and unloved in the darkness, with not a light to be seen.

He heard a car approaching and stood to one side under the cold glow of a flickering gaslight to let it pass.

It was a dark coloured Standard Vanguard, its

260

number EDB 990. He knew that car; it belonged to Edwina. The car pulled into the side and the door opened.

'Pew Weston, is that you?' Weston was elated; his depression had evaporated, gone in a flash. Trembling with excitement, he ran up the road.

'Is that you, Mrs Weatherington?'

'No, Weston it's April, don't you recognize my voice?' She climbed out from the car, ran towards him and hugged him tight while she kissed him.

'I love you, Pew Weston, my Seagull.' She put her finger across his lips. 'Don't say anything to break this magical moment, Pew darling. I've waited far too long for this. Come along, my Seagull, I've procured a month's leave for you from the air force.' She kissed him again long and hard. 'I've the keys to both Rowanberry House and my cottage. We are going to spend a whole month together catching up on what I've missed. Climb into the driving seat, my English Seagull and take me home.'

The End.

Postscript *To Her Eagle was just a*

Seagull

Three years on in time, Paul Edward Weston, for the first time since he'd left the air force, was back in Cornwall. He'd purposely avoided Cornwall, especially Bravemouth, for five very obvious reasons.

However, on this particular occasion, he had no say in the matter; he had to return to Bravemouth to marry his one and only true love: Tamsin Tredinnick.

Even though he himself hadn't been in Cornwall, he and Tamsin had seen quite a lot of each other in the intervening years. Tamsin had procured for herself a job near to where Weston worked, and she had been staying with Weston's family.

Nevertheless, Tamsin's family, the Tredinicks, had insisted quite rightly on the wedding taking place in Tamsin parish. The date and place was the twenty third of May in the Old East Bravy Parish Church, which is situated on a hillside outside the village.

The day before the wedding, Weston, with nothing helpful to do, and feeling in the way, took the ferryboat to Bravemouth to renew some nostalgic memories.

He knew the RAF base at Bravemouth had been closed; however, undaunted, he walked through the town to where the RAF base had been.

The two cottages which had comprised the base

had now been fully renovated and were now someone's holiday home. Standing on tiptoes, he peered through the window into what had once been the C/O's office. In his mind's eye, he went back to the day when he, Peter, Tom and Richard had been marched in by W/O Greenwith to be interviewed by the C/O. Gosh, was that only three years ago? It seemed a lifetime away.

Full of nostalgia and wondering what had happened to Tom and the others, he made his way up the hill to the camp. He smiled inwardly when in his mind's eye he saw Tom and Richard's red faces after they'd carried their kit up that hill. They had been most upset when they discovered his kit had been taken up in the camp lorry.

The gates of the camp, which he'd never seen closed, were now gone. The large notice board which had once stated, "RAF Marine Craft Base B H 12, Bravemouth" now announced in garish yellow painted letters surrounded by bright blue Dolphins:

"Bravemouth Holiday Camp.

Licensed.

Accommodation.

Vacancies."

He thought about the stationmaster and his wrinkled faced sex-starved porter on Polcastle Station. "Marine base boy? Holiday camp? 'Tis same place, boy, 'tis same place."

Very little had changed at the camp; even the box hedge Peter and Digger had planted while 7412 was being rebuilt, and Weston was in police custody, was still there and growing well.

It seemed wrong to Weston that the RAF should move out of Bravemouth, leaving nothing behind to show for all the years they'd been there.

Feeling miserable and wishing he hadn't walked down memory lane the day before his wedding, he made his way to the town quay.

The weather was perfect and very similar to what it had been on that first day he'd spent in Bravemouth; consequently the town quay was crowded with people. However, for Weston, just one group of ladies stood out from the others. In fact they were all there; April, Lucy, Judy, Edwina and Mrs Todmarsh-Rivers, all looking as fantastic as ever. But what shocked Weston was the fact that three of them had a toddler in a pushchair and that the children were at least two years of age.

April, looking as beautiful as ever, was sitting the closest to him, wearing as always a white shirt style dress. He sidled up to her unnoticed and kissed the back of her neck.

'Pew? Pew. I don't believe it, it's Pew Weston? Girls. Edwina, Lucy, Judy, Jemima, look who's here.' She leapt to her feet and before he could utter a word she smacked him hard across the face.

'Don't bother to ask what that was for, because I'm going to tell you. It's for not keeping in touch or letting us know your address, you horrid, horrid man.'

The ladies crowded round while Weston rubbed his smarting face. Lucy hadn't changed one iota; she was the same enchanting tiny Peter Pan, wearing her has usual low cut sundress, this one in bright yellow. Judy was still the same fantastic Amazon; she was wearing beige jeans and a white shirt top at least a size too small, for she was exposing a little more than half of her breasts. Mrs Todmarsh-Rivers hadn't changed either and was as beautiful as ever, but she looked worried and drawn. She was dressed like April but in powder-blue. Edwina was also as lovely as ever, looking all legs in a tiny pair of shorts and a sleeveless white top; however her lovely long red hair had gone, it had been cut short.

Weston looked questionably towards the pushchairs. April saw his gaze and picked up her baby.

'Pew, I would like to introduce you to my son. Say hello to your Uncle Pew, Michael.' There was no doubt the little boy was a miniature Paul Edward Weston, complete with the mass of fair hair and piercing blue eyes.

'Does your husband know, April?'

'Of course he does, they all bloody well know,' Edwina said. 'How could anyone possibly hide babies like these? They're all the same, talk about peas from the pod. However, I think they've all come to terms with it; after all, now Michael and Franklin have heirs.'

'Commodore Michael. He likes that title, Pew, dotes on this little boy,' April said. 'And why not indeed? He is, like Eddy said, his sole son and heir.'

'Good to see you again, Westy, come and meet my son, Paul,' Edwina said. Weston looked. There was no doubt; her little Paul was a carbon copy of

April's little Michael.

'Why didn't you give me little Weston to love,' Lucy said.

Weston didn't answer Lucy but he looked askance at C/O's wife, who had stood back from the others. She didn't look very well; in her arms she was holding a beautiful dark haired brown-eyed little girl, of similar age to the others.

'You also have a baby I see, Mrs Todmarsh-Rivers?' he said. Her eyes filled and she began to cry.

'Yes, LAC Weston. Did you know my husband had passed away?'

'No? No I didn't. I'm so sorry.'

'Yes, out of all the ladies of the Five Leaf Clovers, I was the only one to marry a young man for love, yet I'm the first widow. David did leave this little girl behind for me to love.' She wiped the tears away.

'What happened? He always seemed so fit.'

'He had a massive heart attack. He was a heavy smoker you know, the doctors think smoking had a part in it.'

Judy gave Weston her usual hug and kiss.

'What are you doing here by the way, Pewsy? You've been very naughty you know, not keeping in touch.'

'I had to come back; I'm going to be married. I'm marrying Tamsin my old girlfriend tomorrow at eleven o'clock in the East Bravy Parish Church.'

April's eyes flashed at the news, but she made no comment.

'So, April's Eagle and my Seagull have finally

come home to roost,' Edwina said.

'From the way he's left his offspring to be looked after by others,' Judy said, 'I think we should say the Cuckoo has come home to roost.'

'I believe the Cuckoo in question would have to be a female,' Weston said.

'No, Weston, you're no Cuckoo; if anything you're a wonderful Love Bird,' Lucy said.

Rebecca, back on duty, looked at her wings and thought, These people really do like to compare men with birds.

April joined the others and they talked in undertones for a minute or so.

'It's been decided that you are coming home with me, Pew.'

'No, no way, what about your husband?'

Don't worry about him, he's in London; the old fart's retiring next year. I'm not looking forward to that, having him under my feet all day.' She put her arm around Weston's waist. 'We want no arguments, Pew, you're coming home with me now.'

'What about the baby?'

'The nannies will take care of them. Lucy, find the nannies and tell the others to come along to Rowanberry House in ten minutes. We'll be having a treat. Pew will be making his special Martinis for us.'

Weston glanced to the top of the hedge as he went through the gate. April noticed his gaze.

'She's not there, Pew. She died last year. I never got on with her, but she did tell me one day that you were one of the nicest young men she'd

267

ever known.' Rowanberry House was just the same; nothing had changed. She took him through the drawing room and onto the terrace. 'I didn't think I would ever have the pleasure of having you here again. May I still call you my Eagle?'

'I don't know; do you usually strike poor defenceless birds across the face?'

'Sorry, did I hurt you, my darling? Still, it had to be done; it jolly well serves you right.' She gave him a kiss on the lips. 'Will that make up for the smack, Pew? Will you go down and make five large Martinis and help yourself to whatever you want.' She kissed him again. 'I could willingly take you to bed at this very moment, Pew. I'm still in love with you, you know, and I always will be.'

Weston brought the tray of Martinis up from the kitchen as the other ladies arrived. He looked around. 'I suppose the babies are back with their nannies?' he said.

'Where else, Westy?' Edwina said.

'I see and I suppose the little things will be bundled off to boarding school as soon as they are old enough, like you were?'

'Of course, darling; do you, as the absent father, have some objection?'

'No. They are your children. I wouldn't dream of interfering.' Edwina stood at the end of the terrace.

'Would you all please sit? I want to call an extraordinary meeting of the Five Leaf Clovers.'

Lucy and Judy took hold of Weston's arms and sat him on a chair in front of the assembled ladies.

'Paul Edward Weston,' Edwina said. 'By a unanimous vote, you have been voted in as the only male member of the Five Leaf Clovers. Do you accept the honour?' Weston was dumbfounded.

'Yes,' he said. 'Thank you, but what does it entail? I'm getting married tomorrow.' April ran forward and kissed him.

'It doesn't entail anything, my darling,' she said. 'Except you now have to promise faithfully that from this day on you will always keep in touch.'

Judy came forward and presented him with a small box.

'You must promise to wear this at all times,' she said, presenting the box to him. Weston opened it and inside was a gold Rolex wristwatch. 'Inside the back cover of the watch, you will find the Five Leaf Clover motif together with all our names and phone numbers. Do you promise to wear it always?' Judy said.

'But this must have cost a fortune,' he said. 'Yes I do I agree, but are you sure you want me to have it?'

Edwina walked out and stood in front of him.

'It's your watch, Westy; wear it with pride. You must now kiss each of us in turn to become a fully-fledged member of our group. And remember, you will always be my Seagull.'

'He will always be my Eagle, Eddy,' April shouted.

'Is that so, April?' Judy shouted. 'Well girls, whether he be an Eagle or a Seagull, this is his final afternoon as a free man,' Judy shouted. 'He's getting married tomorrow; however, at this very

269

moment he's still fair game.'

The following day, the 23rd of May, was Tamsin's and Weston's wedding day, and the entire area was enveloped in thick sea mist.

Weston and his brother-in-law, his best man, sat in the bottom pews, awaiting the arrival of the bride. The church was full on Tamsin's side. But there was only Weston's family sitting on his side. Suddenly the sun broke through the mist and the church was bathed in bright warm sunlight. The organist (Tamsin's aunt) was playing Handel's Largo. The vicar arrived, and he shook hands with Weston and his best man. When there was a disturbance at the rear of the church and everyone looked around, Weston was surprised, even shocked, to see moving into the back pews on his side of the church six well-dressed ladies, five wearing different coloured dresses with large hats to match and one lady all in white.

They all in turn blew Weston a kiss before opening their prayer books. The noise level on Tamsin's side grew, and Weston's mother glared at him. 'How many women can you see sitting in that back pew?' Weston asked his best man.

His best man looked around.

'I can see five,' he said. 'Who are they? My word they are good looking.'

'Are you sure there are only five?'

'Yes, why?'

'Nothing.' However, Weston could see six ladies and he knew who the other one was.

She'll really be losing her wings, he thought.

The organ player began to play "Wedding march."

Tamsin, looking lovely in her white dress, walked down the aisle on the arm of her father.

The ceremony started.

When it was over, Weston took a quick look down the church. The top pews were now empty. However, he did see a glimpse of something white hovering above the rear of the church.

Is that you again? he thought in his mind.

'Can you see me? I don't care. I think congratulations are in order to both you and your bride.' The usher came to Weston just as he and Tamsin were going outside to have their photographs taken.

'Those ladies who came in late gave me these to give you. He handed Weston five envelopes. Tamsin was busy talking to her mother and the bridesmaids, so Weston ripped open one of the envelopes. In it was a letter from April and a cheque for one hundred pounds. He quickly slipped it into his pocket. The other envelopes were more or less the same. So with five hundred pounds to spend and five letters concealed in the inside pocket of his morning suit, Weston walked outside. Rebecca looked on, well aware that the powers she'd bestowed upon Weston were still there and they were just waiting to be reactivated.